AuthorHouse™
1663 Liberty Drive
Bloomington, IN 47403
www.authorhouse.com
Phone: 833-262-8899

Cover and illustrations by Heather Staradumsky.
Edited by Kaden Whitman

Published by AuthorHouse 02/02/2021

ISBN: 978-1-6655-1064-6 (sc)
ISBN: 978-1-6655-1065-3 (hc)
ISBN: 978-1-6655-1066-0 (e)

Library of Congress Control Number: 2020924759

Print information available on the last page.

This book is printed on acid-free paper.

HIDEBOUND

A. OLIVER NOEL

authorHOUSE®

This book is dedicated to Tyler.
You will always be my muse.

CHAPTER 1

It isn't until noon that Mr. Connolly announces he's going out. I lift my head from my work, watching as he makes his way to the front door of the shop. He stands with his hand white-knuckled around the knob, squinting out the front window for what feels like too long. His jaw is tight, and he moves with the heavy resignation of a man headed to the gallows. I grip the broom in my hands a bit tighter as he sighs, shaking his head.

"Is e-everything alright?" I'm only stealing glances at him, like if I stare at him directly he won't answer.

He looks almost bored. "Fine," he says, and then my heartbeat roars in my ears like howling wind rushing through my audancers, except... except his mouth is still moving, and I heard what he said, but he can't possibly have said it.

"I–I'm sorry?"

"Don't be. It happens to everyone."

"No, I mean—" I clear my throat, inexplicably nervous. "What y-you said, I di–didn't quite catch that."

He repeats himself, but it takes another long moment for the words to really hit me. His wife died last night. His wife died last night. And he waited until noon to even mention it.

I try to find the right words to express my condolences, but everything feels so hollow, so useless. Mr. Connolly waves a hand as he turns to face me directly, his brows drawn in sullen gray lines. "I wasn't expecting it, either, but everyone goes sometime."

My free hand creeps up to clutch at my necklace before I start sweeping even harder. "I sup–suppose that's one way of l–looking at it."

"My son's coming up today to discuss funeral arrangements. Think you can manage the shop while I'm gone?"

I don't say anything, just give a jerky nod. How could he lose his wife and go about his work the next day like nothing happened? Dreggar... how can he even afford a funeral in this economy? I keep silent and continue sweeping fiercely at the hardwood, gaze fixed on the floor like it might somehow reveal what I should say, how I should feel.

"Artem," Mr. Connolly calls, and I stop. "You're going to wear a hole in the floor."

"Just trying to be- to be thorough!" I wince at how quickly the words rush out of my mouth.

He waits a moment, then heaves a deep sigh. "You've

always been terrible at keeping your mouth shut. Say what's on your mind."

I say nothing, only store the broom in the wardrobe tucked in the corner. The maddening, asynchronous ticking from the various clocks around the shop fills the emptiness until he speaks again. "If your brother died, you'd still come into work. Yes or no?"

My breath hitches a little, and I turn my face away sharply. "Es–Es–Esper's just a kid. L–Let's not talk like that, alright?" I hurry to grab a bucket and fill it in the sink at the back of the workshop. I can't avoid his gaze forever, but I can damn well try. Mr. Connolly thankfully stays put, but I could swear I hear him snort.

"You're in charge. I'll be in tomorrow morning."

The slam of the door as he leaves makes me jump. I carry on cleaning for about an hour, which quickly stretches into two. I spend a lot of time behind the counter, sketching idly and wondering where our usual customers are. Eventually I give up watching the front door and locate Mr. Connolly's blueprints for my audancers: the bulky metal casings that sit on a bolted fixture where my ears should be. The vents and knobs have been loose recently, and I'm starting to worry they'll break down when I really need them. I don't take them apart, just use a mirror and a screwdriver to fiddle around the best I can. Maybe one day I'll fix them for good.

Business has been slow. There's more use for repair work than ever these days, but with the scarcity of work as more places cut corners, people would rather barter for a new pillow than a fixed radio. Even with Mr. Connolly's contract with the skylines, there haven't been many orders from our

bigger clients. Five minutes until close, I get up to lock the front door; no one has shown up, and it doesn't seem like anyone will. As I sort through the ring for the right key, the sign above my head catches my eye: "OPEN". Oh no. No no no.

With growing horror, I flip it back and forth, and my stomach drops. The store has been closed all day. Mr. Connolly is going to kill me. I rub my eyes and try to even out my breathing, clutching the key hanging around my neck for comfort, then flip the sign before going back behind the counter to count the coin in the register. If I can get anyone in the next five minutes, it might make up a bit for the hours of business we've lost.

I've just slid the drawer shut when the door creaks open and a young woman strides in, hair disheveled but every movement purposeful and poised. She releases her ponytail in a tumble of blonde waves, chest heaving with quick, shallow breaths as she flicks a quick glance out the window behind her. Combing her fingers through her hair, she catches my eye, fixing me with a determined stare; before I can react, she has walked over to the counter, undone her jacket, and tossed it, inside-out, atop one of the twin stools meant for seating customers. My eye twitches and I swallow down the lump forming in my throat as she clicks her tongue and makes her way toward one of the radios, perched on a higher shelf than I can reach. She makes her way back to the front desk, and I clear my throat, then falter as her piercing gaze falls upon me. Her eyes are the most startling shade of forest green I've ever seen.

"G-G-Glory be!" Curse my stutter. "So that, r-right there, is o-one of—"

"It's an older radio, right?" Her voice is warm and alluring.

"Yeah." I hold my palms out to take it from her. She hands it over, a smile ghosting her lips.

The door bangs open again. I start to stammer out something about closing up for the day, until I recognize the face: it's Roran, most likely taking a break from his patrol. He's in his dark-blue uniform, the jacket peppered with badges and stripes, and he looks more frazzled than I've ever seen him, sharp blue eyes narrowed, dark hair wind-tossed. He keeps a hand near his pipe balistir, which appears locked but possibly loaded, then startles as he catches my eye.

"Hey, Roran, g-glory be." I stand up on the tips of my toes to try and see him better over the woman's shoulder. "We're actually c-c-closed right now, but you can stop by tomorrow if-if you're looking to p-purchase anything!"

The young woman's eyes widen slightly, and for a moment, her face is full-on panicked. Then, just as quickly, she calms and turns to look back at Roran.

He takes a step to the side to see me better past the counter, and offers me a warm, yet sheepish, grin. "I know. I was chasing after someone, thought I saw her run down this street." Roran looks over at the woman, grin twisting into a scowl. "We had this guy shouting about the proc force being a joke, the standard propaganda against King Lyran. I was supposed to take him in overnight, then some blonde broke into my jitney— a Mycilis Lenzer, just issued— the guy was long gone, and I found her snooping around..."

As he keeps talking, I unintentionally tune out, looking back at the woman in front of me. She's leaning against the counter, but her hand is balled into a tight fist.

Roran is looking for her. My chest tightens at the realization that a potential criminal is standing in front of me. The only reason she stepped in was to hide, because of... whatever she did. Admittedly, I haven't been paying much attention to what Roran has been saying. Still, I keep quiet.

"... point is, I lost her. You seen anyone that fits that description?"

"Can't say I have, procier," the woman replies cooly. Her gaze, when it flits to me, is just as cool. She knows I know it's her.

Roran squints at her, and she runs her free hand through her hair again. "Funny. You kind of look like who I'm after. I never got a good look at her face... where exactly were you two minutes ago?"

The woman laughs, lifting a demure hand to her lips, fingers half-covering a coy grin. "I've been here." Her chin is held high, confident, unflinching. "My radio's busted. I heard this is the right place to get it fixed."

He continues studying her face as she somehow maintains an aura of calm. Compared to her obvious panic only a second ago, I'm impressed. It doesn't look like Roran is completely buying it, though, and honestly, I wouldn't either.

I have nothing to lose turning her in, admitting to Roran that I have no idea who she is, that she just walked into my shop, that for all I know she's a criminal, and a hundred other kinds of bad for my health. Though I could declare my innocence, something holds me back. My eyes dart to his weapon holster. I can practically see the runnels ripping into her, tearing ragged holes into her stomach and chest, her blood staining the hardwood a deep crimson, those green eyes going flat and cold. I can't suppress a shiver.

"I've been here for the past twenty minutes, going over the pros and cons of certain radios." She nods to the set on the table, catching my eyes with a smile.

Maybe she deserves to deal with a proc, but given how most of them strike first and ask questions later, I can't help but worry. Something about her makes me feel like she's not dangerous. Yet I'm still surprised by the words that escape my mouth.

"Yeah, she's be– she's been here." I'm a little dizzy as Roran turns his attention back to me. "Actually, she's m-m-my last client! I don't mean t-to-to be rude, but I do need to close for Mr. Co-Mr. Connolly." Part of me is suddenly grateful for my chronic stutter. While it does get worse when I'm stressed, it's bad enough in general that Roran barely bats an eye at my excuse. The woman's shoulders drop a fraction, the relief pouring off her.

Roran puffs his chest out and shoots me an apologetic look. "Sorry to bother you. Promise me you'll keep an eye out?"

"Veså, kivesh," she replies with a grin and a jaunty salute, before I can even think of a response. W–Was that Sertalin?

"U–uh, yeah," I add. "If anyone else ru–runs in here, I'll let y– I'll let you know."

Roran gives a wave and heads out the door. The woman watches him go, waiting patiently. She turns back around once she's certain he's not coming back, and with a low whistle, searches my face for a good minute. I drop my eyes and hand the radio back to her. She places it back on the shelf where it belongs, then clears her throat and nods to the stool. I fetch her coat and she clicks her tongue as she takes it, still looking me up and down appraisingly. "So, do you just really hate your friend, or are you in favor of overthrowing Parvay?"

"Huh?" My brow furrows. "No, I- I figured you had a reason y-you were lying."

"Well, I can't say prison and proc brutality were high on my list for today." She chuckles, adjusting the jacket in her arms. "I wasn't expecting you to go along with that. You know, lying to a proc is an offense against Parvay and the king..."

I duck my head and scramble to the door, flipping the sign back over as quickly as I can with fumbling fingers. "You can leave through the back, just-just give me a moment." She brushes a lock of hair behind her ear and hums her assent.

I do a quick sweep through to make sure everything is where it needs to be. The stools go back in the corner, the radio I touched earlier gets turned to its old position, and the various objects Mr. Connolly obsesses over being just so are straightened.

The whole time, she stands there, just watching. I feel her eyes on me, as if she were studying me. I do my best to ignore it. Once I'm done, I lead her through the workshop and to the other exit, then wait for her to go, so I can lock up back here and leave through the front. Only... she's not leaving. Instead, she spins on her heel, turning to where I stand on the threshold. My face heats and I tighten my lips. She removes a small square coin purse from her pocket and tosses it in my direction. I fumble and manage to catch it, holding it close to my chest, though my immediate instinct is to throw it back.

"It's not much, but I can pay you more for your help sometime this week," she explains.

"This is— you d–don't have to—!" It's heavier than my own coin purse has ever been, even during a good week. My whole life, payment has been a cool drink of water after a hard run, a reward that feels all the better for how much effort you've put into earning it. But now, standing here, everything feels wrong. I can't take coin for work I haven't really done. "There's n–no way I can accept this!"

"You did me a favor; I owe you."

I almost want to cry. Knowing she'll keep fighting me about it, I weakly nod and stash the pouch in my vest pocket. Maybe I can afford a coat for myself. It's starting to get chilly again, and I had to throw out my old coat months ago.

"I d–don't know what to say. Thank you..." I trail off; I never got her name.

"Hiero," the woman answers. It sounds almost lyrical.

"Ar–Artem," I offer. "Artem Clairingbold."

"Well, Artem." Hiero shoves her hands into her jacket pockets and rocks back on her heels. "Åneysh. Here's to hoping we don't make this a daily occurrence."

She heads down the small alleyway and hangs a right. I stand by the door for what feels like hours. Slowly, I withdraw the coin purse, flipping back the corners of the square pouch. They peel open, and I'm able to take stock of what's inside: coin, lots of coin, more than I make in a month. Gaqĕ. I'm suddenly nauseous.

I quickly pocket it and head inside to lock the exits, only to catch a messenger waiting at the front door. I've already dealt with enough today, but it could be something for Mr. Connolly. I hesitate and open the door. He says nothing, only hands me a single envelope, addressed: To the Guardian of Esper Clairingbold. Inside is a short letter telling me, in no uncertain terms, to head to the school immediately. I can only imagine what trouble Esper has gotten into this time.

I close up shop and brace myself for whatever unpleasant conversation I'm in for. If I'm getting a message from the school instead of hearing about this from Esper himself, it must have been up there with the time he set off fireworks at lunch.

Along the way, I overhear an argument between a proc and a Qorani man, in one of the alleyways along the street.

"I'm just trying to go home, procier!" the man insists, shaking his head.

"Do I need to repeat myself? Turn out your pockets!"

This kind of casual culturalism has long since ceased to be surprising. The man sighs heavily and complies, taking out his belongings. The proc sneers, hand near his pipe balistir, as he practically spits, "That's it. Quarterling."

Violence may have dropped, but it's no secret anyone with dark hair and gold eyes is going to be singled out, especially by procs. It's mostly the eyes that give away where people grew up, or at least have family from. I can argue that I don't have the accent or that I'm not from Qorar, but at the end of the day, anyone with gold eyes is Qorani— or Qorain,

Allowyn's bastardization— and any Qorani is automatically suspect, even in a large and diverse city like Wellwick.

I walk a little faster.

The school isn't one of the nicer schools, but it still maintains a reputation of educating future bankers and procs, though I'd be happy if Esper just managed to find work in an office. It's on the smaller end, holding only a hundred and forty kids at most. This is Esper's third school in five years. I pray there won't have to be a fourth.

Esper sits on a bench outside the main office, swinging his legs back and forth. The moment he spots me, he bolts upright, eyes wide and shoulders hunched. I almost don't want to know what he's done this time. I step closer to him and fold my arms.

"I didn't do anything," Esper whines.

"Clearly."

"No, really, it's stupid and unfair. They just don't wanna deal with me!"

I shake my head and do my best to reserve judgment for now. It's hard to gauge if Esper is telling the truth or not. One of the schools he got booted from proved he had managed to bring in keddin bombs that coated the classroom with clouds of blue smoke. Esper is a wildcard, and he does as he pleases. I'll never understand it, but at the end of the day he's still my little brother, and I'm going to worry about his safety above all else.

As I move to step into the office, the secretary clears her throat. I stop short. "Hello, I'm M–Ms. Clairingbold? I was t-told—" She holds a finger up, continuing to sort through papers. The longer I stand there, the more awkward I feel. Finally, she drops her finger, and without looking up, replies.

"Esper, Ms. Clairingbold— Mr. Larkin will see you now."

"Thank you," I mumble.

Esper trudges in so slowly I have to get behind him and push him along. I'm starting to think whatever he's done is worthy of suspension. He's not into pyrotechnics anymore, and he's never been one to bully other children or outright harm anyone. Could he have stolen something?

The head of the school sits behind his desk, hands folded together patiently as we file in. He's neater than a suit on a mannequin, combover glistening with pomade. The walls are sparsely decorated, mainly with certificates of achievement. On the desk sits a medal of service to the king, next to a statue of a derlyn, the large, two-tailed and tri-horned feline's teeth bared. I gently close the door behind me as Esper takes a seat, slouching as far into it as possible. I must take a little too long, as Mr. Larkin gestures toward the other chair and looks at me expectantly. My cheeks burn in embarrassment, and I do my best to sit down as quickly as possible; my foot catches on one of the legs and I stumble but manage to catch myself. This meeting is clearly going to go well.

"Thank you for finally joining us, Ms. Clairingbold."

Oh boy.

"I came a–as soon as I could. The, u–uh, message you sent me di–didn't reach me until the shop closed."

"Ms. Clairingbold, I feel I should remind you that this is an institution for learning, not a daycare facility."

There's no point in trying to argue. I nod and keep my

gaze down. Esper huffs loudly, and I turn to shoot him a look. He doesn't seem to heed my silent begging for him to cooperate and slouches further. By all known laws of gravity, he should've slid off already.

"What seems t–to be the problem, M–Mr. Larkin?"

Mr. Larkin shakes his head and stands, opening a file. "We've had a number of disturbances in class, problems with classmates, but today overstepped a line we have, Ms. Clairingbold, for tolerance."

"It's propaganda!" Esper shouts.

"Just because you learned a new word in your unit does not mean you are using it properly." Mr. Larkin narrows his eyes. "Mr. Revver was discussing the current political climate and policies approved by the king and Parvay. We do not allow defamation of the Crown, or support of the Airgon anarchists."

"I thought there was supposed to be tolerance."

"That is enough, Mr. Clairingbold!"

Sometimes I can't believe the things that come out of Esper's mouth, but he has a point: shouldn't it at least be a topic for discussion? I don't agree with the anarchists, nor do I necessarily agree with Parvay, but in terms of education, it ought to be discussed, not brushed under the rug. The idea that Parvay— that anyone— is beyond question, is dangerous, to say the least.

I keep my mouth shut and Esper turns his head toward the window. Mr. Larkin sighs and sits back down. There's a moment of grave silence, as the seriousness of the situation sets heavily upon the room, and at last he speaks again. "I'm afraid we have no choice but expulsion, Ms. Clairingbold."

"Ex-Expulsion?" I stammer. Mr. Larkin nods his head. "B-B-But that's insane!"

"I beg your pardon?"

"All he di-did was speak u-up in class! There must be s-some way he could earn-earn another chance. Something th-that can be done other than k-kick him out for something so-so small and—!"

"You do realize what you are implying is treason, do you not? Merely discussing the actions of these criminals is betraying the Crown. I highly suggest accepting the consequences, and perhaps moving him into an apprenticeship trade instead of another institution. Given his record."

I stand up and stare at the carpet until I can find the courage to look Mr. Larkin in the eye. His expression is passive, his mind made up long before I ever walked into the building. There was nothing to discuss here; Esper was kicked out the moment he opened his mouth.

"C-Come on, Es," I manage. "We're g-going home."

Esper hops out of his chair and follows me out. In the hall, he races ahead and holds the front door open for me as we make our exit. We're barely a block away from the school before he starts going.

"I never liked Mr. Revver anyway. I didn't even do anything!" He hops up onto one of the stone ledges separating the houses from the sidewalk and walks along it, extending his arms for balance.

"I think it was h-harsh for them to exp-expel you over that, yes," I start, trying to choose my words carefully. "But it's a touchy subject for a-a lot of people."

15

"Touchy enough to get kicked out?"

"For some people, yes. You know I–I'm more than will-willing to talk about anything with you, Esper, just, th–there's a time and a place for everything. School was apparently... not it."

"Rhine Toberts says you have to question everything." Esper hops down and spins around to walk backwards.

And just like that, as usual with Esper, I'm lost. "Who's Rhine Toberts?"

"The leader of the Airgon movement!" Esper explains. "He's in charge of the whole group trying to overthrow the king. Times are changing and so should Parvay."

I barely know about Parvay to begin with, and barely understand how the system is set up. A bunch of members from the estates meet to discuss motions that can't be carried out by the king. It's meant to maintain a balance of power among the Crown, the church, and people. There are three estates in place to keep that balance: the clergy, the nobility, and the common folk. The noble houses and clergy pay no taxes and get lighter sentences when they commit crimes, while the common folk go unheard in Parvay and generally are treated like scum in the gutters.

"Wh–Where are you even hearing this stuff?"

"...People," he hedges.

"Esper." I shake my head and stop, taking him by the shoulders as we step off to the side. "It's not safe, this whole thing. I–I–I don't want you g–getting involved with the rebellion."

"Why not? They want to take down the skylines. Aren't the skylines trying to take down our apartment?"

"It's complicated, Esper. Please, p-promise me you're n-not going to get more involved in this stuff. It's getting dangerous, and l-like I said, I'm willing to-to talk about it with you, but that doesn't mean right this second, nor that I w-want you sticking your nose into this. I just want you to be safe; it's m-my job to worry about you."

Esper hesitates but eventually nods. I sigh in relief and let go of him. We walk back to the apartment, while all the while Esper manages to talk about everything and anything. Kids. I remember a time when my biggest concern was whether I'd be going to someone's birthday party next month. What are we supposed to do now? I can't get Mr. Larkin's suggestion out of my head: apprenticeship.

Apprenticeships are the one thing I've been trying to keep Esper away from. He seems too young, though he's twelve, the recommended age. There aren't many jobs open for folks in apprenticeships. It's usually unpaid laboring work that'll have him stuck in a canning factory for the rest of his life, or worse.

I only took up apprenticing because I needed the money. I was lucky enough to be offered a position by Mr. Connolly, who used to hire my father for engineering work. I want to avoid that for Esper. He deserves more than working long hours 24/8 for little coin.

When we get to our apartment, Esper is eager to run ahead. The building is overcrowded, even more so since the skyline expansion, and it's always loud, no matter where you stand, indoors or out. A couple is arguing in Qalqora on the ground floor, and the farther up the staircase we trudge, the quieter they get, replaced by a woman singing in a language I don't recognize. The singing comes from my space, of course. It looks like someone has finally taken up the other room in the apartment. When I open the door, she's standing in front of a group of chairs pushed together in a makeshift couch, entertaining the Cavicks family, who live the room over from ours. The walls are peeling, and one of the water stains seems to have expanded right into the doorway of my room.

The room to the right is mine and Esper's. It's cramped, but we make it work. There's not much space to even hold our bunk bed or much else. The suitcases we had piled up as a dresser have been tossed aside— I'm sure I have Esper to thank— and I can only groan as I take in the sight. Esper grabs our radio and climbs up on the top bunk to listen.

Now that we're home, I'm hit with a wave of exhaustion. Today has been... a lot. Taking a small nap wouldn't be the end of the world. I'll sleep for an hour, make sure Esper eats something, then look at the heater in the main room. Maybe once everyone is asleep, I'll take another look at my older blueprints; I won't be bothered in the wee hours of the morning.

The radio announces trade negotiations between Sertalis and Lanrell and the continued expansion of the skylines. The king's son is meeting with Parvay tomorrow to start taking his father's place. Market prices have increased. There's no mention of the riots taking place over the skylines, or the Qorani slowly being forced out of Wellwick.

Everything's fine.

CHAPTER 2

As it turns out, the shop being closed all day wasn't a big concern for Mr. Connolly. I had expected some yelling, but he only waved it off, muttering that I ought to have known better. Somehow, hearing that was worse than getting my pay docked. Now, it seems, being a disappointment has been added more frequently to my reserve of nightmares, at least in the past few days since that incident at the shop.

I rarely sleep these days. Partly because it feels like a waste of time, and partly because my subconscious is out to get me. Most of my dreams are stress-fueled: Esper being taken away, losing my hearing entirely, forgetting how to use a wrench... I've woken up in a cold sweat over too many work-related nightmares. I wouldn't call myself an insomniac— it's just become routine that even when I do manage to knock out for a few hours, I end up regretting the time I've lost. It makes more sense to do something productive rather than wake in a cold sweat from a nightmare where I mop the shop's floor with shoe polish.

The lack of sleep catches up with me now and again. Every other month, I can drift off anywhere if I'm comfortable enough. More than once, I've gone narcoleptic just sitting in front of the heater, surrounded by sketches and bits of metal.

When I open my eyes, the oldest Cavick boy is standing near me, holding two mugs of qosa. I sit up, stretching my back with a couple cracks, and look over at him, adjusting my audancers and trying not to groan at the pain in my stiff neck.

He thrusts the cup toward me, sleep hanging heavy on his eyes, and as thick in his throat as his rich accent. "Aqiil ĕnem?" As soon as the words leave his mouth, he shakes his head and coughs, with a quick "sorry" in Ingwell.

There's no reason for him to be ashamed. For as long as I've lived here and known the Cavicks, they've all relied heavily on Qalqora. A lot of Qorani live here, especially after Qorar's colonization thirty years ago, and often they speak at least some of the language, whether they're first generation or second. We always used to converse in Qalqora— with what I still remembered— and I would translate for Esper, who's never had any interest in learning.

I want to tell him it's okay, but I know why he's balking. He's about fourteen and is finishing up his apprenticeship. More likely than not, his employer has started getting on his case for Ingwell not being his first language. There's probably pressure on him to not respond automatically in Qalqora.

So I just nod and thank him, then bring the mug to my lips. I take a long swig and hold back the urge to gag. It tastes like iron. There's an orange tinge to this qosa, and the consistency is nearing molasses.

He used the water from the kitchen.

The batch is practically ruined, but I rub my face and decide I'll still get use out of it. No one with functioning taste buds should drink this swill. Lucky for me, living off qosa half-killed my taste buds years ago.

Even though it's not my turn to make the qosa, I place my mug on the ground and head to my room. Finding one of the luggage cases with my junk, I pop open the latch and retrieve an insulated mug, qosa grounds, and a bottle of water. The rest of the spoiled batch goes straight into my mug, and the rest down the sink, but before the boy can complain, I dump out the old grounds and pour in my own.

"You ca–can't use that water," I explain.

"We have no containers." The boy turns on the faucet, which creaks loudly in complaint. "And no more qosa."

Deep chestnut water comes pouring out; after a few seconds it eases, turning more orange in color. My stomach hurts at the sight and the mug in my hand feels tainted. Still, I put it down on the counter and shut off the tap.

"We'll use mine."

"It is not enough." He shakes his head, and I sigh.

"It's just for you, right? Your mother is already g–gone for the day, isn't she?"

He hesitates. I grimace and empty the bottle of water into the pot, waiting for it to heat.

"You're still-still growing, you should drink clean water." I pause and look over at him, waiting for him to acknowledge me again, and offer a smile. "Thank you, though."

The idea to fill my mug was an awful one, I realize far too late. I've sacrificed my health to be nice to the Cavick kid. While I finish my qosa, I screw my eyes shut. The key is to not focus on the taste, and convince myself it's medicine to get me through the day. It coats my throat, the taste of iron and blood lingering in my mouth.

I finish making the qosa for him and dump out his old cup, rinsing it out with some excess hot water. He takes the cup and smiles before returning to his room. The moment the door closes, I dump out my mug with a sigh. There will be time to clean it out properly later.

It's only one day I'm cutting back on my qosa intake. It won't kill me. Probably.

Before I head out, I swap out my button-down for a cleaner one, and fold the dirty clothes, leaving them on the growing pile in one of our luggage cases. It's just a reminder that I'll need to do the laundry once I have the free time. I let out a heavy exhale and grip my necklace tightly for strength.

Esper is sound asleep, snoring loudly, and I ruffle his hair until his eyes ease open. With a yawn, he looks toward the window, scowling when he sees the sky is still dark.

"H-Hey. I'm heading out."

He grumbles in response and closes his eyes. "Y'didn't need to wake me up."

"Yes, I did." I shake his shoulder a little. "Come on, Esper. Ky-Kylir can't watch you today. You're coming in with m-me."

Esper huffs and sits up. His hair is an absolute mess. I frown and gently pat the top of my head to check my own. It seems fine. I tug the bottom of my shirt.

He rolls off his bed and lands on his feet. I eye the ladder he could have used, but shake my head and grab one of the few vests from my clothes.

"Mis' Connolly doesn't wan' me around!" Esper yawns.

"She's dead."

"Oh." He tugs his shirt off and starts rummaging through his bin. There's barely anything there, since everything he owns is dirty right now, but that doesn't bother him as he grabs from the laundry pile, sniffs one of his shirts, and then starts buttoning it. "I meant M'ster Connolly."

"He's d-dead, too, on the i-inside." Maybe I shouldn't have said that. I grab one of the neckties hanging around and put it on. Esper looks over and tilts his head, eyebrows raised, but keeps quiet as he grabs his boots.

Once upon a time, Esper used to ask almost every day why I'd wear boys' clothes if I'm a girl. It's not exactly abnormal, so I'd always answer that they were cheaper and easier to find, even if they were all too big for me. Everything I own is large, even years later, to the point I look like I'm drowning in my own clothing. The ties I could never explain, even to myself. Maybe they completed the look, maybe it was because at a glance I'd get mistaken for a boy, and it'd be easier to find clients. He doesn't ask anymore. Instead he focuses on the fact that his own clothes are either too big or too small, and his pants need to be sewn again. We both need newer clothes. Maybe with that extra money I received a few days ago from Hiero, we can splurge a little on a few expenses. Or, luxury of luxuries, on overdue rent.

Esper grabs an apple from our supplies and I take stock of our sparse rations and coupons with a sigh. Once again, I will be skipping breakfast and lunch.

When we leave the apartment and step foot outside, the sun is just beginning to rise. The deep blue of the night has started to fade into a warmer purple, and the moon is out of sight. Lampposts burn dimly, having lost their vibrant flames during the night. For a brief, fleeting moment, the world is quiet. A handful of laborers, mostly apprentices, shuffle along the streets half-awake. Esper rouses slowly, block by block. By the halfway mark, he's wide-eyed and chattering away about anything and everything. If I didn't know better, I'd wonder if he had any qosa this morning.

I hate to admit it, but it's hard for me to share his enthusiasm when he gets this talkative. I care about what goes on in his life, but I'm more concerned with the chilly weather, and just how much farther we need to walk before we're indoors. Esper seems fine, even wearing just a threadbare shirt and no coat. Maybe it's about age, like getting older means getting colder. That would explain Mr. Connolly, at least.

There are a few lights inside the store. Mr. Connolly is stalking around as usual, double-checking everything with narrowed eyes. I've never understood his paranoia; it's like he's convinced someone will break in just to move his stock by a few centimeters. The door is still locked, as Esper finds out when he tugs it, but I'm already tapping against the glass. Mr. Connolly's head pops up, then he trudges his way over to let us in.

Esper races inside as soon as the door cracks open, shouting a greeting while tearing toward the back room. I shiver as the warmth of the shop thaws my cold bones. Dreggar, if it's this cold at the end of Hain, I don't know how Esper and I will survive Darin. Mr. Connolly scowls down at me, silently asking why my brother is breathing and existing in his precious store.

"Remember how I–I asked you earlier this week if Esper c–could come during o–one of my shifts?"

Mr. Connolly shakes his head and jerks a thumb over his shoulder. "Yeah. Make sure he stays in back."

I almost laugh. Keeping track of Esper and having him obedient are nearly impossible tasks.

Nodding, I run after Esper; he's sitting at the workbench, looking at the current blueprints. That's not what interests him, but the colored pencils we use for drafting them. He doesn't have to ask— I walk over and hand him three along with some scrap paper. His face brightens, even when I tousle his hair a bit, and I turn away to start organizing my things.

I've given up on the idea of Esper going down the engineering path like I have, or like my father did. Not that he shows an interest anyway. Technically what I do isn't engineering on the scale I'd like, but the repair work scratches the itch to design and build. If he were to do the exact thing I was, I'd be concerned. The last thing I want him to deal with are long hours of hard labor.

The thing is, he probably won't get a cushy job in an office now that he's been kicked out of another school. I get that schooling is meant to become more challenging with age, but I think if given the chance Esper could have done it. He just never applies himself, and gets bored easily. A lot of kids do, especially at his age. The thing is, it's either get educated for a job in a more professional field, or start apprenticing at twelve.

My circumstances were much different, and had I been given the chance, I would have stayed in school, not started working for Mr. Connolly at age eleven. He's a good man, though a bit crabby and sullen, and I could have had it much worse in terms of employers.

Sunlight creeps its way down the streets and through the windows. Mr. Connolly extinguishes the lamps, and we run over the list of clients who should be stopping by today. There's time before we open for business, so we can get to work on the junk in the workshop begging for repairs. One of the big-ticket items involves an engine for an equestrian automaton, used to pull some of the jitneys in place of pure steam.

The two of us head into the alley out back with the box of pieces; Mr. Connolly took it apart so he could store it inside and not have to worry about someone swiping the thing while it was chained out overnight. After some assembly and a diagnostic check, Mr. Connolly locates the source of the problem: a few loose cogs and an issue with the wiring. We finish right before the store is meant to open. Mr. Connolly goes back inside to unlock the doors while I hitch the automaton to one of the pipes along the alleyway.

It's a normal day, and moves quickly, but as the time ticks by, I start checking the door.

It feels like my encounter with Hiero was only yesterday. I should be able to let go of the incident, forget about it entirely, tell myself she won't come back to the shop and move on. She paid me for helping her out, and her promise of more was clearly an empty one. And yet, around five every day, I glance out the window and wonder if she will pop by. She has no reason to, and I have no reason to expect her to, but still, I watch and wonder.

"Artem," Mr. Connolly calls. "I'm not paying you to fall asleep."

His voice snaps me back into focus. I've been doing my usual sweeping and mopping busy-work after the rush. At some point I must have stopped entirely. The realization burns my cheeks.

"Sorry!"

"Sorry doesn't keep an eye out on the horse," he drawls, waving away my apology. "Finish up and check on it. Client should be dropping by soon."

I shake my head and attempt to mop, only to find it's somehow dried out. Just how long was I daydreaming?

The mopping can be finished later, perhaps before we close. I head to the back to check on the automaton. It's still there; the cogs where its saddle fits turn, and a puff of steam escapes its long snout. I hear a shuffle, and turn my head, but find no one. Odd. I wonder if paranoia is a side effect of regularly replacing sleep with qosa.

Esper looks up from his current project when I come back in. He gave up sketching and coloring a while ago, and is now mashing spare pieces of scrap together to create some monstrosity. Earlier I caught him tossing rocks out back, trying to see if the automaton would respond. I had to shoo him inside and find something for him to do. The junk box was the only solution, and now I'm regretting that, too. Before I can chastise him, I'm distracted by a new voice up front.

Mr. Connolly is talking to someone. A visitor, maybe, inquiring about one of the engines that were brought in. But no, the tone seems... wrong. Mr. Connolly is being more terse than usual, and he's dropped his usual customer service voice entirely.

Despite my better judgment, I creep up to peer through the doorway. A bulky man with short silver-blond hair and bright gray eyes stands at the counter holding a hunk of battered metal. His jaw is crooked, and his nose has been broken at least once before. At a glance, he is possibly the most intimidating person I have met in my entire life, yet when he speaks, he sounds nothing but soft and good-natured. If I had to guess, I'd peg him as Dormyl, born and bred, especially based on his drawl.

"I'm only asking for a moment of your time, sir. Please."

Mr. Connolly shakes his head sharply, folding his arms. "You're having a moment right now."

"I'm here on behalf of Rhine Toberts, leader of the Airgon movement." He pauses to straighten his posture, hardly able to keep from smiling. "We're in need of a mechanic who's for the people, someone who understands the danger the skylines represent and wants to see them gone. I was told this would be the right place." This is most definitely not the

28

right place. I almost laugh, out of nervousness or the sheer absurdity of it all.

"Well, it's not." Mr. Connolly leans against the counter and lowers his voice. "I'm old. I can spot a rebellionist from a mile away. I knew before you stepped foot in here. You don't need to feed me that scrap."

"A rebel, sir?" the man corrects mildly. It only frustrates Mr. Connolly further.

"Rebel, rebellionist; anarchy, reforms. It doesn't matter what you call it, it's all the same." Mr. Connolly waves a hand dismissively and I creep closer. "When it comes down to it, the end of the day is what it is. A rebellion is a waste of time and a waste of lives."

"I'm sorry if I did something wrong," the man tries, but Mr. Connolly won't hear it.

"Walking in here was wrong."

"I thought that you—"

Mr. Connolly holds a hand up to cut him off. "Whatever you want, you're not getting. And whoever told you we're anarchists can go straight to Torny with your Toberts."

A muscle tics in the man's jaw, but he doesn't argue further. Instead, he gently places the scrap heap onto the counter. Mr. Connolly pushes it away.

"You heard me. You're not getting any service from me."

He pushes the metal back toward Mr. Connolly with one hand, expression more hurt than anything. "Forget what I said about that. Completely separate. I need this radio looked at for my friend. You're the only place in town that works quick and does a good job for cheap."

"Cheap" was probably the worst word the man could use.

I hiss under my breath as Mr. Connolly goes an apoplectic shade of red. "I want you and your rebel ass out of my store!"

His voice booms a bit louder than what was probably intended. Esper pipes up suddenly, from where he's crept up behind me. "What's going on?"

With a surprised yip, I lose my footing, catching myself against the wall with a loud smacking noise. Both heads spin in my direction. Esper gasps and dives back into the workshop. Sheepishly, I glance upward at Mr. Connolly. Caught red-handed. Rubbing at the back of my neck, I try to find the words to apologize, but my vocal chords refuse to cooperate.

"Artem, get back to work."

I bite my lip and turn my gaze between the two, every nerve tight with hesitation. But I've very clearly been dismissed. Turning around, I start heading back to the junk box when the visitor calls out to me. "If he's not willing to help me out, you are, right? My friend said this shop was ally territory."

I freeze. Danger. Danger. Mr. Connolly's gaze is a balistir being loaded and aimed. Mortified doesn't even come close to how I feel right now.

"Artem?" Mr. Connolly crosses his arms, scowling. "What's he talking about?"

"We're Par–Par–Parvay owned," I answer meekly, dropping my gaze.

The man's face falls, but he doesn't argue. "Oh." He picks up his hunk of metal and places a bag of coin on the counter. "Either way, I was told to leave this here, so this is yours now."

The sheer amount of change in the coin purse catches my eye. Either all of the rebels are carrying around insane amounts of copper pieces, or this man didn't come here by himself.

"W–Wait." Could I be right? "Wait!"

I take a few steps forward and grab ahold of the man's sleeve. He turns, surprised and confused, but patient. I immediately let go and look away, feeling foolish for reaching out.

"I, um... Hi–Hiero." I swallow thickly and glance back up at him. "Do you know Hiero?"

His gray eyes brighten, and he gives me a large grin, showcasing the gap between his front teeth. It reminds me of Esper's; is it a common trait for folks from Dormyl? Somehow, it's calming, and makes him look like a giant kid.

"I knew you were part of the alliance!" His voice gets louder in excitement. "So this was all a test?"

"No." Mr. Connolly interrupts loudly. "Artem?"

Oh, no no no. This is exactly what I didn't want to happen. I open my mouth to explain his words away, but the visitor cuts me off.

"Hiero sent me in here! She told me there'd be a girl here— that must have been you. She's outside but told me she had something she needed to take care of."

A finger of cold runs down my spine. The automaton. Mr. Connolly shouts out for me as I sprint past him. Esper is at my heels as I burst through the door.

It's gone. There's no metal horse waiting here, only a chain and an open lock. I cover my mouth with trembling hands. My brother just whistles. "What happened?"

Mr. Connolly's all-too-level voice calling my name chills me to the bone. I turn around. He's standing by the threshold to the back room, expression hard.

"I... I–I didn't..." I bite my lip. "What w–will we—?"

"I'm going to say it was unsalvageable." Mr. Connolly jerks his thumb over his shoulder, at the counter. "And that coin is going to buy the client a new one."

I shift my weight from one foot to the other, then walk back to the front, where the man still stands, smiling away, as if oblivious to what's going on. Maybe he really doesn't know. But there must be a reason he's in here, and if Hiero is waiting outside...

I gesture the man toward the door. He obeys and hangs a left, just as Mr. Connolly stalks up from the back. I spin to face him, shaking hands tightly clasped before me. "Mr. Connolly, I'll work o–off book to pay off—!"

"You don't work here." I flinch back at the venom in his voice, heart stuttering to a stop.

"But I—!"

"I've put up with you for so long, and you're gonna bring these degenerates into my shop? Get mixed up with those rousers?" He growls. "Have you been stealing from me?"

"Ne–Never!" I don't know what hurts more: the typist accusation or where this is leading.

"She hasn't taken anything! Half the time she's losing stuff here!" Esper interjects. I slap a hand over my mouth to keep from shouting anything out.

Mr. Connolly doesn't say another word, only points, stone-faced, to the exit. I take a deep breath, then put a hand on Esper's back.

"C'mon." I keep my head down. The two of us leave the shop.

The big man stands paces from the storefront, talking to a familiar blonde, the one whose face I've been searching for in every customer, every passerby. Hiero. She has her hands on her hips and looks vaguely unimpressed as she scolds him.

"Vashtet, you weren't supposed to say anything about the shop being ally territory. Now, things are going to be harder for that poor girl."

"I didn't know," he half whines, shoulders slouching. "I thought that was common knowledge!"

"For us, not for them. People do things without realizing where they stand these days." She crosses her arms, mouth twisting.

"I guess it's too late for that now, huh?"

"A bit. Next time, Tristan, I'll do all the talking and you can make sure everything else goes smoothly."

Hiero spots me and smiles. If I didn't know any better, I'd take it at face value, but such thinking has lost me my job. I can practically feel smoke billowing from my mouth as I open it, ready to tell her off.

"It's been a while. Artem, was it?" Her voice is almost sing-song. She knows exactly what the problem is, yet maintains this facade of innocence.

"Yes." I shake my head. "What are you-you doing here? What the hell was that?"

"What was what?"

"The aut-aut-aut—" I squeeze my eyes shut and ball up my fists. "The horse! I kn-know you took it!"

"She did that?" Esper asks, tilting his head in confusion. Dreggar save me, I almost forgot he was here.

Hiero looks down at him, amused. "And you are?"

"No." I step between them and put an arm in front of Esper. "N–no, you owe me a–an ex-explanation! I–I thought you owed me one. What w–was that?"

Her smile wavers, and she looks between Tristan and Esper with the briefest of grimaces. I press my lips together, waiting.

Finally, she sighs, relaxing, and brings a hand to the ribbon holding her ponytail, retying it as she speaks. "We paid for it. The extra was meant for you. I didn't realize it wasn't your shop. I thought you were a young entrepreneur, owning your own establishment."

The sign out front clearly says "Connolly Repairs and Mechs". I want to argue, but it's pointless. All my words are pointless.

Esper is enchanted. He's hanging off every word that comes out of Hiero's mouth and watching Tristan with awe. He pushes past me, sending me off-balance, and I stumble to catch my footing as he bounces in front of them.

"Are you really with the rebellion? Is Artem helping you out?"

"I–I'm not," I respond.

"She might be," Hiero counters, with a flicker of a sly grin.

He doesn't need this sort of encouragement. Esper starts rattling out questions so fast I can't keep track. My mind is in a fog. I don't get why Hiero couldn't have come in herself to get the automaton if it was truly theirs, or where it could have disappeared to so fast.

Hiero sidles closer to me as the boys chat about the rebellion. I take a step back, but my legs wobble. I'm shaking, and I don't know if I'm more angry or anxious, but either way, I'm anything but stable. Hiero gets the message and hangs back, out of arm's reach. She clears her throat and looks around.

"W-What happened to the aut-automaton?"

"It's been intercepted. There were others besides me and Tristan waiting around here," Hiero admits, tucking a strand of hair behind her ear. "I didn't want to go in and startle you. I figured Tristan would be the friendliest, and you wouldn't recognize him. He'd do his business, you'd get the rest of your money and the correct payment, this would all be a wash."

I want to believe her more than I can admit. She shouldn't be trusted. No one in the rebellion should be trusted. But she seems sincere, and while that's what may have gotten me here in the first place, it sounds logical enough.

A whimper leaves my throat and I do my best to focus on my breathing. Hiero is surprisingly patient, unlike most. Her feet are stationary, hands relaxed, and her expression doesn't show any hint of irritation.

With a heavy sigh, I shake my head.

"Inte-te-tentions or not, I'm out of a job."

Her eyes widen a fraction, but she nods her head sympathetically, pursing her lips. "That doesn't have to be the case."

"Why would I... why would I help you, when the-the last

time I helped, i-it led to, w-well," I gesture with my hands. "This! If I hadn't said anything, I would st-still have a job, I would have a st-steady income, I—!"

"—Would be miserable?" Hiero challenges.

I sputter. "What's m-miserable about ke-keeping a roof o-over my head?!"

"Not about that, about working there." Hiero's eyes narrow as she eyes me over, then clicks her tongue once she's reached her diagnosis. "You looked half-dead when I walked into that shop. You didn't like it there, not really, except for the actual repair work." It's a shot in the dark. There's no way she could actually know that.

But she's right. I don't like the shop all that much, but Mr. Connolly is one of the nicer employers I may ever find in my life, especially as an undocumented Qorani. I'm set back in terms of getting actual working papers, and at this point I doubt he would recommend me when I go through the official process.

Hiero softens up a little, glancing back at Esper and Tristan. I follow her gaze; Esper is dangling off Tristan's flexed bicep like it's a jungle gym. I can't begin to guess at why, but Tristan hardly seems bothered.

I puff out a breath of air, and Hiero slides her attention back to me. "You need to support him still, don't you? I bet I could easily find work for you doing something bigger, give you a chance to do something for yourself. All you need to do is come with us back to our headquarters. Not tonight, of course, but—"

"F-Fine," I answer.

Hiero blinks in mild surprise, but recovers quickly with

a pleased smile. "Then it's settled. I can meet you here tomorrow. But—" She pauses. "It might be best to leave your brother at home. At least for a first-time visit. Not that he wouldn't be welcome..."

"No, I–I get it. I d–don't want him in–involved in any of this." Esper starts running over. "Even if he w–would jump at the chance."

"Who would?" Esper asks, tilting his head.

"Nothing." I ruffle his hair. "L–Let's head home."

As we hurry away on the road toward our sector, Hiero murmurs something that I somehow only process once she's disappeared from sight.

"Tomorrow. Five o'clock."

CHAPTER 3

Most of the night is spent lying awake in bed trying to convince myself to sleep, but it's far easier to tell yourself to do something than to actually do it. Instead I just end up counting every rip and stain under Esper's cot. Every time I get close to nodding off, I wake back up as soon as he tosses around.

Nothing about this is new. I can pass out easily if I'm tired enough, but though I'm exhausted, my brain is wired. Today plays over and over in my mind; I keep imagining Mr. Connolly lurking in the corner. He stands with his arms folded, scoffing at the plainness of the dark room and lack of tools strewn about.

"How long have you been stealing from me?" he sneers, and tilts his head, narrowing his eyes. "How long?"

The sick feeling from before washes over me again, creeping through my veins. There always seems to be a draft in the room, but right now I'm feverish, restless. I kick off my blankets and slip out into the common space. There's no one else up. The mundanity of the space is comforting, and I try to ground myself in the familiar surroundings. The makeshift couch sits next to the woodstove, and the kitchen table stands alone in the dark, next to the oven and ramshackle cupboards. Mr. Connolly is not here. No one is here. For now, I'm alone.

Maybe it's because I'm trying to force myself to sleep when I would normally be up and already at the shop. Maybe if I start working on something, I'll gradually get tired and be able to fall asleep... yet I know without even trying that it won't work. Any tinkering is going to drive me batty, and I keep looping back over and over to the shop and Mr. Connolly and Hiero.

Taking one of the seats, I slump down, burying my head in my hands. Hiero is the last person I should be involved with. She's with the rebellion, she's cost me a job I've held for years, and all she does is talk circles around me. Yet, despite the alarm bells going off in my head, I can't help but want to help her.

And a job is a job. Right now, that's all I can ask for. I don't know how I feel about the rebellion, or any cause for that matter; I don't like change, and I don't like conflict. Tensions are causing enough friction as it is, and getting involved means putting a target on your back for procs. The bullseye painted on me is large and obnoxious as it is: I'm a Qorani woman who's attracted to other women (Dreggar,

39

not that I'd tell anyone that), and who regularly wears men's clothing. Things aren't looking the best for me. At least Roran will— hopefully—always be around to vouch for me and keep an eye on Esper.

Once my thoughts have run in circles long enough, my mind finally tires enough for me to drag myself back to bed. Sleep is still difficult to come by; I roll in and out, skimming consciousness. Soon it becomes too much, and my eyelids grow heavy. But I am not tired enough for a dreamless sleep.

I'm in the workspace of Mr. Connolly's shop, but something doesn't feel right. The lighting is pink, but that's not the problem. Maybe it's that the floor is sideways, or that there's nothing out the back door but a hungry, watchful void. The vents on my audancers open and close with sharp snaps, and a wrench shifts uncomfortably on a table mosaiced with a thousand different nightmares.

The floor writhes in protest. I'm cast into the air; the only thing keeping me from floating away is a heavy work-table. At some point the windows have vanished, leaving nothing but a lamp, flickering with the threat of darkness. The walls sprout a panoply of gears, each rotating in a different direction. The void outside swallows the back door whole, but at the front of the shop shines an orange light. I swim toward it, when gravity suddenly increases once more and I walk through the doorway. The table, abandoned, clangs to the floor and breaks into pieces.

My feet skate across the hardwood. It is no longer a shop but an aerocraft's cabin. Huge and close is an equine automaton, half the size of the room. It whinnies, the loud shriek of a whistle from a qosa kettle, yet the smoke from its nostrils reeks of colfe. My knees knock together as it stares at me, eyes glowing red, and I stumble back to the other room.

The table has reassembled itself. Esper sits on top, swinging his legs back and forth. A girl from my schooling days sits next to him. I stand trying to decide what to say. I want to tell her about the crush I had on her, then remember I already did. The girl sifts through some tools and picks up the wrench, but it melts away in her hand, along with all the others. Only the key from my necklace remains, and she scowls at it accusingly.

The girl looks at me with scorn. Were her eyes always green? Her mouth doesn't move, but her voice echoes from all around me. "Disgusting. Freak." Her voice doubles, triples, multiplies a thousandfold, until I'm surrounded by an army of shadowy figures, all spitting their disgust. They start to move in closer and closer, but before I can run, Esper says it's raining. The ceiling opens and we are engulfed in orange and the taste of blood.

There's a loud shriek of static and a charismatic voice booms into my audancers. I bolt up, banging my head on Esper's bunk. It doesn't hurt all that much, but I hiss and rub my forehead anyway, thumbing my audancers' knobs as I tumble out of bed.

"What time is–is it?" I ask, stretching. My heart is still racing from the dream, from the memory of my first confession... and the violence that followed. I breathe in deep to steady myself.

"Eleven."

I hum absently and eye our makeshift dresser, composed of old luggage casings. Laundry day.

My brother watches as I pool all the clothes together in a pile. The news station continues on the same talking points as yesterday, focusing on the expansion of the skylines. I pause and rest against the pile. "Can you change it?"

A click. Soothing music drifts from the speakers instead. I nod my approval and turn back to business.

It's not the cleanest method, but I suppose I could wash them by hand here. I turn to Esper. "You can ke-keep the radio on, but I'd appreciate your help."

He huffs but climbs down the ladder, then shuffles out of the room, coming back a minute later with a bucket full of clean water from our reserves. I crinkle my nose at the sight of the bagged water, mostly mourning that we could have used the drinking water for drinking, and Esper goes to repeat the process two more times. It doesn't take too long to wash the clothes and let them dry before moving onto the next bunch. By the fourth time through, everything is done. Problem solved. We won't have to worry about laundry for another two weeks.

"When are we going to see the rebels?" Esper asks.

"We?" I shake my head. "Y-You're not coming with m-me."

"Why not?"

"The l-last thing I want is for you to get in-involved with them."

"But that's what you're doing."

He has a point. My involvement, however, is only

temporary. I press my lips tightly together. "I–It's complicated."

Esper leaves it alone and goes back to his radio. Again, he switches it to the news rather than music or one of the story programs. It's his thing recently, and I don't quite understand it. Any news is fluff and half-truths. One time I witnessed a mob gathering in front of the skylines in protest. Procs were aiming balistirs at civilians and orders were given to smoke everyone out. Roran caught me before it got ugly and sent me home, but the radio made no mention of the incident. All that was on was the progress of the skylines, a development in Parvay, and a puff piece on how the king's youngest took his first steps.

"What's h–happening in the world t–today?" I wonder aloud, folding our shirts.

"Not much," Esper huffs. "There's nothing ever good."

I raise an eyebrow. "It's always good!" At least, according to everyone else. I think it's garbage, but it's all Esper will ever listen to, so he must like it a bit. I'd rather not ruin it for him if I don't have to.

"No." He flops onto his stomach. "It's always nice, but not really, you know? It only sounds good."

I don't really know what he means by that. "I sup–suppose."

The rest of my time I dedicate to cleaning our room. I rarely have the time to organize our belongings— what little we have— and do basic maintenance. It's decent-ish after some elbow grease. I don't know what Esper has managed to smudge against the windowsills and floor, but whatever it was is gone now.

I glance at the hunk of metal on the wall that serves as a

clock, gears grinding as the minute hand turns. It's almost four-thirty now. I need to head out. As I straighten my clothes, I debate borrowing Esper's jacket. We're not all that different in size, and if it's swimming on him it'd probably fit me okay. But it's not worth it. Better to get used to the cold now than later.

Esper looks up as I pat my pockets to make sure my keys are there. "You heading out?" I nod and he shrugs. "Okay. Tell them I said hi."

I almost tell him that's silly and childish. No one would know who Esper was other than Hiero— and perhaps that man, whose name I can't remember— nor would they care. Instead, I give a wordless wave and head out.

The streets are barren. I'm used to some folks shuffling through the waxing dawn, half-dead until their first mug of qosa kicks in. Now it's empty, save for small groups of people here and there, rushing about with heads bowed against the freezing wind.

"Spare any coin?" a man calls out. "Simple guy down on his luck."

He holds a sign reading "Homeless Allowyn Needing Help" in ink. The specification doesn't seem necessary, but I know why it's there. To separate him from those "other" homeless, from Lanrell or perhaps Qorar. I don't know how long he's been here, but he's got more coin in his collection tin than I have in my coin purse on a good day.

"Sorry, I can't," I mumble, and keep my head down.

It's quick, and biting, and hardly surprising: "Figures. Quarterling."

I wince but keep going. No one else harasses me, but

no one jumps to my defense either. Everyone is engaged in more pressing conversation, or in making their way to warmer locales.

When I get to the meeting spot, the main street is empty. Everyone is inside, busy with their work and getting ready to leave for the day. The closer I get to Mr. Connolly's shop, the more my chest aches. I duck my head and hunch my shoulders as I pass. There's a part of me that wants to look in, try to explain the misunderstandings and grovel for mercy. Another part of me is curious if he already has another Qorani working cheaper than I was. It's unlikely, though. It's been less than twenty-four hours, and Mr. Connolly was never the sort to actively seek out apprentices, or any company at all. He's a stubborn man, and I've always sworn the only reason he hired me in the first place was out of pity.

It hurts to think about. It wasn't the best, but it was familiar, reliable. I enjoyed having a space I could work in, a place I could improve what skill in tinkering I have. Now that opportunity is gone.

Hiero strolls into view from one of the smaller alleyways. There's no one with her this time, and she seems a little uneasy. I don't think she's used to being alone. She tips her head up briefly in greeting, keeping her hands in her pockets. Before I can speak, she motions for me to follow, and heads further down the street. I follow, mind buzzing with questions.

"What projects have you worked on before?" she asks abruptly.

"What do y–you mean?"

"I mean," Hiero turns her head to look down at me

without breaking pace. "Welcome to the job interview. You ought to have done something that stands out. What projects have you worked on before?"

I stare blankly ahead trying to recall everything I've ever done. A lot of my past experience is helping Mr. Connolly with things, and doing basic repair tasks by myself. "I guess I helped wi–with the skylines,"—sort of— "D–Designing the engine. I've repaired jitneys and aut–automatons, heaters, radios, a–anything I can get my hands on, I guess."

My hand drifts toward one of my audancers out of habit. Hiero hums in approval and leaves the conversation there. After another block, I can't stay quiet any longer. "W–Where are we going?"

"To grab a drink."

I'm uncomfortable at best. We agreed to meet up so that I would meet the folks in this rebellion and secure myself a new job. No one said anything about drinking.

I clear my throat, fidgeting with my hands as I speak. "I'm n–not old enough to d–drink."

Hiero looks back over her shoulder and flashes a grin. "It's a silly rule, isn't it? You're considered an adult at seventeen, yet you're not allowed to touch a drop of anything distilled until twenty. It almost sounds like an excuse."

"An e–excuse for what?"

"A lot of things."

I don't press her about it. What am I supposed to do at a pub I shouldn't be inside? I suppose I could sit there while Hiero gets something. That wasn't the deal, though. The thought sours on my tongue.

Sure enough, she stops in front of a tiny pub sandwiched

between an oversized bank and a bookstore. She holds the door open for me and waits. There's no point in arguing, and while Hiero doesn't strike me as the type to back out of a deal, I don't want to risk it. I need this job. With a deep breath, I step around her and head inside.

If it looked cramped from the outside, it's even worse in actuality. A few booths are set up, and a bar no bigger than a workbench and a half. The bartender looks bored as he wipes a glass clean. As we step through the door, everyone inside, all paired or in a small group, turns their heads toward us.

Hiero glides by me. She's waltzing in like she's the owner of the place, and she might as well be with all the nods in her direction. At the counter, she taps on the wood twice with her middle finger and lowers her voice.

"I'll have a bait and switch." The corner of her mouth twitches up and she leans against the bar, locking eyes with the bartender. "Better make it two."

"I don't drink," I repeat lamely. The bartender lifts the divider up and motions with his head toward the register.

"You do now." Hiero pats my cheek and strolls into the space behind the bar.

I'm confused and wary. Despite my conscience and better judgment tugging at me to turn around, I go after her. The bartender shuts the divider behind me. Hiero opens the cash register, rifling around. With a click, the shelves begin to trundle aside, revealing a hatch in the floor about the size of a window. Metal churns against metal as everything shifts into place, until the hatch flips up. The crawlspace is large enough to squeeze through; some light flickers from below.

Hiero drops into a crouch and slides through, feet thudding against the bottom. She peers up at me through the hole, raising an eyebrow in question. I glance back at the bartender— he just seems annoyed I'm still standing around.

No one in the pub even looks up from their carefully sipped-at drinks. How long has this been going on? Is this even a real bar or just a front? Why haven't the procs caught onto this place?

Now isn't the time for questions, though. I grimace and sit down, then scoot myself through the hole, wishing for a fraction of Hiero's easy athleticism.

It's a short drop, enough to startle me. Hiero waits for me to dust my shirt off, then reaches up to tug at a handle on the underside of the hatch. It slams closed, and then it's just the two of us alone in the tunnel.

There's enough light to make out where we are. A lamp half-built into the wall flickers ahead, and another shines even further along. Once we move out from the cramped space beneath the hatch, the tunnel system is spacious, so much so that I don't need to slouch, though I couldn't say the same for someone much taller than me. There are no other passages, nothing behind us except a wall of hard-packed dirt, meaning there is only one way to go.

"Where e-exactly—?"

I'm cut off with a low hush. "Not here," Hiero warns in a whisper. "Wait."

I've heard stories since childhood of a series of tunnels underground. The rumor goes that one of the kings from long ago had a bunker built under the city, complete with secret tunnels and passageways that stretched for thousands of meters. It was pure paranoia; he was convinced Allowyn would be attacked by any and all of our neighboring countries. After he died, it was said the whole structure was filled with cement and left to be forgotten.

I never questioned the story, and as far as anyone knew that's all it was: made-up nonsense. No one believed anyone could travel beneath the city, except the few desperate enough to hide from procs in the sewers. People stopped doing that, too, once the sewers were bugged with filographs.

It surprises me that no one has gone looking for the tunnels underground, to see if the stories were true. Does that mean we're heading toward the bunker?

The path gradually descends in zigzagging, sharp turns, eventually merging with another, which snakes out of the dark underground to places unknown. Eventually, muffled sounds pick up from somewhere ahead. We stop in front of a circular metal door, a gear-shaped wheel welded to its center.

"This is it." Hiero gives the wheel a turn, and after a series of heavy clunks, the door swings out. A few steps lead down to an iron walkway, which hugs the walls above an expansive hangar. Below, hundreds of people weave to and fro between rooms, carrying various boxes and supplies. The walkway on the far wall is a mirror of this one, with another vault-like door and a staircase spiraling to ground level. The ceiling is gleaming silver, spanned by two hinged panels about the size of a factory.

In the middle of the space sits the half-finished skeleton of a gigantic craft, roughly half the hangar's width. It's about an arm's-length smaller than a lepel, about the size of seven apartment buildings squished together. I've never seen an airship, or any aerocraft, in person, but I'd bet my right arm that's what's being built.

There are no words. All I can do is stumble forward, taking in the view as I grip onto the railing. Hiero stands beside me and crosses her arms.

"It's amazing," I breathe.

"Rhine certainly cleaned up the place." Hiero leans against the railing, one eyebrow raised as her gaze roves over the bunker. "To think, Allowyn had this hiding under Wellwick for years, and no one ever did anything with it."

"How c–could anyone forget about a bunker?"

"Your guess is as good as mine."

I step away and look to Hiero expectantly; she seems lost in thought. From somewhere nearby comes the sound of raised voices, followed by the shattering of glass. Hiero's attention flits from the airship to a room farther down the walkway, and my gaze follows hers. A woman runs out with a quick, irritated laugh as she fixes her ponytail. A similar woman, slightly shorter, follows behind, clutching a clipboard she looks prepared to use as a weapon.

"Christa, get back here!" the shorter one hisses, her voice strained.

"Last I checked, I didn't need a shot of anything other than knackle!" the other snorts.

"So help me, you will be vaccinated."

They could almost be identical. Both have the typical Qorani golden eyes with tan-brown skin, combined with small noses and a dusting of freckles along their cheeks and nose. The shorter woman sports a braid and has a rounder face with sharp features, while the other has fewer curves and more angles.

Spotting Hiero, the retreating woman—Christa?—makes her way toward us, barely glancing in my direction.

"Hey Hiero, mind reminding Runa who got injured during the last protest?" Christa asks, trying to goad a look from the other woman. She doesn't succeed.

"Need I remind you who's older?" Runa strides over, her shoulders pulled back, square and stiff. "I'm sure she's got plenty of other things to do. Not everyone has time to be dragged into your melodramatics."

Christa sticks out her tongue at her sister, and from the same room steps another woman, with vibrant dark red hair. Her every movement is precise, like a step of a dance. Part of me wants to stare, entranced by her beauty, the way I might feel transfixed watching a candle's flame. I'm immediately convinced she could eat me alive.

"A shot's going to keep you from needing a leg amputated the next time you nick yourself on a rusty nail," Runa scolds Christa, scowling as she hugs the clipboard to her chest. "Who's this?" She tilts her head up, the first to acknowledge my presence.

"Yeah, who's the ulqĕluni?" Christa asks.

It's weird hearing the Qalqora word come out so unpracticed and butchered from a Qorani mouth, but I can still make it out. I wince slightly, the word biting even if no one else would know why. It's a term thrown around between those that are Qorani towards someone who looks different. It would be impossible to explain to someone who didn't speak the language the meaning behind it.

"Christa," Runa warns.

"What? It's not like I called her ralvit."

The conversation goes over everyone else's heads, and we fall into awkward silence. I have yet to give my name.

"Artem," Hiero answers for me, and gestures to each of them in turn. "Christa, Runa, and Aether."

The fiery-haired woman— Aether— scowls at Hiero. "Does she not have a tongue? She can speak for herself, I'm sure."

Hiero says nothing, only narrows her eyes. I glance between her and Aether. There's something I'm missing here. Clearly these two have a history.

Runa takes the opportunity to grab Christa's bare arm and stick her with a needle. Christa yelps and shoots her sister a look of betrayed horror. Runa's work is quick and she has a bandage on Christa before she can complain.

"Isn't that unethical? Breach of trust?" Christa asks with a hiss, rubbing her arm. "Last I checked, family can't stick family with that junk."

"You deserve it." Runa's reply is clipped as she steps closer to force Hiero and Aether to make room. "Artem, was it? I'm Runa; I work in the medical ward, just over there." Her handshake is brisk and firm. Christa just gives a nod and half-sheepish grin toward me, then tugs at Aether's arm.

"Christa— I'd stick around, but I need to take care of some stuff, and get far away from this psycho..." Aether murmurs something under her breath and Christa snorts and heads for the stairway.

Too many names and people. My head is swarming with it all. As if sensing my discomfort, Hiero gives my arm a slight nudge. "There will be plenty of time to meet everyone around here."

Aether gives a sharp whistle and Hiero freezes. Slowly she turns her head toward Aether, expression impossible to read. Despite her fiery persona, the air seems to have chilled, and it feels too thick to breathe.

Aether's blue gaze is freezing cold, and so is the small, dangerous smile that tugs at her lips. Her voice is pure velvet. "I was under the impression this was a secret organization... But I'm sure Rhine will be pleased to hear you've moved from petty theft to insubordination."

With a flick of her hair, she strolls off in the same direction as Christa, and with her, like the dark, heavy clouds of a thunderstorm rolling toward the far horizon, goes the frigid tension. I look at Hiero— she's scowling into the middle distance. "Tesht," she growls under her breath. Runa sighs and shakes her head.

I'm not entirely sure what to make of Aether or Christa. Hiero has already made her way further down the walkway, and as I go to follow, Runa calls my name. I pause and look back as she clutches her clipboard.

"I know dehydration and sleep deprivation when I see it." She grimaces as she jots down a couple notes, then stares at me thoughtfully for a good moment. "Don't overwork yourself, especially not for Hiero." I can barely process that; I just nod and make my escape. The smell of oil clogs my nostrils as I take a deep breath.

This whole time I've moved barely three meters on this walkway. I have no idea what I'm supposed to be doing.

Will I be working with the airship? I just hope I don't have to construct weapons.

I scramble to catch up with Hiero, but she's already stopped to lean on the railing and wait for me. "So, what ex–exactly did you want me to fix?"

"About that..." Hiero trails her gaze across the spacious hangar below, the fingers of her left hand dancing along the rail. "It's more about breaking and then fixing."

I blink a couple times, not sure if I heard her right. "B–Breaking? That wasn't w–what you told me. I–I'm a fixer, n–not a breaker. Why w–would I need to break s–something?"

"Revolutions aren't exactly funded by the bourgeoisie. Of course, we have some members of Parvay looking to overhaul the king, but there's only so much that can be donated without arousing suspicions."

She's dancing around my question. And so effectively, I almost forget what the question was. "What do you mean?"

She slants a look over to me. "Let me level with you: Rhine's looking for mechanics. Not everyone can waltz in paperless and on word alone."

"I sup–suppose." It feels rather obvious when she states it aloud. My cheeks heat up.

"You need to prove your worth."

"A–And how would I do that?"

This time the look she slants me comes paired with a grin. "You're going to disable the skylines. Temporarily, at least."

Just the thought makes my head spin. The skylines are huge, used daily by thousands of people, stiff-collars and dirt-collars alike. With airships even more elite and pricey, practically everyone who can afford it uses the skyline, especially when traveling between regions.

I shake my head so fast I get dizzy. "I c–can't do that."

Hiero feigns surprise but just looks amused. "You mentioned working on them before. Unless you were lying...."

"I–I helped Miste— I helped m–my boss with plans for them," I answer too quickly. "I–I've never actually worked w–with any of the skylines hands-on!"

"That's more than anyone else could say!" She crosses her arms and looks down at me. I shrink, overwhelmed, and step closer to the railing.

"I never agreed to... this."

"Didn't you?"

"No!" I cry out. "I d–don't even want t–to be here, to be a–a–a part of t–this, to—"

"—Get involved in a revolution?" Hiero pauses, tipping her head and pressing a finger to her pouting lips. "You did the day you lied to that proc."

Everything about this is messed up. Back at the shop, I did what I felt was right. More often than not, procs abuse their power. At the time I was trying to avoid getting involved in a proc brutality case. I knew Hiero may not have been innocent, but she seemed to have her reasons. I just wanted to help. I never thought it would lead to this.

"I lost my–my job because I h–helped you. You s–said you could get me a n–new one."

"And I will. First we need to build up your reputation."

I'm at a loss for words. Hiero holds up her hands in defense and nods. "Confrontation isn't your thing. I get it. Consider this: you're not only helping get rid of the skylines, but I'm paying you to do so. All you need to do, with what you know about them, is shut one of the carriages down. That's all."

"That's all?"

Hiero hums. "That's all." Her left arm stretches out, hand open and waiting. "Do we have a deal?"

Every part of me is saying to turn this down— the risk and probability of failure are only the first dangers that come to mind. Having my reputation intact is one thing, but if something were to go wrong— if anything were to happen to me— it would affect Esper.

As it is, I don't know how much I can expect from Hiero, or from anyone in the rebellion. The people I've met have been nice— mostly— but kind words and a smile don't speak for reliability. There's no reason for Hiero to help me other than that I helped her. Not many people still operate under a code of repaying debts.

Despite my reservations, I reach forward and shake her gloved hand awkwardly with my own. Her grip is firm, and warm, despite the chill in the hangar. Any words die in my throat as I look up at her. Her expression has brightened, her lips curled into a slight but genuine smile. For the life of me, I can't let go; I just stare dumbly into her eyes. The whirring in my ears is no match for the pounding in my chest.

"North Ayn Station. Three days. Four in the evening. Bring whatever tools can fit in your pocket easily. Is it correct to assume you need an exit visa?"

I blink slowly as she releases my hand. My arm hangs frozen in the air as I process the question.

"A fake one, to be clear."

Oh.

"Yes." My eyebrows knit together in thought. "I don't even h–have normal exit papers."

"I figured as much. You'll have something easy to pronounce, just make sure you memorize the name and birthdate on it in case it comes up. Until then."

"Yeah," I breathe.

Hiero's eyebrows and the corners of her mouth twitch up briefly in amusement, but without sparing another second on pleasantries, she leaves. Her blonde ponytail swishes out of view, and I collapse back, huffing and puffing like I've just run a lap around the hangar. A polite cough from behind turns my head.

Runa stands in the doorway of the medical office as a passing doctor hands her a stack of paperwork. She catches my eye and gestures with her head and a twirled finger. She's clearly caught me staring. My face feels hot, and it only burns worse with the look Runa gives me before retiring back to the office.

How long was she standing there? Why? Maybe Runa is more concerned for my health than she was letting on. Or she's as curious about me as I am her. Runa is the type of person I would want to be friends with, if I had any, and it's refreshing to meet a Qorani who doesn't judge my accent.

"North Ayn Station." The walkway is deserted, so I don't feel as ridiculous for talking to myself. "F–Four at night. Three days." I head toward the exit, repeating the instructions mentally, as if they were a chant or a prayer.

Initially, I get lost. I stand where the tunnels split, not sure which way I came from. Before I can work myself into a panic, I hear someone coming from the right. A scrawny man with large eyes stops short when he spots me, blinking a few times as he looks me up and down.

"Which w–way to the bar?" I ask, clearing my throat. It comes out squeaky regardless.

"Head down that way, all the way to the end," he says, jamming a thumb at the tunnel behind him, and I hurry past with a rushed, "Th–Thank you!"

When I make it back to the apartment, Esper is asleep beside the furnace in the main room. I watch him for a few moments, debating the best way to rouse him and get him in an actual bed. I settle for crouching beside him and ruffling his hair. He rises with a sleepy grumble, tottering back to our room, hoisting himself up the ladder and flopping into bed. The moment his head hits the pillow he's out again, and I'm left alone with my thoughts. North Ayn Station, four at night, in three days. That's not nearly enough time to prepare.

CHAPTER 4

Two years ago, they shut down the old train system. In Allowyn's largest congression in history, hundreds gathered outside the Parvay building in favor of renovating the tunnels. Regardless, the nobility and church made the final decision to create the skylines. All of the railroad tunnels leading to the underground were sealed up, the ones closer to the richer sectors filled in with cement.

I'm not sure why such a reliable form of transport was discarded. We already had airships, which were and still are the most pricey but fantastic way to travel. With the motion to abolish trains, use of airships was restricted to the cities farther north and as a private service to the palace. Then the skylines went up.

I clutch the exit visa in my pocket to ensure it's still there, like letting go might make it disappear. My fingertips run along the thick, folded paper and over the slight embossment of the "official" seal. I have no idea how Hiero managed to get her hands on the most legitimate-looking documents I have ever seen in my life. They're nearly identical to ones Roran once showed me.

Hiero remains calm and collected. She walks casually and with such a sense of purpose that one would assume she works at the station herself. Her head is raised high as she scans the platforms ahead, a shadow of a smirk on her lips. "Try to relax."

"Relax?" I can feel my eyes bug at the mere suggestion. I've never been relaxed in my life, I nearly say, instead sputtering a half-hysterical, "I–I've never been on–on the skyline before, and–and–and you're telling m–me I–!"

"Yes," Hiero doesn't even glance in my direction as she turns a corner, steering me with a tug at my sleeve. "You're too tense. You're going to raise flags."

Relaxing isn't that easy, at least not for me. Especially with her hand so close to mine. Knowing my papers are illegitimate would keep me on edge even sleeping in my apartment. We are about to board the skyline, one of the most regulated transport systems, and all of my documents are forged. If by some chance I run into Roran here while he's on duty, I could wind up in jail or worse. Then who would take care of Esper?

I try my best to be mindful of my breathing and posture; it feels weird to stand upright instead of slouching. I must not look all that natural, as Hiero turns ever-so-slightly to look at me with raised eyebrows. My head snaps forward, my jaw tightening reflexively, and I can feel my cheeks begin to puff out. Out of the corner of my eye her expression shifts to one of amusement before she shakes her head and sighs softly.

If I'm being graded on professionalism, I'm not getting paid today.

"You–You nev–never said anything a–about being on the skyline while we're stopping it!" I try the best I can to keep my voice low.

She tsks. "We're not stopping it in the middle of the track, if that's what you're wondering."

"Then why aren't we disabling it here, wh–while it's already stopped for loading?"

"Because." Hiero tugs on my arm to draw me closer as her voice drops to a whisper. It's hard to concentrate as she invades my space; goosebumps spring up along my neck as her breath ghosts my skin. "It's too obvious. We need to be able to walk away when it's done, not walk on just to walk off. Understand?"

I don't, but I nod anyway. My concern is getting back after, assuming there aren't filographs set up in every carriage to monitor these kinds of activities. There weren't any in the blueprints Mr. Connolly showed me, but we were only tasked with fixing the engine and operating system. Once it was functioning, Parvay could have added anything they like, and I wouldn't be surprised if that included extra security measures, especially with the growing unrest.

A distinctive three-tone chime sounds through the station, followed by a far-too-upbeat masculine voice announcing the arrival of the blue track. Hiero's pace quickens. I stumble trying to match it, clearing my throat as the blood rushes to my face.

The routes, according to Hiero, are organized by color names. Certain tracks are restricted by collar-worker type: dirt-collar, stiff-collar, clergy, and red-collar. For example, no one who works as a representative of the church can ride on the blue track; it is strictly reserved for haulers and traders.

While I'm concerned about my own ability to fit in with the crowd, Hiero has adapted well to her role. Normally her mien is what one might expect from the daughter of a noble— made all the more convincing by her green eyes— and her clothes, while not the most refined, appear to be well-taken care of. Today, however, her ribbon has been swapped for a rope, and her outfit looks almost as shabby as my own. Despite not wearing her usual makeup, her features are still sharp and breathtaking. If we were to run into any problems, it would be because no one who looks like Hiero would be working as a hauler.

A small line has formed in front of the gate. The man inspecting documents slams his stamp down with unnecessary force, and many of the workers get barely a glance before they're let through. Farther down, a couple of haulers are loading boxes onto the carriage-train. Most of their movements are robotic; some look ready to lay on the ground and pass out for a couple of hours. I suspect the majority of them have been traveling on the track since the early hours.

My head pounds at the thought and my fingers trace the edges of my papers again. I can't imagine working for roughly fourteen hours straight...

Except, that's a lie. I used to work at Mr. Connolly's shop for eight hours, and then do the projects he wouldn't take at people's houses, even if the pay was ration tickets. There were more nights than I can count where I fell asleep around two in the morning and got ready for the day before the sun even rose.

All of a sudden, the clockwork movement of the line grinds to a halt. Ahead, a man in well-worn clothes and a brown handkerchief argues with the man checking papers. Their words are lost in the echoey din of the station, but a proc saunters over, clutching the baton by his side, and the laborer is escorted off to the side for further questioning. A weight settles in my stomach. As if already knowing what I'm thinking, Hiero signals behind her back for me to stay put. Râ jĕ qavesii, Artem.

We gradually shuffle our way to the front. Hiero wears a sober facade, lowering her voice in pitch and tone as she answers a few questions from the inspector. After a minute, the man laughs heartily at something Hiero says, and his stamp hammers down on her papers, just once, like the sharp strike of a judge's gavel. She continues through, chancing a look at me.

I step forward, trying to stop myself from shaking. The man is uninterested, more focused on the sheer number of people waiting to board.

"Exit visa?" He waits impatiently as I retrieve my identification and place it on the booth. Remembering Hiero's advice, I clench my fists and will the tremble in my arms to stop. Feeling eyes on me, I rub at my shoulders, feigning cold.

"Name?"

On reflex I almost give my real name, but manage to catch myself. "A–Alair Langley."

"First time hauling?"

"Yes."

"Been a while since I've seen a Qorain on this line."

I bite my tongue. What I want is to ask what he means by something like that, but I already know the answer. Instead, I shrug. The following slam startles me, and I flinch. The man barks for the next person to step up. Ahead, Hiero waits patiently, face so schooled into neutrality that I have no idea what she thinks of the exchange. Part of me wonders if Hiero is so in-character she doesn't care, or if she's just that good at wearing a gambler's mask.

Hiero doesn't waste any time talking and sets out for one of the carriages closer to the back. Behind it sits multiple carts filled with miscellaneous goods shipped from the port in Sertalis.

I had always pictured the skyline to be made up of rows of benches with rounded tables between them, and expansive windows to view the city below. It's dingier than I imagined, especially for a transport as exclusive as it is. There are windows, but they're high up and only big enough to let in trickles of light, much less than that provided by the few gas lamps. One long bench stretches across each side of the carriage, the space between filled with more cargo, strapped to the floor. Only two other people occupy this car, near the front of the left side, both trying very hard to look at anything but us.

I open my mouth to ask, but Hiero beats me to the

punch, once again predicting exactly what I want to say. "A large shipment of bronze and copper arrived that wasn't in the original order. To make room, the back of the skyline carriages can also be used for storage. The carriages on other lines are a bit fancier."

"How do you k-know so much about the skyline but can't di-disable it yourself?"

Hiero doesn't answer, but I catch the faintest snort. She inspects the compartment then takes a seat. It doesn't process at first that she's waiting for me until I catch her pointed stare. I hurriedly sit.

There's something I still don't know about Hiero: what exactly does she do? I know she mainly keeps her eyes and ears open and reports back to Rhine. She's lenient with the label, and I get the idea she does a little bit of everything.

As it is, Hiero not only seems to have a grasp of the skylines and basic conduct, but she blends in well when she wants. Whether for looking suspicious or being Qorani, if one of us was stopped for questioning, it'd be me. Hiero almost looks like she belongs here, a seasoned hauler with more experience than half of them despite being one of the youngest on the crew.

A horn blares from up ahead, signaling the departure of the train from the station. I jolt at the noise, causing one of the others in the carriage to look my way. With a mumbled excuse, I snap my head down, my face heating from the attention. I barely catch Hiero's dismissive explanation to the hauler.

"This one had a problem with the last job we had," Hiero

explains, and I immediately look back up in surprise. "She's a little jumpy, isn't she?"

How did she...? All at once, Hiero's accent has dropped from her usual Sertalin drawl to a lilting lower-class tone like my own. The transition is smooth, effortless, natural. My head spins.

"Will she be alright?"

"She should be."

It's too soon for me to predict if that's true. As the train moves, I'm all-too-aware of the pain in my stomach. I shouldn't be here; on the skylines, in this carriage, working with the rebellion: none of it is right. None of it even sounds like an idea I'd entertain as hypothetical under normal circumstances.

I'm here for a job, and all I need to do is remind myself of that to get through this. Perhaps stopping the skylines is far from my comfort zone, but if the pay is anything like last time... Food prices have only gone up, as has rent. It's not as though Esper and I even have a room to ourselves, let alone an arm's-length of space to call our own. If I can't afford the ratty place we're in now, then what?

We need everything we can get right now, and getting fired leaves us in dire need of income. There are more illegal things I could be doing than shutting down the line. So long as my portrait isn't captured by any of the filographs, I can walk away from this. Because, honestly, I don't know if I want to stay with the rebellion, despite the incredible salary and the opportunity to repair an airship.

The carriage is quiet. One of the haulers dozes off, cap shielding his eyes from the dim light. The other is far more interested in a wrinkled newspaper, though he pauses now and again to eye the cargo in the middle of the room. Hiero stares blankly at the ground, as if fighting off the urge to sleep, herself. I know better; the rhythmic tapping of her fingertips against her sleeve suggests she's far from tired. Other than the constant churning and chugging from the skyline as we move, it's quiet.

It's funny how noisy it is to travel on the skylines after all. Some work was done recently on the switch operation, but improvements were also made to reduce noise and allow for a cozier ride between sectors and cities. Steam power may be reliable, but Mr. Connolly thought switching fuel sources would put less stress on the structure. Then there are the mechanics of keeping the trains moving; unlike the old system below ground, the skylines hang from a set of heavily magnetized tracks. Coal gets it running, and lepel oil keeps it going. Suspension is supposed to guarantee a smoother ride.

Yet all it's done is make things jostle more, causing a fine shudder at the slightest change in angle. The noise from the track isn't impossible to tune out, after a while, but now and again a loud shriek or creak brings the din to my attention all over again. The rest of the time I'm focused on the way my audancer's vents keep falling open with sudden booms of sound. I make a mental note to examine them later.

Without warning, Hiero gets up, making a show of stretching her arms above her head and then in front. I barely notice the tap of her boot against my foot. Should I be stretching, too?

The yawn that escapes my mouth is not for show. I wonder if Hiero thinks it is, that I'm trying too hard. But she doesn't pay me any mind, only heads toward the end of the carriage closer to the tail of the train. She twists the handle, but it's locked. For a moment, I think we're stuck, that maybe this hiccup is enough to keep me from accompanying Hiero on the skyline ever again. Then she slides two slim silver rods from her boot and begins prodding at the keyhole.

Lockpicks. She's carrying lockpicks. It's unsettling, but doesn't really surprise me. At this point, Hiero could confess she was once in a traveling circus and it wouldn't faze me. Well, maybe not. I would still be baffled and awed if it turned out Hiero was an acrobat swinging from towering platforms and juggling fire.

I stand behind her and try my best to cover up what she's doing. Neither of the haulers even glances in our direction. Hiero makes quick work of the door, holding it open to keep it from slamming against the wall. I check once more that the coast is clear, then head toward the exit.

Somehow it never occurred to me exactly how high up we are. Other than the metal joints from which the skyline hangs, the only thing connecting the carriages are two small parallel platforms, each about the width of my foot. Hiero doesn't hesitate as she moves forward, practically skipping as she reaches for the other door.

"Close it!" She tosses her hair behind her shoulder and motions with her chin.

I don't like being out here. Maybe Hiero is fine putting her life in danger, but I prefer being on the ground, not falling to it. My hands are tied. I comply and peer through the thick sheet of glass to see if anyone's noticed us. Nothing.

I cling to the handle for dear life and try to remember that the gap between platforms is only an arm's-length.

The wind howls and whips at us, the world beneath the skyline nothing but a horrible blur, but I can still hear Hiero swearing under her breath. My stomach flips; all the color is probably leaving my face.

"It's jammed!" She tugs on the door a bit more.

"W–We're stuck?!" I'm on the verge of a full-blown panic attack.

"Momentarily," Hiero affirms tersely, before fumbling for her picks again with a hiss.

I can practically see her slipping after a sharp turn, both of us plummeting to the ground. Or, her dropping the tools in her hands, leaving the two of us stuck... until we inevitably slip and... plummet. Either way, the outcome is falling to our deaths.

A jostle makes me stumble, and I curse. "Gaqĕ!" I instinctively reach out for Hiero, grabbing her shoulder. Surprised, she falls hard against the door, palms slapping against the metal. By some miracle, she keeps her balance. "I'm so–so sorry!"

"Sorry won't keep us hanging!" Hiero chides, her tone remarkably light despite her furrowed brow. A loud clunk sounds, and the door swings open. She hops inside, before pivoting around toward me.

Instead my eyes are drawn to the negative space, to the blur of the city, meters and meters beneath us. My heart stops. My legs lock. One misstep and I'm dead.

"Artem!" I can barely hear over the deafening whooshing of the wind, but I look up to find Hiero hanging to the side of the frame. Her hair whips around her head as the bit of rope holding her ponytail back is whisked away by the biting wind. She holds a hand out toward me. "Don't think, just move."

It's either the eerily calm encouragement in her voice or the realization that staying put will kill me that snaps me out of it. I grab her hand and force myself forward, half-leaping as Hiero tugs me inside. I stumble into her, and she catches me against her chest. The door slams shut behind us.

The stillness in the cart is both uneasy and welcoming. Aside from the rumble of the skyline, the only sound in here is our ragged breaths. I look up at Hiero, vaguely aware of my hands clutching her shirt. Her hair is a wild blonde halo, her cheeks flushed and expression flustered. Clearing my throat, I take a step back, turning toward the center of the carriage.

Sure enough, the cart is empty of other people and stocked with more cargo. Boxes line every wall, with only two small walkways surrounding the mass of crates in the middle. Most of the crates hold metals, from what Hiero said earlier. The bulk of it should be steel and copper. The lighting is practically nonexistent, only one lamp on either side of the carriage.

"The emergency controls should–should be in the ba– back." I fiddle with my shirt collar. "I–I can set up an error th–that looks like it needs t–to be examined, and pr–protocol dictates they'd ha–have to s–stop at the nearest sta–station, regardless of th–their destination."

"Right. How long do you think it'll take you?"

"It de–depends."

"Alright then." She quickly finger-combs her hair smooth and pulls it back into a ponytail, fishing her usual ribbon from her pocket to tie it back up. "Let's get to work."

We head down the rows, searching for the control panel I need. When Hiero gives a whistle and stops, I head toward the end of the aisle to cross over. She's managed to shuffle a few boxes around to expose a tiny door.

"This has to be it." Hiero tucks her hands into her pockets and steps aside.

Sure enough, it's what I've been looking for. I could recognize the hatch anywhere, and the small symbol etched above the latch; this is Mr. Connolly's personal work. I crouch down and run my fingers over the inscribed BC. With a deep breath, I undo the lock and inspect the control panel.

It's just like looking at the old blueprints. For a moment I'm back in the shop, with Mr. Connolly standing at my shoulder asking if I can spot any errors in his work. Only he could make something otherwise so boring so organized and aesthetically appealing, from the cuts in the metal to the design of the buttons. Now, though, is not the time to reminisce.

Inside, it's simple enough. The switches and gears are where I remember. This is good. No changes means I do actually know what I'm doing... sort of. I helped and watched, but never came here personally to rig everything up.

I lean back on my heels, forearms resting against my thighs as I clasp my hands together. Turning back to Hiero, I offer a smile. "It's easy e-enough to figure out. I just n-n-need to re-remember which does what. Give m-me a few minutes."

Hiero gestures with a flick of her wrist for me to go ahead. She walks off as I lean back in and remove one of the coverings to get a look at the inner workings. Behind it are a handful of wires, naturally tangled. Mentally I map out the old projects, recall the automatons Mr. Connolly has repaired, his methods in general.

I start to ask how long until we reach the next station, but Hiero is gone. No matter. She must trust me enough to get it done, if she went and wandered off. I know my job is to disable the skylines, but technically the best I can do is register an error and have the lines dock at the nearest stopping point. Anything more than that and lives might be at risk.

With a gentle tug, I manage to disconnect one of the wires, and carefully knot it without touching the end. The wrench I brought with me suddenly comes in handy, as I dig it out and get to work on the bolts. I unscrew the fasteners and cross my fingers as I clip a wire. The yellow bulb in the corner flickers to life.

Satisfied, I close the panel back up. As I stand, I fight the urge to yawn while moving some boxes to cover the wall again. "We sh-should be good!" I call out, strolling down the aisle. "H-How far are we f-from the next station?"

"Three minutes. Nice timing." Hiero's voice comes from the other walkway. Odd.

I go to join her and see what she's been up to this whole time. She's digging into one of the boxes, examining the contents, a bar of refined silver in each hand. The next thing I know, she's stuffing them into her boots.

I recoil. "Wh–What are you d–doing?"

"Securing pay," Hiero responds without splitting her focus. She seals up the crate, only to pop open another. My eyes must be bulging.

"That's n–not ours," I say, stating the obvious once again. "We c–can't take t–that."

She tsks. "And let all of this go to the clergy? Think of the people who might benefit from this more than those crown-lickers. A few bars can go missing, and it'll help someone else out. Me, for one."

"It's still th–theirs!"

"We need all the funds we can get."

I blink in disbelief. Hiero pops open another crate, filled with packages of coin, not only the plain copper daros I'm used to, but stacks of gleaming silver dremers as well. Without any hesitation, she picks up a parcel and inspects it, before tucking it into a pocket inside her jacket.

Is this why she really wanted to get on the skylines? To steal a few things and leave? What was the purpose of this job?

"Wh–Why did you... ask me to come here?"

"To stop the skyline." Hiero seals the boxes, then straightens and stretches her arms above her head, revealing a thin slice of stomach where her shirt lifts up. She slants a bored glance over to me. "What we've been doing."

"W–What I–I've been d–d–doing—" I try to correct her, but Hiero cuts me off.

"We. This was a combined effort. Unless you want to

take all the credit if things go south, then yes, it was all you. Satisfied?"

"No! W–Why are we stopping the sk–skylines?"

"You make it sound like you couldn't have asked earlier." Hiero examines her nails, then looks up, blowing out a breath. "Here's the deal: we plan on completely shutting down the skylines eventually. Part of this is a test run, to see if they can be forced to dock easily without anyone getting hurt. The other part involves a couple pieces of cargo ending up in our hands."

I stare at her. "Then s–some of the haulers h–here...?"

"Aren't haulers, yes. Can we finish this talk when we stop?"

A chime similar to earlier sounds. The line is starting to slow, and a voice announces there will be a delay, due to a routine checkup on the engines. Hiero heads toward the door. I grab onto her sleeve, forcing her to stop, and she glances back, raising an eyebrow. "Yes? Do you want to get caught?"

"Why di–didn't you tell–tell me you were p–planning on r–robbing these people? I–I w–wouldn't have–!"

"It didn't seem important." Hiero pulls her arm away. "Besides, I didn't think it would bother you that much. Considering your background."

"Ex–Excuse me?" My blood begins to boil and my stomach hurts all over again. "Wh–What ex–ex–exactly is that s–supposed to me–me–mean?"

Hiero sighs. "You know, you do a horrible job hiding those aural implants. We both know you lost your ears for petty theft or something, like most Quarterlings. You're not new to stealing things, right? I don't think I've met one other than Runa who didn't resort to it at some point."

I'm not sure what upsets me more: the generalization, the culturalist language, or that she's right about my audancers. I clench my fists and grit my teeth. Hiero is already moving forward, and just as the train grinds to a halt, she opens the door and traipses out. I follow, only to see the door across from us swing open. Before I can react, one of the men from earlier shoves by to enter the carriage, immediately grabbing one of the boxes.

Jumping down, I try my best to keep my thoughts in order. Hiero just wanted me around to help some rebels rob a train. Dreggar, I'm robbing a train.

I catch up with her as we make our way through to the exit. I barely react to the guard, robotically handing him my exit visa to be stamped again. Hiero looks back toward me when we reach the stairway. "About how that came out," she starts. I shove past her to descend the stairs as fast as I can without tripping over myself.

"N–No, I get it. Y–You're as turalist a–as the rest of them."

We don't speak when we reach the city streets. Hiero hails a jitney and mumbles something to the driver, then motions for me to get in. I comply, but only because I need a way back to the bunker, I'm too angry to go back home just yet. The ride is quiet, though my face burns and my heart thuds loudly in my chest. All the while, Hiero's words echo in my head, and I swear I can taste bile.

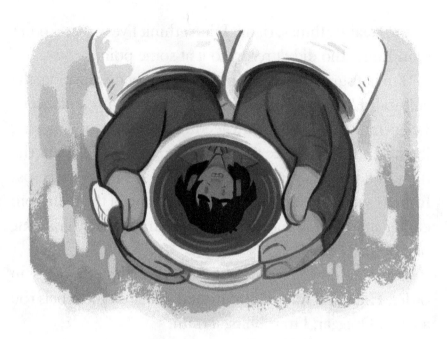

CHAPTER 5

I could go straight home, but I need someone to talk to, someone that isn't Esper. Runa seemed more than aware of Hiero's motives and I feel she'd be the best person to see right now.

Hiero sticks around to thank the jitney driver. I slam the door and march past her into the fake pub. Everyone watches from behind their drinks as I grind something out to the bartender about "a switch and bait." Unfortunately, Hiero is right behind, and as I slide down the hatch, she's too close for comfort.

She doesn't make conversation on the way, which is fine by me. I reach the door first and struggle with it. I stiffen as Hiero reaches over me to turn the wheel-crank in one lazy, fluid motion. She glides past, holding the door for me with a quirked eyebrow. I stomp past her.

The workshops aren't mine to use, so I don't have anywhere to retreat to. I end up storming into what appears to be the medical ward. Ten makeshift beds, stitched together from rusted pipe frames and old mattresses, are lined up neatly in a row on one side. There are two doors leading in and out, and the large far wall is packed with cabinets and a long bureau-desk roughly two people long. Various jars clutter the counter-space, and multiple shelves are hung above the table, filled to the brim with herbs and cotton balls and instruments I don't recognize.

Runa is there, standing by the expansive table, whispering to Tristan. They turn their attention toward me in surprise. Runa is the one who asks, just as Hiero trails in behind me: "Is everything—?"

"Fine," Hiero answers, and I spin around, faster than she must expect. She stops short, almost walking into me.

"Everything is n–not fine." My fists ball up by my sides.

"Is that so?" Hiero tilts her head and clicks her tongue, eyebrows raised. "Funny, I thought we stopped one of the skylines today."

"Y-You robbed one, you m–mean, and you h–had me help!" I squeak.

Tristan tries to interject, but Runa quietly hushes him. Hiero's expression hardens, her eyes narrowing; she takes a step back, hands held up in defense. "Woah, we talked about this back at the station!"

"You t-talked about this back at the st–station! You also c-called me a–a Quarterling!"

"Is that what this is about?" Hiero asks. I can practically feel my blood pressure rise as the world begins to spin.

"A–About you being culturalist? About you n–not being up-front? About you dr–dragging me into something I–I didn't want anything to do with? Yes, Hiero, it's a–about all of that!"

"Culturalist? How is anything I said culturalist?"

"Oh, s–so any Qorain is o–okay with stealing? Do you e–even know what Q–Quarterling means?"

She tosses her head, ponytail whipping behind her. "I assumed it was shorthand for someone from Qorar."

I sputter. "If it w–was shorthand, why is it a long–longer word? I–I'm not even from Qorar! My dad's from–from there, but that's no–not important. What is important, i–is that you're t–turalist."

Hiero crosses her arms and her voice lowers. "So the ear implants are a coincidence, then?"

"E–Excuse m–me?" I sputter.

That damn condescending eyebrow-lift again. "It's almost as obvious as the gold eyes. Thieves get their ears cut off— and which group do you suppose is missing the most ears?" Her voice is the slow, weedling drawl of an adult asking a basic question to a particularly dense child, and when she clicks her tongue again, looking me up and down, I want to scream.

I curl my fists to keep myself from slapping that look off her face. "Th–That's not any of y–your business!" Runa and Tristan both dart forward. Tristan splits us up, and Runa keeps a firm hand on my shaking shoulders.

"Artem, honey, breathe," Runa instructs me, her eyes

darting back briefly to glance at Tristan as she talks. "In for seven seconds... three, four, five..." Tristan shoots Runa a worried, apologetic look as he motions for Hiero to walk away with him. She tears himself from his hold with a huff, adjusts her jacket, and leaves.

It's clear that Runa has family from Qorar, from the yellow eyes and slight accent. I can only imagine how she manages to stay as calm as she does. I'm only half-Qorani and those slurs sting worse than any slap. Her face suggests she's more than familiar with the language being thrown around, and it rolls off her like rain against a window.

Slowly my muscles begin to relax. Runa keeps a hand on my wrist, glancing at a clock on the wall. She mouths numbers to herself, fixated on a button at the cuff of my shirt. I start silently counting the freckles on her hand. Do they stretch all the way up her arms? I've only seen her with long sleeves.

"Easy, that's it." Runa looks me over. "Seems like you've had a rough day."

"H–How does t–that... not make you angry?" I ask, shaking my head.

Runa pauses for a moment, lips twitching as she contemplates how to phrase whatever it is she's thinking. Once she's satisfied, she speaks. "At my age, the words don't feel as heavy. Besides, I rarely hear it in my direction anymore. A lot of people don't want to upset their doctor when their temperature is spiking. Qorani or not, you'd be surprised how much power you earn wielding a syringe."

She guides me over to sit down on one of the cots, retreating to put on a kettle. I recount the journey on the skyline and my reservations about working for the rebellion. Runa never once turns her attention away or interjects. It's nothing like talking to Esper.

As I finish, she nods and rests her hands in her lap. I clutch the cup in my hands and stare into the dark liquid. "Are you s–sure this is qosa?"

"It is, why?"

"Q–Qosa is supposed to hurt w–when you drink it."

Runa blinks, looking as though she wants to say something, but she only peers into her cup. Right. She was talking about something. I shake my head and try to focus. "You w–were saying?"

"Really," she continues, unaware that I haven't been paying attention. "I'm sure doing that for her will give you enough coin to make it to the next month or so, and you can get work elsewhere."

"My p–papers aren't in order." I shift uneasily. "Hiero owes me. B–Besides, now that I kn–know all about—" I gesture around me. "—this, I c–can't exactly walk o–out, can I?"

"Well... no. Aether would be keeping an eye on you."

"What ex–exactly does everyone d–do? I mean, you w–work with medicine, and I assume wh–whatever Aether does Christa does as w–well, or m–maybe Tristan? I don't–– the point is I don't kn–know what anyone does around h–here."

Never one to sit still, Runa springs from her seat. There are papers scattered all over the desk, and a pile of medicines to be sorted. She continues speaking as she busies herself neatening the paper pile.

"I'm a licensed doctor. I could practice, but my sibling

Christa has made their face public with the revolution, so, can't exactly go back to my old office job. Tristan, bless him, knows the proc system inside and out, having gone through the training. After he gathered the evidence he needed to report the corruption going on in his unit, someone higher up got a whiff of it. Blackmailed, kicked from the force."

"I could see him as a proc," I admit. Runa shakes her head.

"For the life of me, I can't. He doesn't have a mean bone in his body." She sighs. "Aether and Hiero are two of the few around here who keep tabs on everything and snoop around. It makes me nervous, to tell the truth. I can't tell what either of their motives are, or just how much they know and don't let on."

She has a point. The thing is, I want to believe Hiero, what she says and how she acts. Maybe that's why she's good at what she does— everyone wants to trust her. Or maybe it's just me, falling for a pretty face like a full-on fool.

Wait... I tilt my head and stare at Runa for a moment. "Sibling?"

"Oh, that." Runa clears her throat. "Christa doesn't identify as male or female, so they go by they/them."

Oh. I get it. In Qalqora there is a third, genderless pronoun, dam, though it doesn't translate perfectly to Ingwell. I take mental note of this as Runa sighs and takes a sip of her drink. I follow suit, with a small hum. It's more concentrated, and far stronger, than the swill I'm used to. Runa looks up and offers a small smile, raising an eyebrow in question. Before I can respond, she's already opened up one of the cabinets and pulled out a familiar brown bottle. My face flushes. "Oh, n–no, I'm not—!"

"Nonsense," Runa scoffs, opening the sugary syrup and pouring in a generous amount. "You can admit it's awful. A little wellum never hurt anyone, I've got plenty."

I don't know what to say. I haven't had wellum in my qosa in years. As soon as I try it, the overwhelming taste of oranges coats my tongue. It's not particularly to my liking, but it doesn't taste bad. I'm just used to the bitter.

By the time I look up, Runa's back to shuffling papers. "Thing is, Hiero's only been part of the movement for a couple months. Aether is Rhine's cousin and acts like she has more pull, partly because she's been around longer. But Hiero has a knack for getting where she needs to be without having her face pinned to anything. They're always at each other's throats."

There's a hiss from somewhere to the side, then, "She lacks any real control."

I jump and turn my head to where Aether stands in the doorway. She approaches Runa, handing over a couple of documents, before taking a seat on a different cot. Runa clears her throat, and I expect her to say something, but instead the noise just hangs in the air.

Aether's eyes dart over toward her before focusing in on me. They're the typical Allowyn blue, but darker, like the sky before a storm. Her visit, though seemingly coincidental, feels timed. Either she's oblivious to the tension in the air or she has an uncanny ability to ignore it. My spine prickles.

"Hiero's miffed she can't talk circles around everyone here the way she would on the streets," Aether says, her voice like silk and smoke. "Regardless of who my family is, I got here by working just as hard as she has, only I'm much more careful. She doesn't plan for the long term, and one day she'll slip. When it happens, I'll be sure to remind everyone who called it first."

I don't know how to respond to any of that, but I find myself slowly nodding along. While I don't know Hiero that well, there's no denying how reckless she can be. None of what I've been dragged into has been well-thought-out.

Aether scowls, narrowing her eyes. She doesn't stare at me so much as through me, straight into my very being. I shiver, unable to keep from feeling sick as she looks down her nose at me, studying me. "You're a mechie, focused in repair, longing to branch out and engineer something innovative and life-changing. What formal training you do have was only in basic repair and now you're—" she smiles slightly— "completely in over your head."

"Wh–Where did you get that?" I manage, baffled, and she tuts.

"Hiero's mentioned a few things offhand, but it doesn't take a genius to see right through you. I can usually get a quick read off anyone, but you're an open book with a handful of dog-eared pages." Aether smirks and props her chin on her hand. "How good are you with security systems?"

I'm not sure what to make of that, and look to Runa for help. She shakes her head and turns away. The gears in my head slowly grind to a halt as I desperately try to follow along. Aether is going into details, but for the life of me, I can't keep up. All I can think about is Hiero and our argument earlier, and how much I wish she wasn't turalist.

Runa attempts to help me out by butting in. "Aether, there are many more willing people waiting—"

Aether cuts her off. "Don't you have someone else to hover over? Christa should be around somewhere if you have a need to fuss."

Runa's mouth clamps shut. She squints, mulling it over as she starts to busy herself again, though she does glance in my direction. The action is so fast I barely get a chance to catch her expression, only the quick slither of her braid as she turns away.

My stomach hurts. I don't know if it's the anxiety or the wellum, but I'm sure neither is helping. Any words that teeter in the back of my throat are filled with salt from earlier, and now coated by the thick, false sweetness of the qosa. Somehow I manage to find my voice again, though it takes more effort than I care to admit to adjust my focus. "I c–can do it. I just don't want to."

Aether smiles again, and it's somehow alluring and terrifying at the same time. "If you can do it, why don't you show me? Unless you can't be bothered to expand your skill set... In which case, what good are you?"

The last part is a husky purr, and I'm suddenly hit with a flush of sympathy for every portin cornered by a karnook. There's a part of me that knows Aether is egging me on, but I can't help but clench my fists. I'm not much use around here right now, nor do I have a single job opportunity or professional reference. Anything at this point is better than nothing, and as long as some sort of coin makes its way into my pocket, I suppose there's not much harm I could do with what little I know.

"It's either help me or help Hiero," Aether says, and her voice is back to being velvet. "Sure, you stopped a skyline carriage, decent work. But that's not going to stick out to Rhine. You heard Runa say it herself: I have more pull. What sounds better, helping Hiero stall a skyline, or helping Aether, his cousin, in taking down Parvay?"

I look over at Runa again. She's keeping her head in her work, every line of her body stiff as she deliberately stays out of the conversation. Aether's not wrong; the sooner I quit running around completing random errands, the sooner I can be recruited for the airship project. Surely that would pay better than these sketchy arrangements. I look back and forth between Runa and Aether, trying to gauge the best course of action.

Right now, I'm furious with Hiero. The last thing I want to do is be around her. Until I get an apology, I don't want to see her face. She's the reason I lost my first job, the reason I'm in a bunker with a bunch of people supporting a cause I never signed up for. If it wasn't for Hiero, I wouldn't be forced into this position.

Runa doesn't trust any of the spies around here as far as she can throw them, and she's been here ages longer than I have. At this point, I'm handing my life over to my gut instincts, just guessing at who I can trust, and I've already been wrong once. Vaguely, I hear my father warn me about never acting out on anger or an empty stomach. Regardless of the risk that might be involved, regardless of how little I know Aether, I hold out my hand.

"You've got a deal."

CHAPTER 6

It probably wasn't the best idea to sign on for another mission with someone I don't even know. Then again, I barely know Hiero, so what difference does it make? I need the money, and I need someone to vouch for my ability to do mech work. Besides, Aether might be easier to work with; she may be smarmy and sly, but as far as I know, she isn't culturalist.

She doesn't want to meet until after moonrise. I don't like leaving the apartment so late, and I'm not comfortable leaving Esper alone. He's asleep by the time I leave, but I still slip some coin to Jynell, to keep an eye on him. The address I was given is on the edge of the Kensing sector, a few blocks from the tavern that leads to the bunker. When I get there, I cup my hands together and do my best to warm them up.

It's one of those nights where I wish I had a coat, or at least a new pair of gloves.

No one is around at this time of night, at least in this sector. This section of town is a lot nicer than my neighborhood, though, and the people tend to be less shady. Overhead one of the skylines zips by, and the ground trembles in its wake.

How long am I supposed to wait? It looks suspicious for a Qorani to be hanging around outside the slums this late. Every time someone walks by, I flatten myself to the closest wall and duck my head. The last thing I want is to be singled out by anyone. Attention isn't great for Qorani.

"When Hiero said she'd found a mechie, I thought she'd hog you all to herself." Yet again, Aether's voice from the shadows makes me jump. I spin on my heel and spot her standing three arm-lengths away. She's got her hair tied back, like Hiero normally does, but in a low bun with a few loose scarlet locks framing her face. She's harder to read than Mr. Connolly's handwriting. I fidget with my necktie as she approaches.

"I don't work with Hi-Hiero." I clear my throat. "I-I mean, I have worked with her, did, but she doesn't, w-we don't, I'm not—"

"You're looking for something more permanent."

I blink a couple times, then give her a jerky nod. "And less dangerous, y-yes."

She examines her nails with a sigh. "Danger, unfortunately, will be involved regardless. That's what happens when you join an anti-monarchy faction."

Aether pulls on her gloves while I stand there trying to think of a response. I could argue that I don't even support the movement, but me being here at all says otherwise. She tilts her head to the side. "If I'm not wrong, you want enough of a reputation to start working on that airship in the bunker." I nod, and side-eye her. Is she going to psychoanalyze me the whole time?

"Then let's get going," Aether says briskly, and starts walking toward the docks.

A lone rowboat tied to a post bobs gently just off the pier, two oars placed neatly inside. A small crate sits beside them, along with a note and a lantern. Aether passes me a box of matches and climbs in. I stare blankly back and forth between Aether and the boat. We're going somewhere in this thing? I wasn't expecting us to leave this part of town, especially not by water.

Aether clears her throat. I fumble with the matches, clutching them tightly to my chest, and take a deep breath, stepping in gingerly. The boat rocks as I take the seat opposite Aether. She doesn't say anything, just nods toward the lantern and starts untying the anchoring rope. My hands shake as I strike a match and open the little glass panel to light the wick. Just as I snap it closed, Aether drops the rope and grabs the paddles, sending us off.

It's... awkward, to say the least. Aether stays stone silent, movements sharp but efficient as we push away from the docks, oars stroking through the water in an easy, practiced rhythm. I have no idea where we're headed, or what I'm meant to be doing when we get there. At least Hiero gave me a vague idea beforehand, though— I scowl— she hardly told me the whole story either. I'm really getting tired of being left in the dark.

"W–Where are we going?" I decide to ask, wringing my hands. Aether's stare moves from the shore to me, and her eyes spark like the harsh flicker of the lantern.

"Lindsor."

"Lin–Lindsor?" I echo.

"We're not leaving Allowyn, if that's what you were wondering."

I suppose I didn't expect us to be traveling to Lanrel, but traveling by boat seems weird; normally one would take the skylines or a jitney to get to Lindsor. But maybe Aether has given this more thought than I'm giving her credit for. After all, I should be avoiding the skylines after the other day.

Lindsor. There isn't a nicer town in Allowyn. Other than the palace, the greatest of the great live in Lindsor, mostly to be as far as possible from Wellwick or the mines up north. Practically anyone who's noble or part of Parvay lives there, including a handful of academics. I've never been there myself, but I've heard stories. Mr. Connolly travels there once a year for a large conference for engineers and artificers, where he obtains some of his larger contracts.

It probably won't be very exciting visiting this close to midnight. We aren't going to meet up with anyone— at least, not that I know of— nor go to any shops. Still, my heart skips a beat at the thought of finally visiting a city beyond Wellwick, one supposedly brimming with the latest technology.

The rest of the trip is silent, except for the oars slicing through the water. I mostly watch the buildings moving past, trying to focus more on the change in scenery than the bobbing of the boat, and absentmindedly fidgeting with the key around my neck. It's roughly an hour and a half before we start heading toward land again. I believe we're close to Lindsor now, but I'm a little surprised by the lack of noise from where we are, the streets clear of people. In Wellwick, the streets are always alive with the chatter of people rushing home or to market or bar-hopping with friends, but evidently the rich don't stand for that sort of public joviality. Most of what I can see is from between large boulders, positioned like fencing, to try and keep people from looking in. Ornate street lamps stand along the stretch of main road, lighting the marble faces of the surrounding buildings in orange and purple. Someone passes in a flash of red between the boulders, but otherwise the streets appear bare. A faint tune hangs in the air, perhaps playing from a padescha in a distant window.

I expected a bustling city, more like the Wellwick I've grown up with, not anything that felt so... secluded. When Mr. Connolly traveled to Lindsor, he spoke of a city resplendent with the height of technology, of bright lights and lavish parties every night. He always hated social events, but lit up with genuine excitement at the prospect of meeting with artificers at these conferences and securing new contracts. From the way it sounded, I expected there to be barely any elbow room, crowds everywhere.

We continue rowing at a steady speed. I'm antsy to say the least, still stuck surrounded by water when we're so close to land. I don't know what's more frustrating: how underwhelming Lindsor is, or being unable to pace.

There are fewer glimpses of buildings between the boulders now, and more greenery. Gradually, Aether's strokes begin to slow, and we change course toward land, easing close to a small beach. There is no pier or dock, just a small, rocky shore. Aether hops out before we're fully aground and pushes the boat along, only stopping once it's fully beached. I grab hold of the lamp and Aether digs through the crate, gathering a few items. Among them are pliers, a pocket-sized spool of copper wire, and the note that was pinned to the crate. She squints at the paper, then reaches over to open the lantern door. In the next moment, the paper is aflame, and she flings it over her shoulder to smolder on the sand.

"Let's go."

I follow her up the beach, to where the sand turns to acres of carefully manicured lawns. Even though the skylines aren't running at this hour, I figured I could at least see them from here. But other than the kilometers of rock surrounding the city, there is nothing but hillside and sand. All the other plots we've passed had huge overgrowths, also meant to block the property from sight, but all I can see here is what appears to be a capitol building. It's intimidating by its size alone. The material is stark white stone, and the architect was clearly a fan of sharp angles.

"This is it," Aether announces.

"We're going into Parvay?"

"Don't be ridiculous," she tuts, her lip curling up in a sneer. "We're nowhere near Wingnal."

"Wingnal?"

"You have no idea how Parvay works, do you?" Aether takes a deep breath and mumbles something I don't quite catch. My ears burn in embarrassment and I turn my gaze to the sand below my boots.

"There are three estates," she starts with a sigh, "and each house has its own building. The headquarters for the First Estate is in Lindsor, the Second Estate's in Brollod, and the Third is in Wellwick, in the Peri sector. All of them meet in Orping." The long-winded explanation makes me feel like a school kid being scolded by a teacher. It's patronizing, especially with the tone she uses, like every word is a physical burden.

Aether eyes me for a second before continuing. "Lindsor's building is called Wingnal and isn't anywhere near the residential districts. This isn't Wingnal. We're not dealing with any part of Parvay directly."

I understand parts of the political system, from my schooling days. I knew the king meets up with Parvay, but not that it happens in Orping. What I do know, at least now, is that the building in front of us isn't for congress. "You mean, some-someone o-owns this place? Someone lives here?"

"This is the Kulkner house."

That's not a house. If anything, it looks like a palace. If this gigantic tract of land and magnificent building is someone's home, I can't begin to imagine just how large Varsiege must be in comparison. I do my best to swallow down my awe. No doubt Aether knows exactly what I'm thinking; she just shakes her head and starts walking up the grassy hillside.

At the top I realize just how expansive the property is. The house and its endless green lawns stretch far beyond what I could see before, the entire perimeter a studded chain of boulders. Marble statues adorn the sides of the house, in the likeness of fearsome creatures I don't recognize, baring sharp teeth and claws, poised to attack. A whirring from the roof is accompanied by the fierce brilliance of a moving spotlight, sweeping a wide track of light across the yard.

The moment Aether pulls out the spool of copper wire, I realize why I'm here, and my pulse spikes. Again, I'm disabling something for illegal purposes. The idea of my name and reputation being spread by word of mouth for future shady work—

Before I can spiral, Aether hands over a pair of bolt-cutters and a hard disk. I look back and forth between the clutter in my arms and the searchlight. Aether clears her throat. Her arms are loosely crossed, the fingers of one hand tapping an impatient tattoo on the opposite bicep. "Do I need to spell it out for you?"

I blink slowly. "No. I'm just th–thinking. I've never had to sh–shut down a security system before."

"How different can it be from the skylines?"

Extremely. I keep my mouth shut, though; my slack jaw speaks for me.

"I talked to one of the other mech-drabblers working on the airship. Meno told me this was all you would need to do it and it'd be simple enough to figure out. While you do that, I'm going to get us inside."

"Why d–didn't you ask Meno to come along then, if this guy kn–knows so much about si–silencing alarms?"

She narrows her eyes at me. "Because Meno doesn't need to prove his worth, and he'd be even mouthier than you."

I flinch away from her gaze and focus on the beam, watching as it passes by and begins to reach the edge of its patrol. Just as the light swings in our direction again, I bolt toward the paneling by the side of the mansion. I'm protected by at least six meters of darkness, but I still hug the wall, heart hammering in my chest, and wait for the loud shrieking of an alarm to go off.

It doesn't.

My hands shake as I grab the bolt-cutters, every muscle straining as I do away with the lock. It tumbles onto the grass with a soft thud, spooking me enough to drop the bolt-cutters and wire and almost lose the disk. Gripping the small piece tightly, I open the panel to get a look at the security system and gauge just how "easy" this is supposed to be.

It turns out Meno was right: the wiring is basic and it's easy to tell how everything is rigged together. I'm starting to think whoever Kulkner is, they were ripped off big-time. My fingers are entangled a few times as I try to work quickly, but before I can stutter through an "I've got it," the light stops, fixed on a hedge a meter from me. I fiddle with the disk, inserting it into the only available slot, and the lights all die, plunging me into almost absolute darkness.

With no streetlights or other buildings nearby, it's hard to make anything out, especially since Aether has the lamp. But the sky-- I'd never noticed how many stars there were, or how they litter the sky like the freckles smattered across Runa and Christa's cheeks. But as amazing as it is, the silence and darkness are more intimidating than anything. The sky is just so big, and the stars only make me feel smaller.

"Artem," Aether hisses. She's managed to open the door, and she holds it open from the inside. There's no trace of her break-in save a window, still ajar. I furrow my brow and hold my tongue as I scurry indoors.

It's abnormally warm for such a large, open space, and I shiver as the cold is shucked from my bones. The main entrance is barren; despite the warm air circulating through the house, it feels clinical, chilling and far from homey. Taking up most of the space is a grand marble staircase, branching off into the two separate wings of the building. Large velvet curtains hang from the ceiling to the floor, covering the majority of the spacious windows. It's like the owner was trying to make the place cozier than it was ever meant to be, like putting a sweater on an eel to make it seem fluffy and approachable.

Like Hiero, Aether wastes no time, immediately heading up the rightmost set of stairs. She doesn't seem to get distracted easily. I suppose if anyone does a job they love, they want to approach it with the utmost focus.

"You and Hiero are kind of a–alike, you know?" I whisper as I creep after her. "Not completely, b–but the way you operate is kind of s—!"

Aether stops dead in her tracks and spins to face me. Her expression had been bored, almost unimpressed, but has turned cold, far worse than the way the wind rips through my threadbare clothes. Her eyes bore into mine, challenging me to finish my sentence. When I don't, she turns back and continues up the stairs.

Maybe... not so similar. Come to think of it, whenever I was nervous, Hiero was almost reassuring, and if she did anything it was to bring more attention to herself. Aether doesn't seem to care one way or another about me, so long as she gets her way.

At the top of the staircase we head down a corridor with almost as many doorways as a train's sleeper car. Animals I don't recognize adorn the door-frames, carved into the wood along with holy farrings and various beasts.

My heart hurts looking at the handiwork. It reminds me too much of the painstaking detail Mr. Connolly put into his designs. I miss being at the shop and having a place I could work; the floor of the apartment common space is no substitute. But I can't go back, especially not if he doesn't trust me after working for him for so many years. I think what I miss more than anything is having security and a routine. Not fearing for my life on the daily was just a bonus.

I probably shouldn't say anything. Yet this house is practically empty, and I have no clue how Aether knows where we are going. Does she have the blueprints of the house, or has she been here before? She broke in much more easily than I expected. "How d–do you know where you n–need to go?" I ask.

"Most houses aren't that different from each other," Aether mutters dismissively, dropping her voice even lower. "This way. Quickly."

She stops at the last door in the hall, turning the knob and pushing inside almost noiselessly. The room appears to be an elaborate study, almost every bit of wall-space covered with the mounted, stuffed heads of different animals. Some I recognize, like the antlered reidor and muskel, but some are creatures I've only heard of in stories. A man sits half-slumped over at a desk angled away from the entrance, scrawling away at some documents.

He must be Kulkner, the owner of this house. I fall back a pace, ready to mouth to Aether that there was a mistake, that we should leave before we get caught, but Aether presses on, stalking with sure steps toward the desk.

"I had a feeling I would find you here," she says, and there's a note of dark anticipation in her voice that makes me shiver. In one rehearsed motion, she produces a cloth bag from her back pocket and slips it over the man's head before he can turn around. The man swings his arms wildly, narrowly missing Aether as she secures the bag at arm's-reach. In one more quick, cruel movement, she slams his head into the desk and pulls his hands behind his back. All he can do is sway in her hold.

What was I thinking, going along with Aether? If I'd known it would come to this— All I can do is stand, still and frightened, watching Kulkner groan in pain as Aether secures his hands to the arms of the chair. She yanks the back of the hood to force him upright once more.

"Wh-What are you—?" I start.

"Shut it," Aether growls.

"Whatever it is," the man begins, sounding much more confident than a man in his position ought, "You won't have. Leave this residence at once, and I won't have you apprehended." His offer sounds good to me, but seems to fall on deaf ears.

Aether whips his chair around to face her, taking ahold of one of his jacket lapels, her voice soft and dangerous. "You really have no idea what I'm here for, do you?"

"I have filographs in every corner of this house," he continues to bluster. "You've asked for it! I'll have you reported to the authorities for harming a panet member!"

Her eyebrows arch up in mock surprise, but since he can't see her the dramatics must be for me. "Do you now? I hope they work with their wires cut. Unless you've got something that records without power?" Again, he whimpers, loudly and pitifully. I squirm where I stand. Why haven't I left yet? There's no reason for me to stay, to have any part of this, yet I can't bring myself to move. Even if I did leave, where would I go? Would I wander through the house until Aether gave some sort of signal? Would Aether even remember to bring me back with her to Wellwick?

"I-I don't t-think I should be here," I say, and it comes out more of a whimper than I would have liked.

Aether ignores me. "Tell me," she hisses to Kulkner, "When was the last time you combed your social circle for spies? Is Parvay so confident that they no longer consider who wants them dead?"

"By the Crown, did Johanas hire you?" he spits, writhing against his bonds. "He's been gunning for my seat for years. I'll die before he gets it."

"Ah, but you dying would take all the fun out of it." Aether smiles, eyes glowing with sadistic glee.

I need a more extreme word for "uncomfortable"; I've reached a new level of discomfort altogether. The usual pins and needles at the heels of my feet are more like gigantic thorns, and the acid in my stomach creeps upward, resting at the base of my throat. It feels like every cell in my body is trying to peel itself away from this cursed place, and I only wish I could do the same. I keep opening and closing my mouth like a dumb fish, wincing with every new jerk from the man in attempt to break free, and shrinking into myself every time Aether smiles like she's having a good time.

Aether gathers the ties to the cloth and pulls them back tightly against his throat, watching his reaction with the sort of detached interest one might give a bug in a jar. The man squirms sporadically, straining against his bonds to reach up to his neck and free himself of the hood. When his choking begins to grow louder, Aether lets go, and his body practically flings itself forward as he gasps for air.

"You could stop things here." She gathers up the ties again, and my stomach churns in sympathy as she draws them tighter. "Just write it up and you might still have some use when we're finished with you." Aether gives a quick jerk to force him upright and he sobs, a short, choked cry. I can't imagine what this man could have done to warrant such punishment. There is no mercy in her eyes. She is having fun torturing this man, and I doubt I will ever know why. No one deserves this, not even the noble crown-lickers in Parvay.

"I've held this position for over fifteen years, I've never been balisted after like this!" The man's voice cracks.

"Maybe if you had, you would be worth your seat," Aether sighs, turning the chair toward the desk as she loosens a restraint. "Since he's so mouthy, I think he can handle a little more, don't you?" She looks directly at me, waiting for some response.

Why— why is she talking to me now? I've been ignored this whole time, hunched in the corner on the verge of a panic attack. I want nothing more than to be done with this whole endeavor. It was hard enough to sleep before; I'm not sure if I can ever sleep easy again after this.

"Johanas will be expelled for this; I have more blackmail on him than anyone else in Parvay!"

Aether laughs, incandescent with delight. "How funny. You wouldn't believe the amount of blackmail I have on you." She starts undoing the buttons along his shirt, and I have no idea where any of this is going but I've never been more viscerally uncomfortable. She produces a knife with a flourish, and calmly dances the edge of the blade against his skin. He tenses, and just as he flinches at a particular nick, she digs the blade in. She makes one 'S' shape, then another, as he cries out in ragged barks of pain. Is she... drawing something? Her motions are fluid, as if merely doodling on a piece of paper.

"Why are y–you doing this t–to him?" I yelp, unable to stay silent.

"Listen, and listen carefully," she orders her victim, continuing to ignore me. "I need you to hand over your panet seat, for— and only for— Sendrick Maloney, effective immediately."

"Sendrick Maloney— my cousin? He put you up to this?"

"Whether he sent me here or not is none of your concern. All I care about is that he is elected."

"He's not getting my seat."

"You sure talk a lot." Her voice is back to that dangerous, velvety purr. "I wonder, how much longer are you going to scream before you realize no one is coming?" Aether fiddles with her folding knife, tapping the bloodied edge with her finger. "Honestly, it's surprising that someone in your position doesn't have a direct line to the procs. A shame, really. I might've had to put in some effort."

I bring both hands to my mouth. I can't remember how to breathe. My legs have gotten shaky. I slump back into the corner for support as Aether's victim continues to shout at the top of his lungs. "He won't get my seat! He won't!"

It's no use. Aether seems to realize this is going nowhere and heaves a deep sigh. She stands once more, heading to the fireplace, then pulls a metal puck and a small, telescoping rod from her back pocket, screws the pieces together, and holds it over the flame. The whole time she stares intently, watching as the metal glows red, then orange, then fiercely, dangerously white.

She turns to Kulkner and drives the white-hot brand into his chest for the longest twenty seconds of my life. He howls in pain, and the smell of burning flesh permeates the air, accompanied by the soft hiss and pop of skin scorching and melting. Her mark, burned into his chest, is deep red and dark golden-brown, the edges bubbling up in half-formed white blisters. She props the brand on the desk and swivels the chair slightly so that I can see for myself: a flame sits branded between his ribs, almost artfully highlighted by bloody swirls and jagged knife-marks. Aether's very own calling card.

"I'm thinking the next one will be a bit lower."

"I'll write you a check! You can take my coin, just stop!"

She tuts. "Coin's not good enough. If you're not going to cooperate, perhaps your daughter will."

"My daughter?" His voice is shrill now. "What have you done with Katlyish?"

Her eyes widen, and a smile curves her lips. "I haven't left my brand on her yet, if that's what you're asking, but I have men ready to collect her at a moment's notice. But you can stop this if you give up that seat..."

"Yes! Yes, he'll have the seat! He'll have the seat, I'll draw up the papers in the morning!" Kulkner sobs, a high, broken sound. "Please, I beg of you!"

Aether twirls her knife, wipes it off on his shirt, then folds it and places it back in her pocket, along with the cooled pieces of the branding iron. She leans down to hiss in his ear. "Twelve hours from now I want to hear that you have opened your position, or I will physically remove you from it."

"It will be opened and given recommendation!" He takes a trembling breath. "I'll cooperate!"

Aether turns his chair to face the doorway and loosens his bonds. With a flourish, she undoes his hood and turns him to face me, then strolls casually across the room, never looking the man in the face as she slips past me and out the door. He pulls the bag from his head; his white hair is disheveled, his nose bloody and broken, and his brown eyes stare into the depths of my soul. They question why I'm here tonight, how I could be party to torture. I don't have an answer. I can barely keep up. I can't tell if I'm nauseous or guilty. It's possible it's a little bit of everything.

I continue staring, unsure what else to do, until Aether calls out and I follow on her heels. Never before have my feet flown down stairs like they do tonight. I keep to myself all the way back to the beach, but by then the turmoil has boiled up inside me, and everything bursts out.

"Wh-Why would you do that? He can't have done any-anything to de-deserve that! Why did you bring me a-along if you could slip inside with-without ne-needing the security shut down? I n-n-never agreed to—!"

Aether cuts me off with a sharp scowl. "What you agreed to doesn't matter. You showed what you were capable of, as annoyingly skittish as you are. Next time, do what you need to do and stay outside of the room."

"Sorry," I squeak.

"Let's get going, before he does something stupid like actually reach out to the authorities with names." I wince. Chances are the guy will remember my face. Aether set me up. I'm attached to a crime, filographs or no, and there's no way around it. At least with Hiero, she made it seem like a team effort, that if something happened to me it would happen to her, too. As much as I don't want to associate myself with a turalist, I would take running errands for Hiero any day over working with Aether again, especially if this is her usual line of work.

The boat ride is silent and drags on for an endless dark eternity. All I want is to go home and watch Esper sleep easy, blissfully unaware that there are evenings like tonight.

CHAPTER 7

It's getting pricey finding someone to watch Esper during the day. As much as I'd like to take him with me, it wouldn't be safe. The last thing I need is Esper getting wrapped up in any more of this revolution junk; he'd fall for it so easily. One dazzling smile and turn of phrase and he'd become a child soldier.

Honestly, I don't know why I'm bothering to hang around the bunker at this point except that I've got nowhere else to go. Hiero guaranteed me work, but I've barely seen her. Ever since our spat last week she's been avoiding me, which is probably for the best; until I receive some sort of apology, I don't really want to see her. Despite that, somehow I still want to get along with her and be on good terms. Part of me wishes she would admit she was out of line and drag me off on another mission... unless it involved more stealing.

The longer I don't see Hiero, the more I worry about securing pay. I don't want to have to go anywhere with Aether again. I hate that it's come down to which I'd rather: culturalist generalizations or borderline homicide. I'm almost out of errands to run and favors to do for people in the bunker. Mostly I've been fixing two-way parmecs for anyone going off on missions, and bastrinas for anyone I hear complaining loudly enough about being unable to send or receive messages. I haven't gotten much in exchange, just pocket change and IOUs.

Occasionally I'll hang by the stairway and watch the construction on the airship. They've finished the framework and started on plating the skeleton of the craft, though it doesn't look that aerodynamic. I mentioned it to one of the guys, Verne, but he waved it off, saying it's the crew's concern, not mine. I know Meno was listening, though, and he seemed to take the comment to heart.

I'm not quite sure what to think about Meno. Given what Aether said about him, he certainly does talk a lot, but he means well. In a way, he reminds me a bit of Esper: too much energy and a knack for getting into things he shouldn't. I don't know what to make of his alleged expertise for breaking into security systems, but as a person he seems okay. I get that feeling about most of the people here, really, like they're good people to know even if they are participants in a violent revolution, and I look forward to catching him during a free moment to talk. He's meant to wire the controls up in the front of the ship, so he's usually around, even if it's just to supervise the construction of the ship's hull.

Today there's not much going on. Maybe the project's been halted, hopefully to reevaluate the structure of the ship.

"Artem?" I whip my head back as Runa pokes her head out of the ward. "If you've got a minute, I could use your help."

If I didn't know any better, I'd say Runa was trying to keep me busy. But it's not as though I have anything else to do. As I walk in I'm overwhelmed by the stench of dust and rubbing alcohol. A few glass bottles sit on a shelf, cracked and leaking fluid. Runa stands by just watching the mess collect in a dribbly violet puddle on the floor, adjusting the shawl over her shoulders and fretting under her breath. The usually warm feel of the room is unable to penetrate the frigid air.

"What ha–happened?" The words leave my mouth in a puff of steam.

"The heater broke, I guess."

"I can see that." I take a step closer toward the hulking machine in the corner. "I was just ta–talking to myself."

This heater is older than anything I've ever seen; I'm surprised it ever worked in the first place. The last time I saw a unit with three compartments was back in Mr. Connolly's around when I first started. All he said was that it would be cheaper to get a new heater entirely and strip that one for scrap. I take off one of my gloves and rub my eyes. With patience and the right attitude, I can take apart each section and hopefully diagnose the main problem.

The chambers have seen better days. Wire upon wire is frayed to the point only bare, tarnished copper is showing, and there are a handful of gears inside, stationary and coated in gunk. Why—? There shouldn't even be gears here, it makes no functional sense! In another compartment, a fan that's beyond rusted is cemented to the structure. I wish I had blueprints to understand the furnace better, but besides some minor adjustments, what it really needs is some love and care. I'm certain some basic cleaning and rewiring will make it at least functional. I stand up and dust my pants off before grabbing my toolbox from its place in the corner.

"I'll see what I can do, but I c–can't promise anything."

"Something is better than nothing."

The ward is quiet. I don't understand the purpose of having a ward in the bunker. I suppose in the long term, it makes sense, with a structure initially intended to house hundreds of people and the likelihood of injury to occur among larger groups. But in terms of the rebellion, I don't see the point in having more than one doctor on hand day in and day out. Emergencies happen, of course, but it seems ridiculous to have someone show up every day.

I pause for a moment to ask, "Do you get paid to be here e–every day? H–how does that even work?"

"It's a little rude to ask questions like that, Artem."

"I–I'm sorry."

"I'm teasing," Runa sighs, crouching to clean the mess off the floor with a dingy rag. "There are funds coming in for the revolution, but not everyone here is paid for what they do. A lot of people volunteer, some get paid in other ways, and the more labor-intensive get funded, such as what you do. Not everyone knows repair work."

"What a–about you? N–Not everyone knows how to fix p–people."

Her eyes don't leave the puddle she's mopping, but the corner of her mouth lifts wryly. "Let's just say Christa and I make ends meet."

There's not much else to add, so I keep my mouth shut. The heater proves to be more beast than machine with the fight it's putting up. I try a couple solutions, with no luck. There's no way around it, I'm going to have to do some cleaning after all.

It takes a bit of elbow grease to wipe the cogs and scrape away at the gunk. There's so much dust and filth inside that I feel more like a chimney-sweep than a mechanic. I manage to waste a good forty minutes just cleaning before managing to get back to the initial problem. After some fiddling around, the heater springs to life once more, and the chill from the room dissipates. Runa brings over another rag and I start wiping at my hands, trying to scrub off the charcoal caked onto my gloves.

"Thank you, Artem. How much do I owe you?"

"N–Nothing," I shrug, putting my stuff away.

"That's quite a way to conduct business," a man rumbles from behind me.

Runa's expression changes, and she goes stiff, tipping a curt nod toward the doorway. I turn to see a polished and well-built individual, two other men standing at attention behind him. He turns his head back, shooting them a look; they salute and disappear from sight. A red handkerchief, monogrammed 'R', pokes from his vest pocket, and his presence commands quiet attention. I can only assume this is none other than Rhine Toberts himself.

My mind goes blank as he steps forward, runs a hand through his neatly combed brown locks, and offers a dazzling but oddly humble smile. He keeps his posture straight and poised, but there's a slight wobble in his shoulders, like he's not yet used to holding the weight of authority.

"At ease," he greets. Even though he attempts to be firm, it's clear the salutes are amusing to him, still novel and flattering. "You must be the mechanic I've been hearing about." The man holds out a hand. "I'm Rhine, leader of the Airgon movement."

I tentatively shake his hand, ignoring the lump in my throat. "A–Artem Clairingbold."

"I'm not interrupting anything important, am I?" Rhine chuckles and looks over at Runa. "We'll be out of your hair. Carry on."

Runa busies herself again, with renewed gusto. I glance between my tools and Rhine, as he waits patiently. I don't know what he wants. I bow as best I can, much to his amusement; he quirks an eyebrow and motions for me to follow him.

We step onto the walkway overlooking the rest of the bunker. Production on the ship seems to have resumed, and clearly they've reevaluated something, because a few mechies are dismantling pieces of the hull with hand-held garmecs. Rhine stops to watch for a moment, then turns to face me directly. My heart hammers under his undivided attention.

"I suppose it's unnecessary to show you around. It looks like you've become acquainted with our base. It's impressive, isn't it? As a boy I heard tales of a space under the city that could hold thousands, a series of rooms and tunnels. Do you know where exactly we are right now?"

I shake my head and squeak out a "no."

"The main bunker is to the right of the river separating the Kensing Sector and the Flooded Sector." Rhine's hooded gaze tracks each worker carefully, and though his posture is casual, forearms resting against the railing, there's a distance to his face, as though he's running sums, adding up the cost of every bolt, the value of each worker. "One tunnel leads close to where the old train station used to operate, and with a little excavation, it's possible to reach as far as Lindsor."

Lindsor again. "How do you kn-know the layout of this place so well?" I ask, daring to step a bit closer. Immediately he shifts his focus and turns to me; I backtrack and stumble over my own feet. It seems as though he is too caught up in the sound of his own voice to notice, or perhaps he simply doesn't care.

"I'm running a base of operations here. It's become my job to know, to familiarize myself with it as much as possible. My father discovered the tunnels himself while he was working with a scribe. Not even the royal family remembers this place exists." Rhine taps his fingers against the railing a few times, expression growing cold as he furrows his brow in thought. His gaze drifts from me, and his voice softens, like he's forgotten I'm here and is just talking to himself. "I spent three years getting the facilities running and found people willing to help get it to where it is now. Over our heads right now is a warehouse at the edge of the Kensing Sector, most likely rigged for sending supplies down here in bulk when the time came." Suddenly, like a switch, he flips back to the charismatic leader persona, and addresses me once more. "The platform is currently covered by our redesigned airship… which is your primary interest, correct?"

I clear my throat and bring my hands together nervously. "I've ne-never even been on a— an—" Pausing for a second, I furrow my brow. The word is escaping me, and at the worst possible moment. "Th-the, um, the… *qes jaq ĕnav?* I-I know what it is, it flies. The *aberqen,* qift, sorry, I-I-I?"

I take a deep breath, trying to focus. *Râ jĕ qavesii.* Flying ship. Air. Airship. That's the word.

"I ha-haven't been on an a-airship, Mr. Toberts. Most of what I used t-to do was repair work and blueprint review for m-my boss' inventions." I wince even more. Old boss, I mentally correct myself.

Rhine rubs at his chin, then crosses his arms and looks me up and down. "You disabled one of the skylines without ever being on them before, from what I've heard. It sounds like you don't give yourself enough credit."

It's giving me too much credit, I'd like to argue, but I choose to drop my hands and be more direct. "I'd glan-glanced at the blueprints once when-when they were st-still being designed. A-And I wouldn't say I stopped them, just de-delayed one."

"And what about airships? Did you ever see anything for an older model?" I grimace and Rhine nods. "That's fine. Most of the people working on it have, but what I need right now is someone who knows engines. I can see to it you're compensated for your time. We may be a rebellion, but even a revolution has its investors."

Who would be funding this rebellion, and why? I know better than to ask, but my mind spins at the gall that having money must give some folks. Giving their coin to a revolution that might well fail instead of saving it for something practical makes no sense. After all, there are procs everywhere doing their best to sniff out their base of operations.

Back on the skyline Hiero had managed to secure a bunch of coin for herself. It doesn't make it any less wrong, but I suppose it puts things into a different perspective if she was just working to help sustain the bunker. But the way Rhine puts it, I get the feeling there's someone higher up than all of us, rubbing elbows with Parvay and somehow funneling coins in the rebels' direction.

In one smooth, quick movement, Rhine pulls a pocket-watch from his trousers and gives it a cursory glance and a nod before sliding it back into his pocket and turning his bright gaze on me again. "Have you seen what we're working with up close?"

I haven't. I'm still an outsider here; I don't feel welcome exploring anywhere other than the medical ward without express permission. I think my face betrays me. Rhine starts to move again, and I stumble as I try my best to keep up with his long strides.

Walking toward the stairway instead of the door is bizarre. I fall behind a bit as I catch myself almost leaving. As quickly as I can, I rush down the stairs, holding the handrail. The whole time, Rhine chats idly to the air about having put quite the planning into this project. I try to keep up as he throws out estimated costs, and facts about the metals being used, along with where they've gotten them. It's dizzying to run in a quick spiral.

"Most of the materials we've been using have been recycled. Fine metals would be appreciated, of course, but there are more important things to be funding right now than just stainless steel. From what I gather, it doesn't make much of a difference between stainless and gray, except that it separates us from them."

Us from them? Does he mean the movement and the Crown? It's not surprising that they're using an alloy. What is, is the fact that the alloy is a mixture of aluminum and stainless steel, of all things. So much for not being fancy or like the Crown. I almost trip over my own feet at least twice before catching up with Rhine.

I've always known it was an airship based on the shape of the armature. The skeleton has been on my mind since day one. In size alone, the potential aerocraft is impressive, larger than most of the ships in service now. There look to be only two main rooms, though, and while girthy, it's lacking in terms of height.

From what I understand, today's airships are built for the comfort of the wealthier citizens of Allowyn. Maybe twenty to thirty passengers are carried to their destination on ships whose upper decks are entirely dedicated to entertainment. It wouldn't surprise me if the king's personal aerocraft also had a study, with a gigantic marble grandio for someone to play as others gathered around to sing. The point is, all of them are meant for extravagance, whereas this ship is pure function. The way everything is simplistic and stripped-back, it's clearly not meant for taking a holiday.

I slowly make my way toward the craft and bring a hand up to run along the surface. The cuts aren't the finest, and it's not the most visually appealing, but that's not my concern. What I'm worried about is how this hunk of metal will get off the ground. It seems Rhine is, too.

He watches me steadily, hands clasped behind his back. "If you're interested in the project, I'd love to take you on as our chief engineer. You seem more than qualified."

Chief engineer!? "I–I've never made a–an engine for an airship," I mumble, but am unable to turn away from the gleaming hull. "Or any flying machine. My o–only experience with engines has been with jitneys, aut–automatons... nothing like thi–this."

He hums thoughtfully. "Unfortunately, that's more than what can be said of some of the men working on this project. If I heard correctly, you brought it to my crew's attention that our previous plating was less than ideal." That's not reassuring, but again, not surprising. I swallow loudly and force myself to face Rhine. His eyes practically sparkle, and he keeps his head high and proud. "You still haven't asked why we're building an airship. Care to guess?"

"It's n–not for transpor–transportation." With a shake of my head, I continue to guess, certain I've pieced it together. "Not j–just tran–transportation, I mean. It–It's meant for even more people, but it's n–not luxury, and you can carry cargo in easier ways th–than airship." Oh, gaqĕ. I look at Rhine, unable to keep the disapproval from my voice or furrowed brow. "This is a–a weapon."

"We need an aerial advantage," Rhine explains mildly, turning to admire the ship's skeleton with me. "Anyone can have ships, utilize the many tunnels, but rather than supply troops with tanks that will never live up to the royal army's, why not go a different route?"

"I'm not even p–part of the movement. I've ba–barely got any experience. Y–You want me to be in charge of m–making sure your ship flies?" I want to make sure I've got this right. It sounds absurd just coming out of my mouth.

He doesn't move, but his gaze shifts to me. "You're committed to this movement on some level. I have enough faith in your abilities, which you seem to underestimate."

I don't know what Rhine has heard to have him so confident. I wonder if Aether actually said something nice about me. Somehow the idea of being talked up is more uncomfortable than flattering.

I shift my weight from foot to foot. Rhine keeps his distance, and one of the men who was with him earlier approaches and mutters something into Rhine's ear. Rhine eyes the stairway, and the other man takes his leave.

The clock's ticking down. Anything else he says goes in one ear and out the other. I'm busy thinking over the logistics, wondering if I can even do what he wants done, if it's even ethical. He must have gotten to the part about pay, as he produces a sizable coin purse, large enough to almost spill from his rather large hand.

"That's i–in advance?" My mouth goes dry.

"This now." Rhine raises an eyebrow. "Negotiable how much a month, so long as you can provide proof of work done. Do we have an agreement?"

I'm unable to think it over as the words tumble out of my mouth. "Three hun–hundred and twenty." He nods his head, barely batting an eye, and I kick myself for not tossing out an even higher sum.

"You're welcome to use any space you need out here with the other engineers." Rhine approaches to place the bag in my hands and holds his right out to shake. "The Airgon movement appreciates your cooperation and efforts. It's been a pleasure to meet you, Artem."

I weakly extend my hand. He practically crushes my fingers, and then I'm left alone on the main floor with a lump sum of coin and my thoughts. Two thick-armed men struggle past me carrying a heavy steel beam between them, and I stumble out of the way. To think, I'll be working alongside these folks soon, instead of watching from the side.

I head off to collect my tools from upstairs, then stop short; standing at the edge of the spiral stairway is Hiero. She's as put-together as always, but looks almost unsure of herself, nervous. Part of me doesn't want to talk to her yet. Another part is clamoring for her attention and wondering why I haven't seen her sooner.

There's no time for me to decide whether to approach her or make my escape; she's already seen me. She walks over, but stops about a foot away, her arms fidgeting and her right hand fluttering at her hip as if unsure whether to rest there. Hiero looks around, taking in the hustle and bustle, before facing me again and looking down. She's biting her lip, and something shudders through me at the sight. Bad Artem. You're still mad at her.

"I see you've already met with Rhine."

"Yeah, he sort of just... sh–showed up." I grimace. "I was starting to think I'd n–never meet him."

She lets out a breath. "Good. It was hard finding a time he could meet me down here to see you, but I guess he decided to show up a bit earlier than planned." Hiero huffs lightly, casting her gaze off to the side. "Just as well, I don't think we're exactly on the best terms."

I blink a couple times, not sure I heard correctly. Was Hiero going to meet Rhine here and then approach me? I thought Aether might have reported to Rhine and inquired about a position on the airship for me, not Hiero.

"You t–told Rhine a–about me?"

She blinks, surprised, and her gaze finally swings up to meet mine. "Of course. It was part of our agreement, remember?"

"But I–I thought—!"

"What, that I was going to leave you high and dry?" Hiero looks away again, still nibbling at her lip, though the slightest grin ghosts her features.

I don't answer; my silence is enough. She nods, and we stand quietly for a few moments, both of us just watching the workers buzz around the airship. It's not that I thought Hiero would back out of her word, it was more how we parted on such uneasy terms. The last time we spoke, she was incredibly culturalist and seemed not to care how much it hurt me. After working for Aether, I'm starting to think culturalism might not have been the worst thing, but that doesn't make it less painful.

Hiero closes her eyes and takes a deep breath. I want to

117

leave, but I'm interested in what she has to say. Maybe she can explain why it took so long to talk to Rhine about me. Actually, no, I can guess for myself that Rhine Toberts is a busy man. Getting any audience was probably more difficult than it sounded. Still, I find myself hanging on her pause, waiting.

"I don't want us to have this..." she gestures vaguely, "... air between us, and I've given it some thought, what I said and what you said and everything that happened." She's less polished than usual, less practiced. I didn't think Hiero even got nervous. She stuffs her hands in her pockets, looks down at the ground, and then directly at me again. I find myself trapped in the emerald of her eyes, locked into place. I don't quite want to leave, and I don't think I could if I did. Does she know the power she wields with her gaze alone? That she could force anyone to stop in their tracks by a mere glance?

Well, it's Hiero, so. Probably.

"I'm Sertalin, and that's not an excuse, but the thing is, I don't know what your life is like or what it's like to be anything but Sertalin. I didn't realize what I said was wrong, was... cruel, and I've taken some time to think about it and talk to some other people. What I said hurt you, whether I was trying to or not, and I'll... work on it."

I'm fairly certain that Hiero hasn't had to apologize very often throughout her life. She's uncomfortable and having a tough time maintaining eye contact, having to look away now and again whenever her voice wavers. Nonetheless, it's one of the most genuine things I've ever heard, and something in my chest flutters, not from her words but from the effort she's put in.

She clicks her tongue, fingers drumming against her leg before she continues. "I'm sorry. *Kashø*. You don't need to say anything, just, I'll work on how I've been phrasing things and what I say. If it happens again, please just tell me. I would rather know I've done something wrong so I can correct it than think things are fine between us when they're not."

"I ac–accept your apology."

The tension leaves her body all at once; her shoulders drop, and the tightness of her face smoothes. "...Thank you." She releases the words in a husky sigh, and a shiver runs over my skin. With that, she brushes past me, to walk around the ship, all the way to the opposite staircase. I tilt my head and watch her as she goes. Why she couldn't use the same stairs she went down is beyond me. Hiero's regular theatrics, maybe.

Before I move to leave, I reach into my pocket, finding a new weight. My fingers wrap around a small pouch that hadn't been there earlier. I manage to undo the ties and peek inside. Various tiny tools and bits of high-grade metal rest inside, a bit jumbled but in decent condition. Hiero must have dropped it into my pocket as she walked by. She couldn't have just handed them to me?

Right. Theatrics.

I slide the pouch back into my pocket and find myself smiling as I head up the stairs. Maybe this will work out after all.

CHAPTER 8

The head of construction, Gewells, gathers together the crew working on the airship. No one seems thrilled about the interruption. I'm assuming it's to make an announcement about the newest addition to the team: me. Never in my life have I enjoyed being the center of attention, and this is certainly no exception. All eyes are on me, standing beside Gewells. "Waste of time," one guy grunts loudly to the fellow beside him. Out of habit, I adjust my tie and try to swallow my anxiety.

"Alright, settle down, settle down. We've got everyone, I think, so I want to make this quick. You've seen this young lady hanging around the past week or two; this is Artem, she'll be joining the project as a chief advisor working with the engine."

Everyone is stone-faced, blinking back at me, and I am suddenly alone, despite Gewells standing next to me. My palms are sweating, my shoulders tense.

Gewells waves a hand at the gathered crowd. "Alright, announcement over. Everyone get back to work."

No one seems to be paying any real attention. Each man turns and disperses to his usual spot. I can relax. It's all just business as usual. Yet I'm unnerved by just how quickly everyone dismissed Gewell's announcement. Maybe they just don't care.

I catch Verne and Meno talking off to the side and perk up. They're the only two I've really talked to, though mostly just in passing. If I can make friends with anyone, it's probably Meno. He always seems friendly and willing to talk. I walk over, catching the tail end of their conversation about supports.

"I see you guys to–took my suggestion!" I greet them, and they stare blankly at me. "F–For the ship," I clarify, trailing off uncertainly. "W–With it n–not being aer–aerodynamic, and, um, st–stuff." Dreggar.

"Oh. Hey, Artem, right?" Meno asks. The smile he shoots my way is quick but genuine.

Verne scoffs. "Listen. Just because you've done some work before doesn't mean you're in charge. Got it?"

I never claimed to be in charge. My shoulders slump.

"C'mon, Verne." Meno gestures vaguely. "She's doing engine stuff, it's not our concern."

"I hav–haven't ever actually w–worked with an en–engine," I pipe up. "I'm excited to–to try, t–though!"

I instantly regret saying anything. "Try?" Jesault, one of

the haulers, stops mid-stride to interrupt in his low, drawling voice. "There's no trying here, we're doing a job."

Verne looks incredulous. "Wait, back up, you've never even worked on one of these ships, and suddenly you're chief engineer?" Any words of defense leave me, especially when he follows up with a snide, "Who'd she screw to get a job playing expert?"

That's my cue to leave. I give a weak wave, jerking my head away to hide the growing red of my cheeks, and retreat to one of the side rooms. I'm here to do a job, so I'll do my job, coworkers be damned. Pulling out some of the paper lying around, I get to work sketching out designs and initial blueprints, just as Mr. Connolly would have. I swear I hear a snicker or two in my direction, but I do my best to pay it no mind, my hand drifting down to the bag of materials Hiero gave me yesterday. She believes I can do this.

Meno stops by, hanging by the doorway for a moment. It takes me longer than I care to admit to notice him. He coughs; with a slight jump, I turn in my chair to look over at him, offering my best smile.

"Don't draw too much attention to yourself," he says by way of hello. "Everyone will get used to you."

So much for making friends. I nod sharply and Meno grabs some bolts before ducking out again. I'm left alone in the room, with just my prints and drafting pencils. How can I get along with these guys? I'm already at the disadvantage of joining the project late, but I shouldn't have admitted to having no experience with engines. I guess technically it's not true, as I can handle jitneys and automatons, but airships are a different beast entirely. There's not a single other girl around, either; I can't remember the last time I met another woman who worked as a tinkerer, engineer, or inventor.

Maybe I'm doomed to be awkward in every work environment. Making friends is hard, but forming bonds with coworkers is even harder. For the life of me, I don't even know how I managed to become friends with Runa— but I guess that's not such a shock. She's one of the friendliest people I know.

Did my father have as much difficulty fitting in when he was hired for contracts? He must have at least won over Mr. Connolly; their connection was the only reason he took me on in the first place. But he was likeable from what I remember, and always had friends... friends that conveniently disappeared after he did.

I don't know how long it's been, but it feels like I've spent hours just sketching. I pack up most of my belongings and tuck them away in a corner. Grabbing my knapsack, I head out, with a small wave to the workers who remain, then head up the spiral staircase and through the tunnels. I need to pick up Esper from Kylir, and head to the market before it closes.

While I would love to leave him alone at the house, every time I do I end up regretting it. Last time, he was caught messing with fireworks near a storefront and broke a window. The only reason he didn't wind up in a cell or with a few fingers missing was because of Roran. I already feel bad about how much he's helped us in the past, and the last time I saw him I was still working for Mr. Connolly. I don't know if I could handle another run-in with Roran right now, especially if Esper is committing minor vandalism. So no matter how frustrating he makes it to run errands, I have no choice but to bring Esper along.

Kylir lives a block away from the big market in the middle of Brunsel sector. She used to live in the same complex as us, before she married a baker. Now she does fairly well and spends most of her days helping manage the finances. Sometimes I ask her for help with Esper, but she doesn't like to. No one does. Kylir is usually my last attempt for a babysitter.

As soon as I knock on the door, Kylir answers, crossing her arms as Esper trudges out. I must be late. I put a hand on Esper's head and offer a sheepish smile. "Glory be. S–Sorry I'm r-running a little—."

"It happens," Kylir says, cutting me off with a sigh, then holds out a hand. "That'll be two ration tickets."

"Tw–Two rations?" I choke out.

"Yes. Two ration tickets. For bread."

Those aren't cheap. We only get a handful of rations for certain items a month, mostly because Esper is still underage and we can't survive off just water and cans of beans.

I don't know why Kylir would want the ration tickets—she's married to a baker. One ration ticket already seemed much as payment for watching Esper, but I chose not to complain about it.

"You u–used to ask for one— why two now?"

"You know, bread isn't easy to come by. There's a lot of work that goes into collecting the wheat and the grinding and sifting and baking of it."

"But why w–would you need the tickets?" I ask, tilting my head.

"Unless you have twelve in coin..." Kylir trails off, lips pursed. I know that look. I hate that look. 'Gotcha, poor girl, I know you can't pay.'

Ugh. I wish Jynelle had been free. Rummaging through my knapsack, I pull out the thick coin purse I got from Rhine. Esper's eyes widen and I feel him tug on my sleeve as I carefully count out the twelve coins and hand them over. She snatches the coin from me and hums in approval before tossing a goodbye to Esper and slamming the door on us.

There's no use in arguing. Judging by the sun and the sky— because, of course, my pocket-watch just broke, and all my tools are in the bunker— it has to be close to closing time for the merchant stalls. We need to get going. I pat Esper on the back and lead the way.

"Was that from—?" Esper starts, but I shut him down.

"I-I got paid to do a-a job. That's all."

For the end of the day, it's busy. I'm used to coming by in the morning, when it's still early and the crowds don't show up until I leave, twenty or so minutes later. There must be a good forty people milling about, asking about prices and trading goods. The sun hangs low, casting shadows everywhere and hanging, blinding and inconvenient, over the market signs. I squint the best I can at the nearest stall, selling bundles of carrots and potatoes. Somehow prices have gone up by thirty percent. Five daros for a half-rotted vegetable is outlandish, but far less so than the prices in the shops.

Esper tugs at my sleeve. "Can we get peaches?"

I look at the sign and wince. "I don't t-think so, Es." I adjust my arms. "We're k-kind of on a tight b-budget."

"It doesn't look like we're on a tight budget..."

"Th–That's for emergencies."

Arguably, we could splurge on groceries this week. The advance from Rhine is way more than I'd make at Mr. Connolly's shop. However, there's no guaranteeing the pay I'll get next week, or any of the following weeks. A rebellion isn't what I'd call... financially reliable.

"I can pay for it!" he insists. I chuckle at the offer. More than likely he'll pull out a little stash he's been saving to help out. I would never let him pay for it anyway.

"With what money?" I ask.

On cue, Esper produces a large coin purse from his shirt. He thrusts his haul toward me, wearing a huge grin.

I stare at the pouch in his hands. My mouth goes dry, my voice low. "Wh–Where did you get that?"

"I found it."

"Where d–did you find it?"

"Lying in the street?"

"...T–That makes t–two of you." There's far more ice in my voice than usual. Esper's stealing things again. This is worse than swiping some fruit off a vendor or a trinket from one of his classmates. No, this is straight larceny.

I push the bag of money back at him slowly while fighting back my urge to panic. Esper scowls, on the verge of arguing. "You need t–to put that b–back right now." My voice wavers. "For Dreggar's s–sake, w–why would you do that? We've talked a–about this!"

"It's for a good cause, right? The rebellion says—"

"F–Forget w–what the rebellion says, y–you can't j–just take coin from people!" My heart leaps into my throat. How has he managed to take anything while he's been by my side this whole time? "Okay." I take a deep breath, bringing a hand to my head. "What el–else did you steal while we've b–been here?"

"Nothing."

"E–Esper," I warn.

"Nothing, seriously!" he huffs, raising his voice. "Why can't you just take my word? You never believe me."

I raise my hands and try to get him to lower his voice. No one seems to be paying attention, but that doesn't stop me from glancing in every direction to make sure. Not a single proc nearby is looking our way. "N–no, no, I mean, I just worry. Let's t–try this again: w–why are you taking things?"

"We take stuff all the time, though, don't we?"

"N–No!" Not exactly. "Esper, taking things that don't belong to anyone, th–that's different. Taking things that already h–have owners, that's stealing."

I'm not in the mood to debate ethics with a pre-teen. I also don't know where he started getting such a mouth. Once upon a time, I took care of a boy who didn't question everything and apologized when he was wrong. Now he's getting moody and everything is suddenly a personal attack. "That purse has an o–owner. You are going to p–put this nearby w–wherever you took it, and y–you are going to walk away. G–Got it?"

He looks like he wants to argue more, but instead huffs and disappears. I bring a hand to my chest, my heart hammering against my ribcage. I expect him to come back grumbling any second about finders-keepers and the like. Just in case, I start prepping the speech I've had to give twice now, about time and place and ownership. Rummaging through a dump for salvage is different from taking someone's coin purse. I learned my lesson years ago; I don't need him learning the same way I did. I can barely maintain my own implants, I don't need to try constructing new audancers for him. And if he lost fingers or a hand? I'm not sure of my ability to make a functional prosthesis. There's a dull ache near the base of my audancers, and I clasp my hands together to keep myself from cradling the implants defensively.

Someone clears their throat behind me. All the blood drains from my face as I prepare to meet whomever owns that coin purse. I spin on my heels, only to look up at a familiar rough-stubbled face.

"R–Roran!" I gasp. "Glory be!"

"Glory be, Artem." Roran furrows his brow, looking behind me for a moment. "Lose Esper again?"

"N–Not r–r–really, he's just—" I sigh.

"Yeah, I remember when I was that age." He laughs and rubs the back of his neck. I find myself copying his motions and looking down at my feet. It feels wrong to be talking to Roran after what happened at Mr. Connolly's shop with Hiero. He was just doing his job, chasing after a woman who released his latest arrest. Yet, without even knowing Hiero, I chose a stranger over someone who's done so much more for me.

Even now, I don't know why I acted the way I did. A flash of Hiero's astonishingly green eyes pops into my head, but I shake it away. At the time, my goal was justice. The proc system is far from merciful with vagrants, and as nice as

Roran has been to me, I've seen the way he's treated other people— and other Qorani— on the job.

He flashes me a smile. "Actually, Artem, I've been looking around for you recently. Haven't seen you over at Mr. Connolly's in a while. What's going on?"

I choke on air. "I-I was let go."

"What?" Roran's arm drops to his side. "How did that happen? I thought Mr. Connolly adored you!"

Adored is quite the overstatement. "That, um, that's..."

He waves a hand. "It's alright, you don't have to talk about it if you don't want to."

A wave of relief washes over me. I nod and leave the explanation there. He's confused, but doesn't push it, opting to clear his throat as he looks around.

I gesture toward him, trying to think of something to say, but my voice catches in my throat when I spy the sword by his side, instead of his usual club. Sure enough, he has another on his back. He must have been promoted. Immediately my arm drops back to my side and I nod a couple more times. I silently beg Esper to come back.

Roran clears his throat with a low hum. "Anyway, now that I've found you, I had a favor I wanted to ask."

"Oh?" My lungs fill with lead.

He quirks me a reassuring grin, his eyes crinkling. "Yeah, it's kind of stupid, actually."

I can't imagine what he wants, but I owe him quite a bit at this point. It's not that I don't want to pay him back, but something in his tone doesn't sit well with me.

"I'm supposed to be going to this gala over in one of those Lindsor houses. It's mostly on-the-clock stuff, but I originally said I had someone going with me and she sort of backed out..."

He trails off with a half-laugh. I just look up at him, fighting the urge to twist my lips together and shake my head. His story doesn't sit right. Roran knows plenty of people, I'm sure, and if I didn't know better I'd think he was asking me on a date. There's no way this was a spur-of-a-moment type thing; Roran has tried to ask me out before. But I'm just... not into guys.

Before I can respond, Esper crashes into me. I stumble but manage to find my footing, sputtering all the while. He looks around wildly, only to glance up at Roran and bolt upright.

I don't need to wonder what happened.

"Out of my way! Somebody catch that thief!"

Without thinking, I take a step in front of Esper and hold an arm out to block him. The man is easily two heads taller, on the lanky side, but looks like he's been in a fight or two. Roran juts his chin out, stony-faced as he turns to the man, hand hovering by his sword. "What seems to be the problem here?"

"That kid," the other man spits, pointing a finger toward Esper. "Stole my coin purse!"

"I found it! I was giving it back!" Esper protests. The man tries to push closer, and Esper jolts back, huddling behind me.

It looks like his plans to return that coin purse didn't go as smoothly as I thought. I told him he should have just left it nearby, not return it to him personally. Roran looks at each of us and takes a moment before addressing the man directly. "There must be some misunderstanding. If you wish to file a complaint, I will be happy to walk you through the necessary steps. In the meantime, I'm going to have to ask you to step away, sir."

He's a bit red in the face, ready to say more, but he huffs and walks away. I hear him mutter under his breath a slur I'm far too familiar with. Roran gives a short, barked, "Move along!" then turns to my brother. "I swear, kid, keep it up and I'm gonna have to give you a tour of the cells," Roran warns Esper, though his voice has grown softer.

"I didn't steal his dumb coin purse!" Esper sniffs and turns his head. "He dropped it and I gave it back to him."

"Uh-huh." He looks me in the eye. "You're lucky I'm prone to looking the other way for you."

He knows. My head starts to spin. Roran knew— or at least suspected— who Hiero was, and walked the other way. Was it because I got involved? Did he think we were friends? Esper's just landed me a date that I don't want to go on. There's no way I can turn down Roran's invitation now.

I take a deep breath, close my eyes and gather my thoughts. I'm tired in a way no amount of qosa can fix. "When is t-the gala?"

His grin is back, but there's a cold triumph in his eyes that makes me sick. "It's on Larns. I'll be by at six. We can take the skyline into the Sector, then a jitney from there."

"I'll n-need to find s-someone to w-watch Esper." My shoulders slump. "It sh-shouldn't be a p-problem. Do I n-need to-to find a dress?"

"If you can." Roran tilts his head in thought, then gives a wave and heads off.

Esper snorts loudly. "You? In a dress?"

I couldn't agree more, but I let it go and look at our groceries for the week. As if things weren't tight enough, now I need to probably find a dress for a fancy event full of people I shouldn't be around.

Reluctantly, I pull out my coin purse and take quick stock of what I brought with me today. We have more than enough, but that doesn't mean I'm not uneasy spending some of it. Last I checked, the price of corn has gone up even higher than the last time we were here. There's no way I'm going to be able to swing this trip, buying a dress, and paying rent for the month without feeling guilty. Maybe I can borrow a dress from one of the neighbors...

Esper groans as I start toward a merchant with an abundance of cabbage. Despite everything, I dig a coin out and thrust it into his hands to get him to stop complaining. His eyes light up and he speeds off toward the nearest fruit stall. I shake my head and wonder if it's worth getting qosa this week. Then again, with everything I've gotten myself into... how could I afford to go without it?

CHAPTER 9

I'm running out of places to stow Esper during the day. We keep receiving letters inquiring about apprenticeships and opportunities in the factories. I don't want to know how anyone knows about Esper's situation, especially since his papers are expired. The situation with Kylir is less than favorable, and I'm left with two options: leave Esper home alone, or bring him to the bunker.

It's not that I don't trust Esper... I just don't trust his impulse control. As much as I'm sure Rhine or Aether would have my head for bringing along my kid brother, leaving him at the apartment is asking for trouble. He'll probably run off and do something stupid out of sheer boredom, like throw rocks at proc MLs or start hanging around with the Terwin kids. I really don't want Roran at my door with Esper again, especially after what happened in the marketplace the other day.

Esper swings his arms wildly as we walk, and he only stops to adjust the oversized cap on his head as he looks up at me. "There's really a city underneath Wellwick?"

"W-What? No. And keep your vo–voice down, maro," I urge, shushing him. "Rosh jul, you're g–going to be the d–death of me."

Esper makes a face at the term of endearment but keeps quiet. I shiver as a strong wind tears by, and rub my arms out of habit. I really wish I had a jacket for this weather. At least Esper is nice and warm, even if his clothes are too big. I can't remember the last time either of us had clothes that fit properly.

We get to the faux-pub and Esper looks at me, confused. "Are you an alcoholic?" I'm already regretting this.

"For Dreggar's s–sake," I mumble, and push him inside.

Heads turn in my direction. I feel my face burn as I ask for a "b–b–bait and switch." The bartender eyes Esper but steps aside and lifts up the divider. Esper stiffens as I walk past him and pull the lever.

"I don't want to go in there," he whines as the hatch opens.

"It's just th–this once, then you won't have to come back here again." Hopefully. "Don't worry, y–you can hold my hand."

"I don't need you to hold my hand!" Esper puffs his chest out, though he falters by the entrance. I slide in first to demonstrate that it's safe. Slowly he follows after, darting his gaze around the tunnel. The hatch closes and he steps closer to me, the slightest tremble in his frame.

"This w–way." I rub his back gently and lead on. He walks alongside me, head turning at the slightest sound. I remember being just as wary the first time I walked through these tunnels. It's funny, in a way, how quickly they went from being scary to familiar.

When we reach the giant door, I struggle with the handle, grunting as it eventually gives way. Esper stands frozen in shock, taking in the hustle and bustle of people skittering up and down the set of stairs on the opposite side of the room. He quickly runs to the rail to look down below, unable to contain his awe as a "wow" tumbles past his lips. Spinning around, Esper practically jumps and starts spitting questions. "How does this place exist? Is this really under all of Wellwick? How far down are we? Why hasn't the roof caved in? What's that giant door on the ceiling? Do you always have to go through the tunnels to get here? Can we check out that big thing?"

"Woah, s–slow down, Es!" I shake my head. "I–I don't know. I need to–to go to work downst–downstairs."

"On that thing?"

"Yes, th–that thing."

"What is it?"

"An airship," Runa answers for me, heading over with a washcloth in hand. "Which is not safe for young boys to hang around." I feel my cheeks burn at Runa's tart warning. It doesn't feel like it was intended to be a dig at me, but it stings nevertheless. I don't get a chance to defend myself as Runa rubs her hands with the washcloth and looks Esper over with a wide grin. "You must be Artem's brother, Esper. I've heard so much about you!"

Esper watches carefully as she extends a hand, and warily accepts her handshake. "Who are you?"

"This is Runa," I answer quickly.

Runa nods. "I'm a medic. I take care of people who get injured working on things like that airship."

"Cool."

"You know, I could use an extra set of hands, today, Artem." Runa casts me a sympathetic look. "Mostly filing, but it'll keep him out of your hair."

"I'm right here, you know!"

I feel my shoulders relax, unaware how tense I was. "Pasha, e vâlĕ-qev'niin ĕnem."

Runa blinks a few times, looking surprised— did she assume I didn't know Qalqora? Many Qorani automatically assume that based on my accent. But her surprise comes from a different place, it seems, as she clears her throat and tucks a stray hair behind her ear. "I don't speak Qalqora."

"You don't—" I tilt my head to the side, secondhand embarrassment burning on my face. "B–But you're—"

"I know bits and pieces, just like my siblings, but," Runa explains, shaking her head. "My parents wanted us to learn only the common tongue."

"Oh, w-well, I said thank you."

I don't quite catch her response, my head still spinning. Someone who's Qorani that doesn't speak Qalqora? It shouldn't bother me, but it does. Christa called me ulqĕluni— essentially, someone trying to fit in too hard. I've tried harder than most to fit into some sort of background, immersing myself in Qorani culture as was silently expected of me, and it still isn't enough for most of them.

I shake the agitating thoughts away and make my way down to the engine room to start drawing up new blueprints. Mr. Connolly mentioned something once about more than one engine being ideal for an airship. In his blueprints, he was working with an engine he claimed worked better than steam power. At the time I had just laughed, incredulous, but as I look at the skeleton of this monstrous aerocraft, I can't help but wonder if maybe I should use two different types of engines: one to get it off the ground, and one to power the rest of the ship.

There's an empty spot by a small desk with a lone stool, rickety as can be. I sit down and brace myself on the edge of the desk until I get a better feel of how wobbly the chair is, then grab a few pieces of paper and start sketching. The lines are atrocious, but I get a basic idea of what I want from them, and make a mental note to use a ruler on my next go.

"Two engines, huh?" A tongue clicks near my ear.

I wobble on the stool and sputter as I try to keep my balance. By some miracle I do. I know from the smell of spice perfume and leather exactly who it is, but can't help but scold myself for knowing as the name tumbles from my lips. "Hiero!"

"I would personally go with three, but what do I know about mechie stuff?"

"H-Hiero, what are you—" I stop, fiddling with my audancers. How did I not hear her come in? Was I that focused on my work, or are my audancers acting up? I haven't had a chance to work with them, even with the spare parts Hiero gave me.

She cants her head in silent question but doesn't say anything. Instead her eyes narrow slightly, and she looks me up and down. I clear my throat, fiddling with the switches on my implants. "Sorry, I didn't, uh, h–hear you come in."

"Did those parts not help? I didn't really know what I was grabbing, but--"

"Wait," I hold a hand up. Actually, maybe I don't want to know if grabbing means stealing. I take a deep breath and exhale sharply. "I wouldn't know. I–I haven't had five minutes to myself."

"I'd imagine, with your brother and all."

He can be a handful, but I don't admit that aloud. I'm sure anyone who knows me automatically assumes Esper is trouble. I tend to wellumcoat it more than I care to admit, but at the same time... he's just a kid.

"Were you the one who adopted him?"

"Huh?" I blink. Hiero gives a half-shrug, leaning back against the table. Dreggar, it's so hard to focus when she's this close.

"Well, correct me if I'm wrong, but you don't seem to be in the best financial state. I'm guessing it's just the two of you, no parents, and you look, well, completely different. He's obviously adopted. But if you adopted him yourself, in spite of everything... well, that's just interesting."

The word falls from her mouth like a silken caress, and I can't help a little shiver. This is an extremely personal topic, but for whatever reason I'm not upset. It seems to be coming from a place of genuine curiosity. "I a–adopted Esper." I look down at my hands. "Wh-When my parents died, I had no one. Except for Mr. C-Connolly, that was, but... I-I don't want to get into that. I-I met Esper, a-and we connected. A-As far as I'm con-concerned, he's my brother."

"Is that why you're a mechie? Because it's an easy way to make ends meet?"

"I w-wouldn't say it's easy, b-b-but... honestly, I don't kn-know what else I'd be d-doing if I could. My dad was a-a mechie. It's all I-I know. A-All I want t-to do."

She tilts her head back, the long fall of her ponytail brushing against the desktop, lips pursed in a thoughtful moue. "I can relate."

I furrow my brow, pulling my gaze away to fidget with the necklace under my shirt. "How so? D-Don't you ch-choose to steal things?"

"It's all I know," Hiero echoes. "But unlike you, I know what I'd want to do." She's still looking up, into that thoughtful dream-space, but the frown's been replaced with a soft smile. "I'd be in the trader business, transporting cargo on my own airship."

That's... surprising. I suppose it's not unlike Hiero to be piloting an airship. I could see her as a captain with a crew, flying to different destinations and hauling on her own terms. Or a pirate. Hiero would make one *hell* of a pirate.

She rocks back forward, moving away from the table and toward the door, and I can almost physically feel every inch she puts between us. "I mean, I'm here to try and get an airship for myself. Once this revolution is over, it's gotta go somewhere, right? Then, who knows. I might need a mechie to help with the engine." She spins back to face me with a wink.

My face burns. "I sh–should be getting back to w–work... what e–exactly was it you w–wanted?"

"Nothing, poshi-må." Hiero hangs by the doorway, the slightest smirk playing on her lips. "I just find you interesting."

That word again. Interesting. With one final wink, she glides away, and I'm left to my own devices once more. It's even harder to focus now, though. All I can think about is when I adopted Esper. Does he remember anything about his parents? I knew mine for longer and I can barely remember them. I can't even remember what color my mother's eyes were, though I think they were blue, typical for Allowyn. All I remember were her hugs, the warm velvety tone of her voice, and her potato stew. My father I remember less of, mainly just how silly he could be and how scratchy his beard felt against my cheek. But I remember more clearly how upset we were when he disappeared, and how lost I was when my mother fell ill, and that dredges up the more recent memories, the ones I don't want to think about.

I end up abandoning my work to check on Esper in the ward. He's occupied with helping Runa sort out some things, and seems to be in a good mood. I watch for a little while to clear my head, and when they notice, Esper rolls his eyes and starts going through one of the boxes with more vigor. Runa gestures for me to join, and I accept, but my heart isn't in it; I can only think about my parents, and how little I remember. Who would I be if I'd never lost them? Would I still be allowed to be young?

CHAPTER 10

Esper stares at his bowl as I dole out a generous helping of stewed cabbage and beans, screwing his face up and jabbing at a lump with a spoon. Before he can argue, I bring the pot in my hands closer in silent warning that I can and will give him more. He slumps in his seat a bit and scowls.

"Oh, c–come on, Esper! You liked th–this a month ago." I scoop up a bowlful for myself and leave the pot on the counter for anyone else who wants it.

"That was a month ago," Esper says sullenly.

"That's w–what I'm saying."

"No, I mean, I've gotten sick of it." He lifts a spoonful of broth and dumps it back into the bowl. "It's gross."

"We c–can't afford to be picky. Eat your food."

"You're not my mom," he snorts. Still, he drops the

argument and begins shoveling as much stew as he can into his mouth, no doubt so he can get to something sweeter as soon as possible. I don't blame him. The cabbage passed its date before we even bought it; it's far from appetizing.

I could live off bread and Griplem apples for the rest of my life, but Esper's a lot pickier, and as it is I can't get more than one loaf a week, if we're lucky. With how much work goes into making it, the price has increased dramatically, and the only solution to combat the rising prices has been to hand out coupons dictating how much bread a house can get a month.

The reality of the situation is there's only so much I can buy for groceries each week, so most of the time I skip the market and instead buy cans of beans. Canning used to be a big deal back in the day, and anyone over thirty-five still gushes about what a handy thing it's become, particularly for beans. I hate canned beans. But we all do what we must to survive, and sometimes that means cracking open a metal tin and heating up sludge for dinner. I try not to skip meals in front of Esper, and I don't want him thinking we're doing as badly as we are, but there are nights I would happily miss a meal if it meant eating something else a few days later. Instead, it's hot beans for dinner and a meal straight out of the can on busy mornings.

Technically, we're better-off than normal, with the coin I've been getting from Rhine. However, there's this nagging voice in my brain that tells me we can't spend more at the market. It could just be paranoia from getting involved in the rebellion, or simply paranoia from being poor my whole life, but I can't shake the feeling something's going to happen, more so since Roran's heavily coerced invitation to the gala.

A knock sounds at the front door. Jynell gets up from one of the chairs at the other end of the room. As she greets whoever's there, I hear a familiar voice and start to choke. I can practically hear fate laughing at me, mocking me. Esper gives me a funny look as I cover my mouth, coughing.

Standing there is Runa's sibling, Christa, and a lean, keen-eyed man in a dark-blue scarf I vaguely recall seeing once or twice in Runa's ward. His hair is dark, almost like soot, typical for an Eoten, but his skin is almost sickly pale. I try to remember his name, but I don't need to as Christa pushes past him. "Arek, it's fine. We're not intruding, the woman said we can come in." They stand with their hands behind their back, like a soldier. Jynell rolls her eyes but otherwise says nothing, retreating back to her spot across the room like she wants to be as far from my uninvited guests as possible.

Arek hesitates, closing the door behind him as he adjusts his scarf to free his mouth. "Let's make this quick. Artem, right?" Chestnut eyes lock onto me as he speaks.

"Can I-I help you?" I ask automatically, getting up from my seat. Come to think of it, I've never told anyone in the rebellion where I live. My blood runs cold. "Wait, how did you know w-where I l-live?"

"Do you think anyone with the cause goes under our radar?" Christa snorts. Right. Spies.

"You're with the rebellion?" Esper asks.

"Unimportant." Arek's eyes narrow. "We don't have time. How fast can you pack?"

Pack? Like, everything?

I stand dumbfounded, trying to process his question. We barely have anything to call our own, but I don't see why we would need to pack. Most of the tools I use are back in the bunker, and Esper doesn't have anything of use.

"Where are we going?" Esper scoots his chair out, bowl in hand.

"We?" Christa asks.

"H–Hold on a s–second."

I resist the urge to bury my face in my hands and instead look directly at Arek. He seems like someone who might explain things better than Christa, but he just fidgets impatiently with his scarf and eyes the door. "Ask later."

Picking up on his body language, Christa heads back to the entrance and presses their ear against the wood. They look at Arek while they speak. "Grab important documents, anything you can't live without; clothes aren't needed."

"Except what you're wearing," Arek adds. Christa snorts again.

This is... beyond sketchy. Is this some sort of setup? A precaution? I know what happened with Aether at the Kulkner house was a close call, but I highly doubt we'd need to leave the apartment over that. Roran would never come after me, even with my recent involvements... would he?

Christa remains in their spot by the door, listening intently. Arek looks around the room like he doesn't know what to make of it, like maybe he's never been in such cheap living before. His eyes never stop moving, his shoulders curled in as his natural confidence gives way to wariness. "Get packing," he urges when he catches me staring. I hesitate.

Anxiety gets the better of me. Without further debate, I head for my room and dismantle the makeshift dresser. Esper grabs one of the cases and searches through another. I gather the papers under the bed and flip through them for anything that sticks out, anything important.

"What's going on?" Esper flings a case aside and starts ripping through the next. I suppose now isn't the time to snipe at him about making a mess.

"I d–don't know." I grimace as I shove all the letters from under the bed into the case. "I-I wish I knew. I h–have a bad f–feeling about t–this."

"But why do we have to go?"

We own so much less than I'd thought. I end up just stuffing what small trinkets I can find into my pockets. I ignore what they said about the clothes; most of mine get shoved into one of the smaller cases, the dirty mixed in with the clean. Esper's packing is as unorganized as mine, but less chaotic.

Outside, Christa and Arek talk in semi-hushed tones. "No one mentioned bringing along a kid!" Christa hisses, and I peek around the doorway to watch them.

"You know Hiero: never enough important details."

"My job is to make sure Artem is in one piece; no one said anything about a package deal." They move their head from the door and press their back against the frame.

"Would you abandon Runa?" Arek challenges, and Christa falls silent. They push his chest to make some distance and turn their head from him.

"You know I'd never actually leave him behind. It just

wasn't part of my plan, you know? Grab the girl, get out. Not grab girl and little brother, get out."

There's no straightforward way to interrupt, so I settle for clearing my throat. They both turn their heads toward me, but otherwise Christa goes back to listening at the door. Arek looks on the verge of pacing.

"We're all ready to help the revolution," Esper jokes.

Arek brings both hands up, eyebrows jumping up to his hairline. "Quiet, the walls are thin."

That's right; we're not underground where we can talk openly. There's no telling how many of the other tenants are listening in. Most of them would turn me in for treason if it meant more rations.

With a hiss, Christa walks briskly away from the front door and heads into my and Esper's room. I follow and so does Arek, tugging Esper behind him. Before I can ask, Christa shuts the door behind us and leans against it. Arek goes to the window and yanks the bedding from the top bunk. He's already started stripping the other bed when I hear the footsteps.

It's a loud thudding, multiple people in a hurry. Next door, in the other complex, a door slams open, and someone shouts for help: "Qa visaq! Maro qa visaq!" Slowly the gears in my head begin to turn. Procs. There are procs in the building, and they're looking for something. Or someone. My heart hammers in my chest, and I wonder if the others can hear it.

Arek remains stone-faced, quickly knotting the sheets together. He starts to tie on a pillowcase when Christa snaps, "What happened to being quick?"

Arek huffs and pushes his hair out of his face. "I'm open to suggestions."

"It'd be easier to jump."

"Jump?" I squeak.

Arek throws down the sheets. "Fine. Rappelling is easier, but I've climbed from higher."

"Are they looking for us?" Esper interjects. For once he looks genuinely worried, shifting his weight from foot to foot.

"No." Arek tosses the sheets onto the bed and nods in my direction. "They're looking for her. C'mon, kid, you're with me."

The voices are getting closer. The procs are leaving the neighbors' place and are no doubt heading for ours. "Are y-you in-insane?" I ask.

"He'll be fine," Arek insists. He grabs Esper, who gives a small yelp, and heads for the window. In a blink, he's gone.

I rush over to the window and look down. Arek hangs one-armed from the windowsill, muscles barely trembling even as he holds Esper tight with the other. He manages to swing his body over and latches onto the drain pipe, practically sliding down as he finds footing in the loose brickwork. Esper doesn't scream or cry, merely hangs on for dear life to his case and to Arek, all the while looking up at him in awe.

It's impressive. That doesn't mean I'm not petrified. With a sigh, I bring a hand to my chest and clutch my shirt. There are four stories separating me from the ground. No sane person jumps out of a window at such a height.

An insistent push on my shoulder forces me to turn my head. Christa nudges me again, trying to get me to go, but my legs lock and my mouth goes dry. I'm not Arek, and I'm not Hiero. I don't blindly leap into things, especially not athletic... things. They lean around me instead, dropping my luggage out the window. It falls with a soft thud, narrowly missing Arek and Esper.

"Just don't fall," Christa says. "If you do, loose legs, roll back into it. Better to fall on your ass than break your ankles."

"I–I–I can't ju–just—" I start, but they cut me off.

"Do you want to get shot? I don't. Go!"

I scramble over the ledge, trying to find some footing, but my balance is atrocious. I start slipping. At the last second, I manage to grab onto the edge of the window instead of plummeting to the ground. I hang on as tightly as I can, feet dangling helplessly while I try to dig them into a gap in the crumbling brickwork.

My head snaps up at the sound of a whistle to my side. Christa has managed to climb down without stepping on my hands or getting in my way. They jerk their head to say "follow my lead," and I watch as they propel themself onto another windowsill and drop down, catching themself. There's no way I can do the same thing. It's difficult enough to think of even letting go, let alone try to catch myself. Maybe the fall won't be awful if I follow Christa's advice.

Except I can't remember what they said to me before I practically leapt out the window.

As they descend, I hear the front door to my complex slam open. There's no time left. I grit my teeth and prepare for the worst as I let go of the edge.

For the life of me, I don't know how either of them can

climb so gracefully. Years of practice, certainly. Somehow my flailing helps me grab onto another ledge. The force is tremendous, and I hit the wall hard enough to almost lose my grip entirely. My arms scream in pain, begging me to let go.

Râ jĕ qavesii.

I look down to see the ground is a lot closer than I remembered. I could drop from here easily. Arek's expression is unreadable, and I can't see Esper, but Christa stands ready to take flight. I let go again. My feet hit the ground, and I stumble back while reaching up to massage one of my shoulders. The force is enough to jar the loose switches in my audancers, and I struggle to reset them while every step knocks them back out of place.

The sound of a door slamming open forces my head up. Arek keeps his voice low as he urges us to keep moving. A head pops out of an open window and searches below, then starts shouting as he spots me.

I grab my case and start running. Arek leads the way, Esper— still clutching his suitcase— tucked under his arm. Christa stays behind me, urging me to hurry up as they keep lookout for any pursuers. By the looks of it, they're limping, a lot more than usual, and I can't help but wonder if it had something to do with the fall. My mind is a mess, and I barely notice when Arek skids to a stop and bangs twice against a door. A bright light glows from behind us, and the smell of flames and burning wood fills the air, accompanied by screams and shouts.

The building I had lived in for years with Esper is burning to the ground before my eyes. I clutch my necklace tightly, unable to think of anything but Jynell and the rest of the Cavicks and the Petersons and everyone in that building. Most of the procs have been drawn to the fire, and only a few men keep pursuing us, most turning back as someone cries for the fire containment squad.

The door in front of us swings open. Arek hunches his shoulders and heads in. I've lost my train of thought and can barely move; Christa ends up pushing me forward, hissing under their breath to keep going.

It's a small house, the entrance leading straight into a parlor with a narrow hallway branching off into two other rooms. A man, seemingly unfazed, stands close by. He locks the door, pointing wordlessly down the hall. Arek nods and slows his pace. I consider thanking the man, but it doesn't seem to matter; he acts as though the intrusion is a common occurrence.

How many people are involved with the movement? The procs make it out to be a heinous crime, but more people seem to support Rhine's ideas than I thought. How can so many aid the rebels without worrying about being apprehended?

Esper unknowingly voices one of my thoughts. "Is everyone with the rebellion?"

"No," Christa answers, their tone much softer. "We needed an escape plan, and we found enough people to help."

Arek clears his throat, a gentle reminder not to dally. "This way." We make our way to a closet in the corner of the kitchen, and I bring my hands together, tentatively debating speaking up. He simply opens it up and removes a panel from the back. There's a crawlspace, half Esper's size, leading into darkness.

My questions are left unanswered as, one by one, we make our way through. I crouch and keep my hands close to my body, pushing the case in front of me. The tunnel is lightless and cramped, and I'm immediately claustrophobic.

I don't know how Arek and Christa found out where I lived. From what they said, Hiero sent them to get us. How could she have known procs were going to show up? Was it a lucky guess or did she overhear something? What about the fire? Who started it? Why would anyone set an apartment filled with innocent people aflame? Could it have been Christa or Arek? They seem far from the sort to do that, but what do I know anymore? Every rumor I've heard about the rebellion has been disproven, and it's getting difficult to tell who can be trusted.

I fumble around, bumping into Esper a couple times. The sound of another panel being moved brightens my spirits, and light begins to filter in. The crawlspace leads out through another closet, though this time the door is open for us. A different gentleman waits nearby, helping us clamber out.

We're close to the tunnels now. A street-lamp flickers warmly outside of the fake pub. A jitney drives by, and someone dumps their trash into a bin with noisy abandon. There are no procs surrounding the place, no one after us, just the distant sound of a siren, getting fainter as it heads away.

Inside the pub are a couple of patrons, all paired off in their usual twos and threes, huddled against each other. A few heads turn when we walk in, even more as we nudge Esper toward the bar. He stares with wide eyes at the bartender, who's shooting a particularly dirty look in my direction. I duck my head and push Esper forward as the man lifts the divider.

"Artem, I don't want to—" Esper starts to whimper.

"It's fine," Christa says.

"But—"

They hush him gently, crouching to get closer to eye level with him. "Your sister's with you, and we're here to make sure nothing happens to you. You've been here before, right? I promise, it's still safe."

He seems to perk up at their words, and Arek scoots by to lead the way. There's no hiding Esper's undiminished awe as the lever opens and the tunnel is revealed down below. Arek goes first, then gestures for Esper to follow, helping him down into the tunnel.

I'm touched by Christa's change in tone with Esper. Before I can say anything, though, they cross their arms and tip their head toward the hatch. Right. Now's not the time. I slip down into the tunnel and put an arm around Esper as we wait for Christa to join us, the entryway sliding closed behind them.

I hold Esper's hand as we walk through. He doesn't speak, taking his cue from the rest of us. The tunnel shakes every time a particularly large jitney thunders by overhead. Esper squeezes my hand tightly and I rub comforting circles on his hand with my thumb. The farther underground we go, the fewer disturbances can be heard from the outside world. In the dim light of the tunnel, I can't be sure if Esper is still okay. His expression is indecipherable.

Runa stands waiting at the door and opens it for us as we approach. Christa groans loudly, but waits until we are all inside and the exit is shut to complain.

"What were you doing out there?" Christa asks. Runa scowls in response, grabbing Christa's arm and turning it over, then doing the same to the other. Methodical, practiced, she checks every inch of her sibling, grabbing their head to check their eyes as she speaks.

"Why do I have to find out that you're on a mission from anyone other than you?" Runa's voice comes out harsh.

"You'd be too busy worrying about me to do your job." Christa tugs themself out of Runa's grasp, and Runa plants her hands on her hips, glaring.

"It's my job to worry about you, since you don't have the sense to do it yourself."

"Can you stop fussing over me and check out someone else for a change? I think Arek cracked his head on something."

"You're hilarious," Arek says dryly, then clears his throat and lowers his voice. "I might need bandages." He holds his hands out; one's red, covered in scrapes and trails of dried blood. It must have happened while he was carrying Esper down from the window. He never brought it up, and not once did I notice him flagging behind. My stomach churns.

"You were awesome!" Esper pipes up. The compliment seems to roll off of Arek's shoulders, but he grants Esper the barest wisp of a smile.

"I don't think your sister would forgive me if I let you try that yourself."

"I'm sure we could teach you to do it too," Christa adds.

"Really?" Esper's eyes widen.

"Uh-uh." I want to nip this in the bud immediately. I tug at the bottom of my vest and frown at Christa. "Don't en–encourage h–him."

"A conversation for another day, when we're not all on an adrenaline high." Runa pats my shoulder and shoots me a sympathetic look.

The talk about scaling stops. Runa examines Arek's hands, mouth twisting, then moves on to Esper. He squirms, but keeps quiet as she checks his hands and face. Finally, she looks me over, scanning my arms and hands for signs of injury.

I'm unscathed, but that doesn't stop Runa from squinting while examining my eyes. She doesn't say what I know she's dying to: Have you been sleeping? Instead, she gestures to the cots in the ward. It makes sense that we would be staying here. As far as I know, there aren't many beds in the bunker. Any housing was probably gutted once Rhine began organizing his rebellion. There's not room for much of anything, especially with the airship taking up most of the main floor.

"They're not the most comfortable," she says softly, "but I have two cots you can sleep on until we find you something better."

I mumble an awkward thank-you as I strip off my vest and tuck my shoes under the bed. When I glance over at Esper, he's opened his case, revealing his most important belongings, among which sits his radio, nestled into a messy stack of clothes. I bite my lip to keep from saying anything about it. Once he's satisfied that everything is in place and undamaged, he slides the luggage under the cot and settles in.

Thankfully, the ward is empty. I don't know if that's necessarily good or bad; Runa should have people to look after, otherwise she's wasting her time. On the other hand, patients would mean people are getting hurt. A flicker of fire dances at the edge of my memory and I let out a low hiss of air through my teeth. Right, people are— people are getting hurt all the time. Because of the revolution? Because of me?

Arek and Christa bicker back and forth as Runa secures some bandages around his hands, then he draws away to talk with Esper, crouching by his cot. It's a nice gesture, though I should be the one making sure he's okay, especially after such a traumatic night.

I hang by the doorway, looking over what's visible of the airship in the few work-lamps still lighting the bay. It's stopped looking like a metal skeleton. Part of the interior is finished, and I can make out a large cockpit and sizeable main room. I focus on the lines of the craft, tracing out a blueprint in my head in a vain attempt to block out my conscience reprimanding me for what I've done.

But I can't ignore that little voice. The one pointing out that Esper could have gotten really hurt tonight. That I've taken away something stable from him, one of the few things he had. He's not only lost a school, but now a home, and probably a trust in me I'll never get back. There's a burning in my throat, as if my thoughts were dying to get out and make themselves known. Slowly I make my way back to the cot, footsteps heavy, unable to lift my head even as I sink back into the mattress. My chest aches, and the weight of the evening hits me all at once. I can't breathe. Esper could have died tonight. And it all would have been my fault.

I barely hear Runa call out my name as she crouches to my level. I try to keep it together, but when a warm hand rests on my back, the tears begin to fall. I cover my eyes with my hands and choke back a sob. "It-It went u-up in flames. A-All of it," I manage.

"These things happen sometimes."

"Not to-to-to n-normal people! And how m-many are hurt? Did you pl-plan for that?"

"Of course not!" Christa raises their voice, sounding defensive and a little annoyed. "If I knew the place was going to burn, I would have gotten out of there sooner!" As nice as it is to get some confirmation the fire wasn't them, I can't help but start shaking. How many people are dead now because of me?

"Ever sin-since I-I got wrapped up in-in all of this, I-I'm just..." I shut my eyes and swallow, trying to keep my voice from wavering. "I-I keep lo-losing places I thou-thought I-I could c-call mine. I c-can't save them, they're just g-g-g-gone and th-that's the e-end." Runa starts making a hushing noise. I vaguely hear Esper say something, but I can't hear him over the heartbeat echoing in my skull.

"I-I need to st-st-start looking a-at genqii housing again, a-and without a g-good word from an employer, o-or a st-steady income, o-or papers— Dear Dreg-Dreggar, the p-p-procs are after me, th-there's no way I-I-I can g-go to that gala, and I-I did-didn't want to b-but not like this a-and—!"

Runa smoothes a hand over my hair, just like my mother

used to, and I suck in a shuddery little breath. "Everything becomes a lot easier to manage after a good night's sleep."

I almost laugh. Sleep. Gaqĕ. I'm probably just going to stare at the ceiling, tortured by my own racing thoughts.

Arek walks over and kneels beside her, grabbing one of my hands. "It's not your job to worry. I'm heading back over to investigate. Listen to Runa, get some rest."

"You're heading back?" Runa lowers her voice. "Arek, it's late, you should—"

"I'll be fine." He slowly stands back up, letting go of me and heading toward the door while adjusting his scarf into a tight loop around his face. Runa grimaces, but holds her tongue, her gaze following his back out of the room. After a moment, she drags her attention toward Esper, nodding at the other bed. I hiccup and stare at the ground for a few moments, collecting myself.

As Esper gets ready to call it a night, Runa grabs us two glasses and a bottle of water, divvies its contents, then drags over a makeshift side table to place between the beds. I'm beyond worn out, but my mind is restless. Where are we going to go? What are we going to do now? Why are the procs after me? What about Esper? But as the adrenaline wears off, I'm helpless to fight the fatigue that replaces it.

The last thing I see is Runa, braced against a table in the corner, letting herself cry where she thinks no one can see.

CHAPTER 11

In all my recent dreams, I've been airbound. Aboard this ginormous aerocraft, larger than any airship, I'm far above the city, leagues beyond Allowyn and the rest of the world. Esper sits beside me, uninterested in our journey to who-knows-where. The seats are red leather, soft as a cloud. A small table sits between us, strewn with various blueprints and a notebook filled with Esper's doodles. There are dozens of rows in the cabin, yet no one else is there besides the two of us. The skies are green, and even higher a few stars glitter in a vaguely familiar constellation resembling a boat. I study it, tempted to draw it out myself as it starts to change shape. Esper yawns loudly; I turn my attention to him as he speaks.

"How long have we been falling?"

I jolt awake. The ward is as cozy as could be expected from an abandoned hangar, but even with the makeshift beds and obnoxious hum of the heater, it's welcoming. It's not home, though. In the back of my mind are the remnants of a half-remembered lullaby, but it fades into oblivion with my dream.

Esper is sprawled out on his cot. He's managed to kick off part of his blanket, showcasing two holes in his sock. I sit up and observe him for a few moments, watching the steady rise and fall of his chest as he dreams. His snoring stops as he practically flings himself onto his side, then starts up again.

We can't stay here. Not just in this building, but with the rebellion. I never wanted to be part of a revolution. The blood in my veins makes me enough of a target, and being associated with an uprising isn't ideal for keeping a low profile.

Runa walks in carrying a load of blankets. As I swing my legs to the side, she tsks and motions for me to stay put. She approaches Esper and places most of the bedding on an empty cot before gently tossing another blanket on top of him. He sighs softly in his sleep, turning again, and huddles into the covers. Runa uses the back of her hand to check his forehead, then glances over to me with a frown. "How long has he had a cold?"

Dreggar. I didn't even know Esper had a cold. He never complains of not feeling well, so it can be hard to catch when he's sick. Other than a slight sniffle, he had seemed fine to me. "I-I don't know."

"He's not running a fever, but he's congested and fighting a chill. It seems as though neither of you gets enough rest."

"I co-couldn't get him to e-even if I wanted." I rub my nose. I'm not his parent, as he often likes to remind me, and he insists he can take care of himself. "You know h-how kids are."

"Exactly— he is a child and needs to sleep more. The same goes for you."

"That I n-need sleep?"

"That you're still a child." Runa walks over to me and checks my temperature as well, pressing her cool hand against my forehead. "And that you need sleep."

My face warms. Runa certainly makes me feel like a child. Am I really, though? At seventeen, I'm considered an adult... but I don't feel like one. Kids don't have to worry about bills or where the next paycheck is coming from, and especially not about hate crimes or arson.

Okay, technically Esper would know the last part, but he's a special case. Most kids don't juggle pyrotechnics for fun.

Runa says nothing else, just busies herself with other work. Taking that as a sign everything's fine, I get up and start stripping the sheets from the bed. She glances over, and I catch her biting her lip before returning to taking inventory. It's odd having someone worry about my well-being. Anyone, really. I'm definitely not used to Hiero and Arek's quiet concerns, nor Runa's more vocal urgings to improve my health. I haven't been able to decide if it's nice or frustrating. Meanwhile, I can't help but feel awful knowing that Esper has a cold, and I hadn't even noticed. My mom was a master at catching a cold before it developed into anything further. She could catch almost any illness. Except for the one that killed her.

What kind of a guardian am I? Not a good one, clearly. Some days, I wonder if it'd be easier to hand Esper over to someone else, though I know I could never go through with it. I'm pretty sure he'd wind up in an orphanage and have to age out of the system.

I shake my head to dispel my thoughts. I have an engine I'm supposed to be working on, and I'm still in the blueprint phase. Attempting to build an engine inside of an airship rather than as an external hanging fixture, like most older models, is proving difficult.

I make my way downstairs to my makeshift office; the floor is silent, dead. No one is supposed to come in today, and normally I work best when left alone. Yet, despite the relative peace, I keep focusing on the little things, any and every noise getting my hopes up that someone is coming down to join me.

Throwing my pencil down, I collapse onto the desk with a groan and bury my fingers deep in my hair. It's gotten messier, bedhead rearing its ugly face, yet somehow the extra sleep does nothing for my constant dark circles. I muss it even further, squeezing my eyes shut and taking a couple deep breaths. All I want is some qosa and for my brain to not feel so heavy and fogged-up. None of this seems real, and the more I try to ground myself, the more I'm convinced I'll float away.

The sound of footsteps forces my head back up. Could it be one of the guys, coming in despite it not being a scheduled workday? Have my half-formed prayers been answered? I expect to see Hiero but find myself staring at Christa. They hang by the doorway, hair down rather than pulled back in its usual wavy ponytail. The longer they stand there, the faster I find myself calming down again.

"What's up?" I ask, as if I wasn't on the verge of a breakdown.

"If you have a moment, I wanted to ask you about something you said last night."

I raise my eyebrows and look around the empty workspace, quietly emphasizing that no one else is around. Christa's not amused. They grab themself a stool and sigh heavily. For the first time I start to realize just how similar they and Runa truly are, from the way their cheeks are littered with freckles— Christa's more prominent— to the traces of wrinkles developing in the same spots. If I didn't know any better, I'd think they were twins. Perhaps they are, and Runa's just been aged by her occupation.

"What did you mean before about going to a gala?" Christa furrows their brow. "No offense, but you don't strike me as the type to live it up at a fancy event. I'm not even sure how many dust-jacket workers you're going to find there."

If it were anyone else, I'd be a little hurt. But Christa is right, and if anyone could get away with saying it, it'd be them or Runa. While Runa's not a dust-jacket worker, and Christa isn't exactly either, I get the implication. It's a matter of cultures. It's always a matter of cultures.

I push my work to the side and spin in my seat to face them. "I was in–invited by a–a friend of mine."

One eyebrow lifts. "You must have some impressive friends."

"He's a-a p-proc. He's sup-supposed to be w-working at the event."

For some reason, Christa seems unfazed by the information. After what we went through the other night, I expected them to be wary or upset. Instead they scratch at a sore on their arm, mouth twisting in a little moue.

"It's n-not like I can go now, though. Not with the-the fire. He's bound to-to know what happened, and it s-sounded like he knew ab-about Hiero w-when—" Christa doesn't know that story and doesn't need to know. "—I wasn't ex-exactly asked. It s-sounded like he k-knew some things that he sh-shouldn't."

"What rank is he?"

"B-Brigario, I th-th-think. Just promoted."

Is it possible he turned me and Esper in? It wouldn't make sense if he did. One moment ask me to go with him to some fancy event, and the next rat on us for conspiring against the king? I don't think Roran even knows about my involvement with the movement, considering how small my contributions really are in comparison to some of the others working for the cause.

Christa folds their arms. "That's not the special forces."

"The-The special forces?"

"The MPs, they're the ones you need to look out for." They sigh and straighten their back, rolling their shoulders. "A proc is a proc. MPs work more for the king and higher echelons of Parvay. They're the ones trying to sniff out where the bunker is and squash the movement before it can escalate even further."

It makes sense. I suppose I could see the point of having

a special force within the procs dedicated to stopping the rebellion. There are plenty of other things that still need to be taken care of; they could hardly put every proc on the case.

So that means it's just the MPs that know about me. Roran wouldn't have any idea, unless he was friends with an MP and my name came up. Though I highly doubt I'm that important. There are much bigger players in this revolution, and only Rhine Toberts could be singled out by name alone.

Christa gazes thoughtfully in the distance, then looks me up and down and stands up. They step closer, and my stomach clenches in anticipation. They want something, I just don't know what. It looks like they're about to tell me either way.

"I need you to go to that gala."

I can feel my eyes bug. "Ex-Excuse-Excuse m-me?"

"I need you," Christa repeats, a bit slower, like I'm dumb, or a small child, "To go to that gala."

Are they insane? If the gala has a bunch of procs on the scene, who's to say someone from the MPs won't be there, too? Wouldn't the Lindsor sector be dangerous after the last time Aether and I went together?

Aether. That has to be how I ended up on the MPs' list. When we were at the Kulkner house, she took special care to show my face to the man she was torturing. Surely he said something to the authorities. Aether made me an easy target to come after.

I try to take a few deep breaths and collect myself. The last thing I need is to start shouting and causing a scene... even if it's just the two of us. "Are-Are you n-n-nuts?"

So much for collecting myself.

"Ch-Christa, I-I can't." I bring a hand to my chest as it rises and falls rapidly. "I can't, I-I c-can't do that. You said yourself, I'm-I'm not the type to-to go to the-these things! My apartment was burned d-down last ni-ni-night! I don't even kn-know who or-or why it hap-happened and I—!"

"Hey, hey." I force myself to stare back into their eyes, gold against gold.

"I can't do th-that."

Christa drops their voice down a bit. "Don't make me beg."

"Wh-Why do I-I need to go?"

"Think of it this way: it's keeping up with appearances, which sometimes is all we have. You'd be hiding in plain sight, and, I never said this, but I know the team heading over there is going to need a tinkerer."

Team? More rebels are going to be at this event? Just how big is this gala anyway, and what's the importance behind it? Like anyone would ever give me a straight answer. It's odd though, seeing Christa like this. They seem genuinely antsy about the gala, ditching their tough facade and reminding me of how Runa was behaving last night with Arek. Honestly, the similarities between the two can be uncanny. Or maybe it's the idea of still having to go to the gala. I'm not quite sure, but this conversation is freaking me out. Everything's beginning to spin, and it's getting harder to breathe. I need to get out of this room.

Shaking my head, I get up and walk out the door into the open workyard. Christa follows right behind, but keeps some distance between us. I want to say that I'll think about it, but that's not true. I don't want to think about it, and I want absolutely nothing to do with this gala. I didn't before, and I really don't want to now, especially if I'm being sought out by the MPs... having to wear a dress for the event just adds insult to injury.

Christa keeps after me. "There's a handful of us going to the gala, mainly the spies, because the gala itself is a distraction; there are some letters and plans Rhine wants intercepted. I'm not going, because of a conflict of interest, but Tristan is going to be there."

"If a–a fight happened, Tristan could–could definitely han–handle himself," I mumble, heading into the airship. "I'm just o–over six facs, and l–l–less than fi–fifty-two canils, barely able to c–carry around a wr–wr–wrench."

"That's not what I mean."

I stop wandering around, standing between some marks designating where the walls for the engine room will go up. Christa leans against one of the braces and sighs heavily. "There won't be a fight, or any conflict, if it can be helped. My problem is, he tends to blurt whatever comes to mind, and he's the clumsiest man I've ever met. He has past connections with the procs, and if he gets to chatting with anyone, he's going to be recognized."

"Then w–why is he e–even going?" I ask. "Why n–n–not have him stay o–out of it?"

Christa scowls. "Because he's muscle, and Pythan forbid he ever listen to me when I tell him not to volunteer himself for these things.»

Pythan? That's the god according to the Church of Ptholy. I always expected them and Runa to be Siqhadran too. I guess it's wrong for me to assume these things. Runa doesn't speak Qalqora, and I've only heard Christa curse in it a few times. I just assumed they were more in touch with their Qorar roots then they seem to be. Still, the Church of Ptholy is considered an offense to the Church of the King and "official" religion, so at least they're not being hypocrites.

"Look." Christa takes a deep breath. "I know they're going to need someone like you. Hiero can pretend she knows tech, and Aether can bypass a handful of security systems, but from what I've heard you're the go-to mechie."

I freeze. I stopped really listening after the word 'Hiero'. Hiero is going to be at the gala. If anyone can help get me out of this, it's her. It must be obvious that I'm starting to consider it. Christa gets a look on their face, and tilts their head upward, squinting at me. "She'd never say it, but I'm sure Hiero would appreciate the help."

"I-I guess..."

Christa shakes their head. "I asked Runa to help find a dress for you to wear. We don't have anything cutting-edge, but you should be fine. The gala is tonight, correct?" They take a few steps toward the exit, then turn on their heel as I call after them.

"W-W-Wait. Why would y-you have to–told her to f–find a dress if you did–didn't even know if I–I'd go?"

"I took a wild guess." They pause, then head back out, calling over their shoulder. "It doesn't take a spy to see it."

I'm not quite sure what they mean by that, but they're gone before I can ask. I'm left on the empty floor of the hangar, the metal beams curving away around me like the ribs of a leviathan. I plod back to my blueprints in the other room. There's no use standing around getting more worked up, and at this point I'm just retracing old lines making sure my measurements are correct.

I spend the next few hours dragging heavy pieces of metal into the soon-to-be engine room, then sitting in the middle of the mess and sifting through which parts I need and which I don't. At this point, it's more busy-work than anything. I start blocking off where the engines are going to sit, before scurrying into the back room and hammering out scrap for the casings. There aren't any pistons or exhaust ports that are going to be big enough to fit what I'm picturing, and on top of that, I can't use parts from older engines because nothing would work. I'm going to have to try something new— this is going to be a tri-engine design.

Before I can pop on my goggles and get to work, Esper jumps into view, waving his hands in my face. I push my things to the side and close my eyes, waiting for the inevitable.

"Runa says you need to go upstairs now."

"Right. Th–Thanks, Esper."

My feet drag as I make my way back up to the ward, each clanking step heavier than the last. As soon as I step foot inside, Runa rushes over with a lukewarm face-cloth and starts scrubbing at me. I sputter, trying to squirm out of reach, only to find Runa looking down at me, her face all scrunched up in an exasperated scowl. "I had a feeling you'd be covered in gunk. I was right."

"I n–never signed up for th–this!" I complain loudly. The cloth continues to assault my face, and Esper snorts, the bed squeaking as he hops onto it.

"That makes two of us getting baths today!"

"This does not count as a bath!" Runa argues, horrified. "Don't tell me this counts as a bath for you guys."

"It can be."

"Esper," I warn.

I guess it's a good thing Runa isn't busy with anyone. No one's around but her and Esper, and he watches my hair get attacked by a brush with gleaming eyes. This must be some sort of revenge on his part, payment for the times I've tried to comb his hair and get him to wash up before breakfast and after dinner each night. At least he's enjoying himself.

Runa pauses her assault long enough to pick up a dress that was laying out on one of the beds. It's thrust into my hands, and I glance back and forth between the fabric and Runa. She stands expectantly, ushering me toward the exit and to the toilets. I spend a good minute working myself up to take off the slacks and button-down. There's another five spent putting on the dress part-way, getting overwhelmed and stopping, then trying again. I catch a look at myself in the mirror before heading back to the ward.

It doesn't quite fit right, like most of my clothes, but it's at least less baggy. Normally I wear a vest to secure my too-big shirt, and a sash seems to be doing the same job with this blue monstrosity Runa's given me. My grimy boots don't exactly go with the outfit, and I can't stop my limbs from shaking. I look like a disaster.

Esper seems to agree. The moment I shuffle back in he starts howling with laughter. Runa beams, and Christa, who has made a reappearance, seems... concerned.

"You look ridiculous!" Esper shouts.

Runa throws him a chastising look. "I think she looks nice. It's a pleasant change, doesn't need to be permanent."

"I'd hope not," Christa interjects, earning their own stern glare from Runa. "You look uncomfortable."

"I am un–uncomfortable."

"Maybe we should just get rid of the dress—"

"She'll be fine for one night," Runa insists.

I don't really have much of a say in the matter. I groan as Christa hands me a pair of flats, and sit down to slip them on. Why would anyone want to walk in anything other than boots and socks? It feels weird and vulnerable to put on shoes that don't cover the tops of my feet.

I haven't even gotten to the gala and I already want to leave.

Christa nudges me to follow them. I give Esper a wave, trying hard not to grimace, and make my way to the surface once more. Meandering back through the tunnels and up through the hatch proves to be more difficult than usual. Christa now and again shoots me a sympathetic look, and stops in front of the skylines to fix my shoulders a bit.

"Dresses aren't for everyone," they sigh. "Like Runa said, it's one night. Just try not to panic, and once everyone is ready to leave, you can probably duck out with your date shortly after. Tristan told me that procs only need to serve a minimum of three hours at these events."

"He's n–not my d–date," I mumble. "And thr–three hours is a long time."

"It'll fly by. Just keep an eye on my boyfriend."

"Who, A–Arek?" I joke.

"No, my other boyfriend," Christa snorts. "Tristan can

take care of himself, but he's kind of a dope. Just promise me you'll make sure he doesn't get into trouble."

Overhead, a green light flashes, signaling the arrival of one of the skylines. Christa squeezes my arm, then heads off in the other direction. I take a deep breath and make my way up the stairs. Roran said he would meet me here with a guest pass in front of the check-in. The sooner I meet him, the sooner I can get this evening over with.

CHAPTER 12

When we disembark from the skyline, we're greeted by a jitney, paid for by the proc service. I don't listen to much of Roran's explanation, just bow my head when he opens the door for me. I've only traveled by jitney a handful of times. They're all pretty generic, cushioned with plush purple faux-leather, the backrest stitched into patterned bumps. It's dark and cramped, a small window with tinted glass to either side letting in the only light. Between the front and back is a small partition, with a window to converse with the driver and see the front of the jitney, though the view is mainly taken up by the galloping backside of the automaton. I sit stiffly, still rattled from the skyline. Roran joins me, and as he closes the door, the jitney takes off.

He turns his eyes to me. "That was your first time on the skylines, wasn't it?"

I almost laugh. I wish I could tell him I'd ridden the skylines before and jumped between cars at high speed. Trusting my life to giant magnets is unsettling enough. Recalling my first experience on the skylines just made my anxiety worse. I end up nodding my head a little too enthusiastically. "I–It's very high u–up. A bit bumpier th–than I expect–expected."

"Oh, it wasn't always," Roran sighs. He reaches up to tousle his hair, but stops short before he can muss his carefully gelled locks, dropping his hand with a sheepish smile. "They've been messing with the lines ever since one of them shut down in the middle of service. Can you believe that?"

I make some sort of strangled hum of agreement and lean in to peer through the small window in the divider that separates us from the jitneer. "So h–how long have you be–been operating jitneys?" The man grunts out a number I don't quite catch, and the ride turns silent for a few minutes before Roran coughs and proceeds to fill the silence with one-sided small talk.

As the ride bumps along, I glance over at Roran; he's actually shaved, and without his normal stubble his jaw is defined, his cheekbones jutting out. He's in his usual dark-blue uniform, though it's been fitted with a gold sash and decorated with medals. As much as I hate leaving Roran in this silence, I don't think I could talk right now without breaking down. My apartment has been burned down, I'm probably wanted by the MPs, Runa's spending her valuable time babysitting Esper, and I'm wearing a dress. Each time we pass one of the mansions as we travel down the endless winding roads, I wonder if it's the Kulkner house. After that night, I don't exactly have fond memories of Lindsor.

"Where is th–this gala?"

"Frenlis, I think."

"I'm sorry I'm n–not more t–talkative," I fib. "It's intimidating, b–being in Lindsor. I–I've never been, n–not that I'd have a–any reason to be, be–be–because why would I–I ever be in Lindsor?"

Dreggar save me, I'm going to prison.

"Not even for one of those conferences with the Artificers? I thought you would be all over that." Roran laughs. "I always pictured you as one."

"A–An Artificer? They work with–with procs, don't th—?"

"An Artemficer." He's wearing a huge, goofy grin, just waiting for my reaction.

For the first time since the fire, I find myself laughing, a small snort snowballing into a series of genuine chuckles. "That's th–the dumbest thing I've e–ever heard!"

"You mean genius."

I feel bad for sometimes forgetting that Roran can be a great guy. I can't even count the times he's talked Esper out of trouble and kept me from needing to bail him out of jail. I miss having friends that understand what it was like to struggle. Kylir's married and left the gutters, Roran's risen through the ranks, and I have no idea what's happened to Lycan. I'm the only one left struggling in the dark. Roran doesn't understand that, and I know he can't connect the same way when he's barking at a woman for hassling a vendor to give her rotten food for free.

My audancers ache at the thought. Has the penalty for larceny changed in the past six years? Roran can be merciful, but I know if it came down to it, he, too, would chop off someone's ears for stealing an apple.

We pull up to one of the mansions and wait in a line of jitneys inching closer to the entrance. Everyone is taking a jitney tonight, it seems. What a waste of coin.

Roran gets out first. I start to follow suit, but he makes a noise like a shout, and I freeze. He comes to the other side and opens the door, offering me his hand. I acquiesce, adjusting my dress slightly and dusting it off as I would a pair of pants. With his help, I step down from the carriage and onto the cobblestone drive.

Everyone before us walks arm-in-arm as they head up the steps and into the grand hall. Roran offers me his arm and I take it, though I keep my grip loose and my eyes down. The marble statues by the sides of the stairs resemble twin tarlyns, one with its mouth open, showcasing foot-long fangs, and the other with one paw raised, all six toes flexed, ready to pounce. Two men stand by the entryway, dressed in fancy black suits; they pull open the doors for us in a smooth, synchronized motion as we approach. Roran nods his head in acknowledgement and I follow suit. There's nothing I could think to say other than "thank you," but it doesn't seem like the couple before us did. Maybe that's just not a thing people do at these parties. I feel bad for the men; surely it can't be fun to stand there the entire night just letting people in and out.

This place is even larger than the Kulkner house. A grand staircase branches off in two sections only to meet again near the third floor, with a balcony overlooking the entrance. A proc occupies each side of the stairway and three more pace the balcony. Whatever is being showcased must be more important than I realized, though it also feels like just an excuse to throw a lavish party. Everyone is wearing suits and satin dresses, aside from the procs in uniform. To the right is where most of the guests seem to be gathered, to the left a small cluster of people smoking pipes in the foyer. A woman stands at a podium in the entrance hall with a pen and a book, scribbling down names. She looks over expectantly as Roran clears his throat.

"Glory be. Brigario Procier Roran Burke. And guest."

"Glory be, sir. All guests are to head into the right wing."

We step away from the woman and I wrest my hand from the crook of Roran's arm. He tilts his head in confusion, and moves as if to take my arm again but stops himself and nods ahead, following at my shoulder.

There must be at least two hundred people in this house. The room we walk into is overcrowded, filled mainly with women holding fancy glasses filled with green liquid. Most of the walls are decorated with lavish tapestries and elaborate portraits of doughy, sneering nobles. Several ornate, rose-tinted crystal chandeliers laden with glass upon glass of colorful liquor hang at waist-height throughout the room. In the center of the hall, a large banquet is set up along an enormous rectangular table steaming with fresh, hot food, from roasted baves to a huge bloodmarvin fillet. My stomach grumbles at the sight.

Except... there are no plates. The only flatware is what the food is resting on, and no one seems to be carrying anything but flutes of alcohol. Maybe it's just not time to serve the food? Yet, just as I think it, one woman walks over to a roasted bave and picks up a serving fork, a slice of meat already skewered at its end. She lifts the cut up to her nose, inhales deeply, then puts it back with a satisfied expression.

I— has Roran been to something like this before? I turn to him with a spike of anxiety. "When d–does the food get served?"

"It doesn't."

My heart drops. "What?"

"It's not customary to eat at these things," Roran explains offhandedly, and I work hard to keep from scowling.

"Why h–have food pre-prepared if no one is g–going to eat it?"

He shrugs. "It's a sensory thing, from what I gather. Everyone can smell the food prepared and leave it alone to drink instead."

My stomach churns; I've lost my appetite. Something about not eating gorgeous arrangements of fresh food makes me sick with anger. The spread would have been enough to feed everyone in my apartment for a month. Back when I had an apartment.

How can the host of this party afford so much food and preparation, only to let it go to waste? What happens to it all? Does it get thrown away? Can the workers at least take some home afterwards? It's cruel, almost inhumane, to let so much good food go spare. We starve and fight over scraps, and they waste a feast worth more than I've made in my lifetime? No wonder Hiero hates rich people.

My throat burns, and I swallow heavily. Roran seems to interpret this as thirst; he grabs a drink from a passing waiter and places it in my hand. Up close, the emerald liquid sparkles with bubbles, and the glass is freezing cold. I'm mesmerized for a moment, caught by a fluttering feeling in my stomach that's more than nerves, and the memory of a color, an emerald color.

Eyes. Hiero's eyes.

Where is she? Is she even here? Christa said she would be, but as I scan the crowd— as best I can, given my stature— I don't spot her. It wouldn't be like Christa to lie, though. I can't see Tristan either, but they insisted he would be here too.

"Once I talk to whoever is watching the front balcony, I'll need to take their place for most of the evening," Roran explains, then points over to the other room. "Why don't we do something together? Then I can point you to where the artwork will be showcased, and maybe see if I can find something for you to do to avoid mingling."

That's kind of sweet and thoughtful of him. But I don't know what he means by "doing something together," other than dancing. That's the only thing going on in the other room. I set the glass, untouched, on the tray of a passing waiter.

"I'm not r–really much of a–a dancer..." I trail off as he takes me by the hand.

"One dance? I won't bother you about it for the rest of the evening. Unless you want me to."

I don't want to dance at all, and really want to turn down the offer. But there's a lot of pressure on me to be nice tonight, and it would be rude to say no when he invited me. If the dress hasn't killed me yet, neither will a single dance.

He takes my silence as consent and escorts me to where all the other couples are dancing. A wave of nausea washes over me as we approach the dance floor. It's crowded, and the band plays a slow tune I don't recognize. I feel even worse as Roran places a hand on my hip and attempts to lead. I move his hand back up to my shoulder with an awkward cough.

The only dancing I ever learned, other than swaying back and forth, was a waltz. My father used to dance with my mother to any song played on a jehkrim, and I'd beg him to teach me how to dance. Most of the time I'd stand on his feet, but I've learned how to follow a decent lead, even if it has been years. Surely it's like learning to tie your laces, something you don't ever really forget.

That is, unless your lead doesn't know how to lead. Roran's steps are rigid and a bit clumsy. I don't mind all that much; I'm just as clumsy, and I do my best to laugh it off. He smiles the whole time, enjoying himself even when he narrowly misses crushing my toes. Eventually he seems to get the hang of it.

Nothing I do feels right. If I try to be like everyone else here, I'll just feel awful about myself. If I even try to talk to anyone, it'll be obvious I don't belong. No one else's first instinct is to discuss the lighting fixtures. I want to get out of this dress. I want to disappear. I want to leave.

The song winds to an end and Roran blinks down at

me. "I hope I didn't step on your toes too much. It's been a while."

"I c–can't even remember the l–last time I danced," I admit.

Roran clears his throat and tilts his chin upwards. "Perhaps when I get a break later, we can try dancing again?"

"M–Maybe." I don't know. Dancing with Roran isn't exactly fun. I'm trying to enjoy myself, have a good time, but it's nearly impossible. I'm only here for the sake of appearances. Between the MPs looking for me and the way Roran is looking at me, all I want is to get away from this place.

As if sensing my distress, a familiar blonde approaches, weaving between groups of people in the crowd. She's dressed in a gauzy gown of pale yellow, her hair tumbling down her back and over her shoulders in loose waves. In her hand is a glass full of fizzy purple liquid, her knuckles white around the stem.

"Hier—"

"—'s to a lovely gala." Hiero raises her glass a bit higher, neatly covering up my slip. Her smile is still poised, but a bit strained around the eyes. "Glory be."

Roran immediately tilts his head upward and squints. They're both smiling, but it's not by any means friendly. It's obvious they recognize each other, and the air thickens as they size each other up. But neither will back down from this game, playing their respective parts to keep the peace. They don't know I know.

"Glory be. I couldn't agree more," Roran says slowly. "You look rather familiar."

Hiero gives him a sharp, inscrutable smile from behind her glass. "I've needed to call a procier here and there. You're stationed somewhere shabby, aren't you? Wellwick?"

"M-M-Maybe! It's easy to-to mix up faces and p-p-people. I do it a-all the t-time!" I get louder with every word, until I'm almost shouting, face burning at my own awkward obnoxiousness. Forty minutes in, and I've already panicked. They both look at me for a moment; Roran clears his throat and Hiero takes a slow sip from her drink.

"Well, there's no point in keeping you," Hiero says. "I'm sure you've got plenty to take care of this evening."

Roran furrows his brow, jaw tight. He clearly has something he wants to say, but he keeps it to himself. He heads to his post on the opposite side of the room, but not before stopping and catching me by the arm, his voice low. "I'll find coverage in a bit. Try to enjoy yourself while I'm gone." His assurance burns in the back of my throat. As he puts more distance between us, it gets a bit easier to breathe, if only for a few seconds.

Hiero gestures toward the dancing couples around us, silently asking to cut in where Roran had been before. She tips back the last of the purple liquid, then sets down her empty glass on a nearby tray, offering me her other hand. Despite my discomfort, I find myself following her lead. She glides with ease, her steps confident and graceful— though perhaps it's not surprising that she's good at yet another thing— and I start to forget where I am.

"Wh-What are you d-doing here?"

"I could ask you the same question."

"I was i–invited." Blackmailed and coerced. "Why are y–you here?"

"Invited as well. Technically. But you, I don't—" She hisses out a breath, slanting her sharp gaze to the side, somewhere beyond my shoulder. "You being here isn't part of the plan."

I've never seen Hiero so shaken up. Her movements betray nothing but confidence and her face is a mask impossible to read, but her voice always gives her away. I can just barely catch her eyes darting quickly between the band playing and the crowd of people lingering around the edges of the dance floor.

"You're not supposed to be here." If her words weren't so soft and worry-laden, they'd sound like a threat. My mind races back to the fire and the procs looking for me, and clearly it shows on my face. "Sayev, calm down, you'll arouse suspicion."

I consider biting my tongue, but the words leave faster than I can rein them in. "And t–two women dancing doe–doesn't?"

She cants her head and twirls me, expression still inscrutable, the green of her eyes the cold, impassive glitter of jewels. "You'd be surprised how common it's become in higher circles. Noble women with lazy husbands. Passion has to be found in other places." Hiero pulls me closer and shoots me a cheeky smile. Oh. My face burns; while some eyes are lingering over us in disgust, many of the occasional looks in our direction are of excitement and scandal, whispers behind hands. Still, I hope nobody runs to the procs.

My knees wobble, and on cue, Hiero dips me, leaning in until her mouth is the barest whisper from mine, her hair cascading in silken curtains around my face. "So sabi taknik," she purrs, and I shiver at the sensuality of her rumbling accent. Enveloped in the scent of jasmine and honey, her eyes dark beneath lowered lashes, I barely make out her next throaty whisper. "Are you following me?"

Dreggar, I forget how to speak when she's this close. It isn't until she pulls us from the dip that I can breathe again, or think any word that's not her name. My cheeks are blazing by the time I can form a reply. "Well, y-you're the one le-leading, s-so, by pr-process of elimination—"

She sighs and leads me back into the dance, sharp gaze flickering over my head, then back to me. "I meant here. This gala."

"N-No." I blink. "How could I-I do that? Besides, if an-an-anyone is fo-following anyone, you're foll-following me." It's a bluff, and I'm waiting for her to call me on it. Part of me being here is circumstantial, thanks to Roran, and part of it isn't, thanks to Christa. If I wasn't starting to feel bad about it, I'd try to have a little more fun in knowing that she, for once, doesn't know everything.

"Hiero, why sh-shouldn't I be h-here?"

Hiero falters, and I stumble a step. It barely registers; I've almost forgotten where we are and what we're doing. Is this even the same song we started dancing to?

"You need to leave."

Right. That. "Why?"

Again her eyes are shuttered by the sweep of her lowered lashes. "It's not safe here."

"With the procs? Ob-Obviously, it's n-not safe for you, e-either."

"No, I mean that something is going to happen." That's vague, even for Hiero, but my heart skips a beat. Seeing Hiero step away from the suave mask she dons and be sincere is almost moving. On the outskirts of the dance floor, I'm vaguely aware of a giggle or two, but I can't tear my gaze away as Hiero continues to struggle with her words.

"W-What do you m-m-mean? What's go-going on?"

"I need you to keep your voice down." She hisses the last part through her teeth. "I just got wind there are two groups here from the rebellion: I'm with the first one. The other wasn't sanctioned. There's talk of bad things happening. Dangerous things. You need to go."

There's no way I can leave. Roran was my ticket in, via an incredibly long and awkward jitney ride, and he knows Hiero keeps suspect company. As nice as Roran is to me, something tells me he wouldn't hold back from arresting me for my connection to the rebellion. I wrack my brain for any other escape plans, but they all involve alerting Roran and proving my guilt. Hiero is right: I shouldn't be here, and I never should have come in the first place. I'm trapped.

We've stopped dancing; I only realize it the moment Hiero starts walking away. The music kicks up again, and around me other couples resume dancing in dizzying, synchronized whirls, gems flashing and skirts billowing as they fly by me. There's an ache in my chest, and my feet are leaden weights at the end of my legs.

I manage to steel myself and push forward, trying my best to catch her. She knows I'm following, from the way she darts to and fro, winding and weaving and trying to blend in with the crowd. I bump into a couple folks and mumble apologies but keep going, eyes straining for a glimpse of pale yellow cloth. I don't want to lose her. Our conversation and her sudden disappearance has made everything feel empty, meaningless, like reality has been suspended until we continue where we left off.

Eventually Hiero stops trying to evade me and pauses by the entrance to the kitchen. "I'm serious, you need to—" She sighs, leaving her thought unfinished, and shakes her head, waving me onward. I follow her as she pushes on, past counters heavy with baked goods and roasted vegetables. In the kitchen pantry, we find ourselves face-to-face with Arek, Aether, and Tristan, all dressed to the nines.

I don't know what I was expecting, but the three of them, Arek dressed in a fine black suit with tails and white gloves, and Tristan bulging out of a too-small, patched monstrosity, both with their hair slicked back, were certainly not it. Aether and Arek barely look up, though Arek offers a hum of acknowledgement. Tristan brightens at our arrival and grins. "Hey, I didn't know you would be here, Artem!"

"What is she doing here?" Aether hisses. She's wearing the slinkiest cocktail dress I've ever seen. I wonder how many knives she's managed to fit under it.

"I don't know, but I'm glad she is." Arek abandons his position by the wall, revealing a tangled nest of wires hanging from a pried-open keypad beside a locked door. "This one's beyond me."

Aether's shoulders tense and she ducks her head. I crane

my neck to peer over the best I can, but Aether shuffles over just enough to block my view.

"Wh–What are you trying t–to do?"

Arek rubs the back of his neck and glances to Hiero for help, but she only shrugs in response. "We need some documents upstairs, but the area's restricted. Some kind of alarm that triggers if you don't have a badge. Which we don't."

"Where are t–the cooks?"

"It doesn't matter." Aether cuts Arek off, finally stepping away from the keypad. "This is pointless. I told you it'd make more sense to gain entry to the roof and work our way down."

"This way is safer," Hiero counters, furrowing her brow.

"It's ridiculous."

"Maybe I–I can look?" I offer.

Aether takes another step away and gestures unceremoniously to the mess of wires hanging out of the keypad, then tosses me a screwdriver she's pulled from Dreggar-knows-where. I glance around out of habit and give it a look-over. I've never tried to do anything like this before, but it shouldn't be too difficult.

Arek and Tristan keep watch as I start fiddling around. Aether and Hiero's eyes are heavy on my back. One set feels encouraging and curious, while the other is frustrated, demanding I hurry and not screw everything up. I fumble with a wire and almost drop the screwdriver. Aether starts to hiss something, but Hiero gives a warning hush, coming closer and offering a free hand. I quietly push it away, mumbling my thanks, and turn back to the panel.

As I set the last wire in place, the door beside us unlocks with a sharp click, and Aether flies up the stairs in a flash of black silk. Tristan beams proudly as I step out and close the door behind me, while Arek crosses his arms and tilts his head upward.

"Nice." He gives an approving half-nod, something like a smile on his lips. "Glad you ran into us."

"Yeah, Hiero told me you were good with mechie things!" Tristan adds.

My face warms, and Hiero clears her throat. "I believe your jobs are done. I'll stay behind to wait for Aether, you two head back to the boat."

Boat? How'd they get a boat over here? Is the backyard like the Kulkner house, with its own little beach? Are all houses in Lindsor the same?

Arek mumbles for Tristan to follow him and Tristan nods enthusiastically, waving goodbye to the rest of us. I hang around, not sure what else to say. Hiero glances in my direction than back at the stairs. The absence of cooks and servants during a party worries me. Did something happen to them?

"It'd be best if you found Roran and convinced him to take you home early."

I shake my head, even though she's not looking at me. "N–No, I don't t-think so."

"Artem."

She turns back to me as I shake my head again and make firm eye contact. "I'm alr–already in a b-bad position. Yo-You said yourself: I shouldn't b-b-be here. But I–I am, and

I have no st-straightfor-straightforward way to g-g-get home without raising s-suspicion."

Her eyebrows are so high they might fly off her face. "Sometimes I think you really do support the cause. Sometimes I think you like a little danger."

"I don't." Not danger, at least.

Hiero's lips quirk upwards in a smile, and I find myself smiling back.

Footsteps sound near the doorway. I whip my head around in a panic, but Hiero only takes a half-step closer to me, until she's almost too close, and winds her arms around my waist, fixing me with the full, heady heat of her stare. She's so close, we're— We're going to get caught. What is she doing?

"Excuse me, guests are not allowed back—" Roran stops, going silent as he stares us down. My heart seizes in my chest, and time starts to slow down. "—Artem? What are you doing back here?" His eyes narrow. "And you, miss?"

"W-W-We were ju-just..." I bite my lip.

Thankfully, Hiero jumps in, turning her face to him lazily. She tucks an errant lock of hair behind her shoulder and tugs me even closer. "Doing what most women do when they leave a party together."

Okay, maybe not so thankfully. My cheeks burn as my jaw goes slack. I look to Hiero, scandalized. Her expression is all coy delight, and I try to beat my mind into shape as it wanders into dark corners with hypothetical Hieros.

Roran's eyes dart uneasily between us, but he puffs his chest out and tries to assume control. "There is a time and a place for humor, and here is not it. I'm afraid I have to ask you to rejoin the party, or I will have to provide force."

There's shouting upstairs. I glance up. The mechanisms in my audancers have slipped again; I can't make out what's happening. Hiero is tensed up, and Roran is glancing wildly between Hiero and the stairs. There's the light thudding of someone running down the stairs, and Aether appears, clutching a file under her arm.

She locks eyes with Roran, and we all turn to look at her. A call echoes down the stairwell after her: the alarm bell isn't working. All the while Roran keeps eyeing Hiero and me, putting two and two together.

"Roran, it's not—!"

"No," he interrupts me, his voice unusually soft. "Don't."

"B–But I—!"

An explosion goes off in another room. I jump at the sound, as does Hiero, though I could swear she was expecting it. Screams pour from the direction of the party as people begin to panic. An adrenaline rush sets my limbs to shaking and the world seems to sway as I glance around wildly, trying to see where the crowds of people are gathered. Is everyone okay? Did someone get hurt? Who set off a bomb and why?

The same shouting from earlier cries, louder than before, from the floor above. "Sound the alarm! Secure the doors!"

I look toward Roran, unable to come up with anything to say. All I want is to apologize: for coming here, for not being the friend he deserves, for, well, everything. "Glory be," I manage, the words tasting as bitter as they sound.

Hiero's arm slides off my waist and she grabs my hand in a firm yet gentle grip, grumbling something into one of my audancers. I don't catch it, and the jostling only knocks something else loose in the devices. As I'm whisked past Roran and the kitchen, the shouts and screams of panic all melt into a whisper. Roran just stands there, deflated, as Hiero drags me through the guests and into the backyard.

Outside, beyond a small rocky patio, slopes a hill supported by loads of dark, jagged boulders. Arek waits in an engine-powered skiff along with Tristan, Aether, and a man I don't recognize— the boatsman? The boat is ready to take off. Hiero boards quickly, practically jumping in, and extends her arm to me. I take it, and the moment I sit down, the skiff lurches forward.

Behind us, people are trying their best to escape the building, a crowd of them swarming the drive at the front of the house. Smoke billows from the windows that are open, before giant metal plates propel down, sealing the doors and windows as the procs who made it outside search around.

The voices around me are muffled, like I'm hearing through a long, echoey tunnel. I'm paralyzed, unblinking, watching the house even as it grows smaller and smaller in the distance.

There's no going back.

CHAPTER 13

The ward is eerily quiet this morning. I guess I was expecting to wake up to another proc attack, or the whole place burning down around me again. Instead I wake up craving a cup of qosa, confused that I'm not on an airship.

I don't know what to make of last night. There were parts that were... okay, but mostly the evening was a disaster. The major radio stations are probably avoiding it. The station that Esper's recently been tuning into, one Arek recently mentioned, seems to delve into the grittier topics, without putting some spin on it; they'd probably have more information.

I switch on Esper's radio, waiting for the charming yet clearly uncomfortable broadcaster to speak. His program is on, but the conversation seems to be about the skylines. All anyone seems to want to talk about are those damn skylines. What about the fires? The explosions, the people getting hurt? Why is it that even Leonard Kitts won't talk about the important things?

My head hurts. I bring a hand to my forehead and close my eyes, practicing my breathing. In for seven seconds, out for eleven. Or, is it in for eleven seconds, out for seven? Now my chest hurts too.

I can only imagine where Hiero is now, or Roran, for that matter. All I know is that a bomb went off and people were injured, which is the same thing I know about the fire in the apartments. Some of the rebels are clearly proving to be arsonists. What was the point of setting off an explosion anyway? To send some sort of message? I'm just glad Tristan and the others didn't get hurt. Just how much did everyone know about the second group at the gala? Is there anyone here I can really trust?

As much as almost every part of me argues against it, I feel like I can trust Hiero. Yes, she's technically the reason I'm stuck with the rebellion now, but there's something about her that makes me want to believe she's trying to help me. I do think that she means well, even if I don't agree with most of the things she does.

Last night, while Runa checked everyone over for injuries and Christa harassed Tristan for details, I made a beeline to the ward to check on Esper. He was sound asleep, blissfully unaware, yet again, of the hell I've been through. I returned to Hiero, eager for a moment alone with her, but the second I turned around, she was gone. Christa brushed it off with a shrug when I asked where she went. "It's just like her to slip off."

I didn't get a chance to ask them to elaborate before Arek, free of Runa's overcautious administrations, spun on them, eyes narrowed. "What do you know about the bomb?"

"Nothing," Christa scoffed. "I overheard that the splinter group was going to be there. Beats me how that even got started. You accusing me of withholding information?"

It's all the same thing: there's some faction within the resistance causing problems, and Christa and Hiero just happened to know about it. I wish I knew more about the group, like who they're working for and why they're doing what they're doing. Maybe they're the same people behind my apartment going up in flames.

Until I see Hiero again, I'm stuck at the bunker, and I'm going to worry about her.

Arek and Tristan come often enough to the ward, Tristan because he keeps getting injured and Arek because he just wants an excuse to stop by and see Runa, not that they get much privacy. Esper is always desperate for interaction, and especially likes to bother Arek or Hiero.

I head out of the ward and onto the walkway. Over by the vault door stand Arek, Runa, and Esper; as soon as I walk over, Runa pats Arek's shoulder, her hand lingering on his forearm for a brief moment before she heads toward me. She looks me over with a smile, as if making sure I'm still in one piece. "Did you sleep well, Artem?"

"Not t-too bad," I lie.

She doesn't buy it; I can tell from the way the sides of her eyes crinkle. But she doesn't press the issue, just slips by me. I watch her walk back into the ward, pressing my lips together. Runa worries about everyone a little too much.

"Artem!" Esper shouts. I spin back around. Esper's eyes have gone wide, practically lit up from excitement. Arek seems vaguely amused, but it's hard to tell past his usual annoyed expression.

I find myself missing Mr. Connolly any time I interact with Arek. They don't look alike, as Mr. Connolly is as Allowyte as they come, while Arek is clearly Eoten. It's that they act so alike, both concise and to the point. Maybe it'd be easier to say that Arek reminds me of a grumpy old man. His default mood is brooding, though he at least seems capable of displaying an emotional range larger than a thimble. It still doesn't make me miss Mr. Connolly any less.

Arek crosses his arms and leans against one of the braces near the door.

"A-Any more information?"

He shakes his head. "Only more of the same."

"You mean the gala?" Esper asks, bouncing impatiently. "It sounds boring."

The gala had been anything but boring, but I don't want to get into more detail. The less Esper knows, the better. "You'd un-understand why it's not b-boring if you were older." I run a hand through my hair.

Arek sighs. "It's just a splinter from the cause. I don't know who ordered it, I don't know how Christa or Hiero found out, and I don't know who was part of it or who else knew."

Esper jumps, as if he can't contain himself any longer, and starts talking in one breath. "Arek said that he's going to do stuff for the rebellion and it sounds cool and I want to go with him and he said if you said it was okay I could go so can I? Please?"

Jaq? I blink a few times and Arek lets out a chuckle. "Slow down a second." I pause. "St–Start over?"

"I mentioned we have recruits his age and offered to let him follow me for the day. I didn't say you'd agree."

"She agrees to anything if you say it fast enough!" Esper quips.

I don't really have a response for that. Admittedly, I've said "yes" before to Esper when he starts spouting off, and nine out of ten times I end up regretting it, but when he starts talking so fast it's hard to keep up. I can't even keep track of my own frenzied thoughts, so paying attention to Esper requires a level of skill that I don't think I'll ever achieve.

This isn't the first time Esper has bugged me about this, and it won't be the last. Honestly there's not much keeping me from giving him the go-ahead other than wanting to keep him safe. I went into this rebellion expecting that he could stay safe at home while I tried to figure out an apprenticeship for him or get him back into school. The thing is, I don't want him going off doing the types of things Aether does, or even Hiero for that matter. I trust Hiero, though, and that's saying more than for most of the folks here. I don't even know what Arek does other than sneak around places and look good in a suit. I suppose if there was anyone I'd let watch Esper other than Runa or Hiero, it'd be Arek. Perhaps doing something, instead of sitting around bored out of his mind, might be helpful for everyone. Well, everyone except Arek.

Ignoring the alarm bells ringing in my head— because, to be honest, they never really stop— I close my eyes and take a deep breath. "Alright, f-fine, you can g-go with Arek, as long as he-he's okay with it."

Esper starts shouting and pumping his fist in the air. Arek raises an eyebrow and turns back to me. "Are you sure it's alright?"

"I'd like to-to be able to get some wor-work done, and I th-think Runa would like the p-peace and quiet. Just... promise m-me he won't be doing anything da-dangerous."

Arek huffs a short laugh. "What kind of work do you think I do?"

I have no idea, only a vague one at best. What does that say about me? Being so frustrated with Esper that I'm willing to hand him over for the day to someone else when I have no idea what they do. "Sneaking-around-ty-type stuff?" I ask, wincing as soon as the words leave my mouth.

Arek shakes his head. "It's more walking-around-the city-type stuff. Don't worry, I'll make sure he stays out of trouble."

"No promises," Esper adds with a wicked grin.

There's a part of me regretting this already. The other part is more concerned for Arek, who I'm sure has not yet realized what chaos Esper can wreak. I suppose I'll need to stop fretting over my brother eventually and trust him with other people... today is a big step toward that. Arek opens the door and motions for Esper for go ahead of him. As they leave, I hang by the door waiting, until I can no longer hear their chatter.

I remember when Esper was younger and didn't want to

leave my side. I'd drop him off at school and he'd wail for me to come back, and when I picked him up at the end of the day he'd cling to my legs and beg me not to leave him. He's not a baby anymore, though, and nowadays it's like he wants to spend as little time with me as possible.

I observe the structure below for a few minutes. No one else is working on the airship yet. Most likely everyone is only just heading to the bunker now. My internal clock guesses it must be almost half past seven. Understandable, really, that no one else is around. And yet, the lack of mechies rushing about is unsettling. I drum my fingers along the rail until I can't stand it anymore and propel myself across the walkway.

Once down the spiral staircase, I duck into one of the rooms in the back where I've been keeping my tools and papers. Sticking out from behind a desk are the rolled-up plans I need. I tug them out and unfurl them across the length of the table, pinning them down with my toolbox on one side and a wrench on the other. I pick up a nearby pencil and twirl it between my fingers, the gesture mindless and familiar.

It's rare I get any time to myself. Back in Mr. Connolly's shop, if it was one of the days I opened or closed, I'd either get there early or stay late to have some peace and quiet. That was back when Esper was still in school and I could trust him to walk home with the other kids in the building and be watched for a little while by the Cavicks.

Out of habit, I abandon my station and search around for a broom or dustpan. Tucked in the corner is a ratty old thing, with more broken bristles than not, and I grab it. Something about sweeping calms me down; right now it might dull this aching in my chest. It's by no means the shop, and Mr. Connolly would never step foot here, but I can pretend for a few minutes that everything is back to the way it used to be... the way I wish it still was.

I spend more time than I should trying to tidy up the space, even though barely anyone uses it for anything but storage. As soon as I finish, I start fiddling with my blueprints for the engine room. I've gone over them more times than I care to admit. Mr. Connolly's voice nags at the back of my head, tutting to always triple-check measurements before proceeding with a build.

Slowly, people file in and out, throwing a coat onto a table and grabbing a tool box, or going through the communal collection of screws and bolts. It grows noisy and soon, outside, there's shouting from every direction, and the clanging of metal. So much for playing pretend.

It's not necessarily how to build a steam engine that's been holding me back on this project, more so, how am I going to build something the right size for an airship? From what I've been told about how the ship works in general, a steam engine is the only thing that can do the necessary work, besides the gas, and now I'm looking at building three.

I catch a glimpse through the doorway of someone walking past the airship toward me. For a moment my hopes soar, thinking it's Hiero, wanting to talk to her about the other night, but once I spot red hair, I realize I couldn't be any more wrong. Aether glances around appraisingly, and for some reason a chill travels down my spine.

Of course, she isn't here to observe the structure. She pauses by Meno, who points over to the room I'm in. As soon as Aether's eyes meet mine, I whip my head back toward the desk and pretend to be busy scribbling away.

Even I wouldn't fall for my bad acting.

Aether stands in the doorway for what feels like minutes though it probably is more like a couple seconds. She sighs and lets herself in, hovering over me as I pointlessly scrawl on spare paper. Sweat beads at my temples.

"Hard at work?" I wince at Aether's drawling tone and spin around in my seat.

"T-Trying."

"You certainly are."

I gather my materials together into a neater pile and do my best to look anywhere but at Aether. Before I can ask why she's over here, she holds out a bundle of papers. I hesitate, and she makes a face. "They're not explosive."

I'm starting to wonder if I'm just entertainment for people like Aether and Hiero. At least with Hiero I don't feel like I'm mocked as openly.

"What are th–these?" I ask.

"Papers," Aether replies drily.

"... I c–can see that," I start cautiously. "I mean, what kind of p–papers?"

She heaves a dramatic sigh, like just standing here talking to me is an enormous strain. "Legal papers. New name, new fake address, new history. Traveling papers. They're papers."

I turn them over in my hands to look through them. Sure enough, it's my picture, dark circles and all, paired with a name that couldn't sound more Allowyn if I tried: Emie Stroud. It doesn't really fit. Esper has some papers as well, in the name of Asher. They're nearly identical to my old documents, with minute differences: they're not out of date, for one, and Esper's picture is recent.

"I had some f-f-fake papers before, I d-don't know why I-I can't just use those." Except Esper didn't have anything. That and I don't know what even happened to those fake papers. I guess I answered my own question.

"They've updated protocol on what needs to be on them. Your old papers are garbage. Hiero thought it would be a clever idea for you to have these so you don't get all of us busted."

Aether has talked to Hiero since last night? My head spins, wondering why she'd talk to Aether, of all people, and not me. Is she mad at me? Did I do something? I don't think there's any bad air between us, not since she apologized, and especially not with the way she was acting last night.Where did Hiero even get papers so quickly? How does she keep getting them at the drop of a hat? Did she know I would need them? I'm unable to contain myself, and ask outright: "You've seen H-Hiero? Where is she?"

My shoulders drop as Aether scowls. "Uck, no. I haven't seen Hiero in a while and I'd like to keep it that way. Someone else passed these off to me and made me errand boy."

"Oh." So much for seeing Hiero. Maybe it isn't personal, after all.

As if reading my thoughts, Aether continues. "I wouldn't go searching for her. She disappears sometimes and waltzes back into things like she was never gone."

And does she waltz...

"Hey, base to Artem, do you always zone out in the middle of conversation?"

Had I been zoning out? I shake my head to dispel whatever look may have been on my face. When I look back at Aether, she continues to stare. The only thing I can do is blink, waiting for her to say something else. Suddenly her eyebrows lift, and she gets a look on her face as if I had done something interesting, or someone offered her a purse full of coin.

I don't think I want to know what's on her mind. Placing the papers on the desk beside me, I clear my throat and clasp my hands together near my chest. "Sorry," I mumble. "Th-Thank you for b-bringing these to me."

Aether says something that falls short of my ears, like she's whispering down a long tunnel. I mess with the dials on my audancers and hold up a finger. "Wait, what did you sa—?"

It doesn't matter. Halfway through my sentence she spins around and gives a salute before continuing on her way. Probably off to the torture chamber.

CHAPTER 14

I spend the bulk of the next few days testing one of the three engines I want to use for the airship. I avoid working on the steam one, as I know it'll be easier; I haven't decided what the third will run on yet. I can't only use gas, and steam isn't going to cut it for the power that's going to be needed behind everything. I'm feeling less and less confident about coal, especially after some of the looks I receive from the engineers who will actually listen. Verne claims coal will lead to the whole ship going up in flames. I get it, but I really want to avoid working with an engine I don't know how to build.

Not much has been happening in the bunker. Esper has gone off with Arek again, though I swear I overheard Runa asking Arek to take him for my sake. It wouldn't surprise me if that was why Arek offered in the first place. He strikes me as the kind of guy to do whatever Runa says to keep her from stressing out.

I take a break to go upstairs, grab some water, and clear my head a bit. The bunker is nice and all, but I can't help but get stir-crazy in here. There's no real fresh air: it's all stale, coming from the filters constantly chugging, and the lights scattered along the walls are harsh, and dimmer than true sunlight. As smoggy as the air felt back in the apartment, I miss being able to hear the launauts chirping when the sun rose, and the neighbors singing in Dormylin.

Runa is one of the few people keeping me sane at this point. Meno is a comfort while working, but Runa has been more than helpful with Esper. She's like a mother, checking up on my sleeping habits and if I've eaten anything during the day. It's a little annoying, but touching nevertheless.

I wish I knew more about her. Sure, I know that she's Qorani from what little she's talked about, and that she got involved with the rebellion to protect Christa, but other than that I don't know much. There's a part of me that doesn't understand how Runa doesn't speak Qalqora. I've heard Runa mumble in it once, but neither her nor Christa have any real working knowledge. But Christa and Runa both follow the same god that the rebels do, and speak only passing phrases in Qorani. It's odd, as I'm used to speaking Qalqora with the Cavicks and celebrating the same things. I grew up assuming it was an identity I had to embrace. It just made sense that if you had gold eyes you had to identify as Qorani and you had to speak Qalqora and follow Siqhadra, worshipping Siqhadmar and the prophet Dreggar. I went out of my way to embrace the culture just to try and fit in.

My hand grasps at the necklace hiding beneath my shirt, clutching the fabric and metal tightly for a moment. It's a messy path, mentally, going down this road. It only makes me think of my parents. I take a deep breath, try to gather my thoughts, and steady myself. Slowly, I let go, and head inside the makeshift medical wing.

"... why a splinter was even there, but—" Hiero stands near the other doorway, pausing mid-speech to glance my way. She smiles, her eyes landing on me for a second before she turns back to Runa. "But we can continue this conversation later, when I figure out what exactly is going on."

Hiero is back! After days of wondering where she's been or what she's been up to, she's here and in one piece. Part of me wants to start asking as many questions as possible, but I'm sure Runa's done enough checking up on her. Instead I cough and wonder what I'm supposed to do with my hands to not look awkward.

Trick question: no matter what I do, I look awkward.

I settle for crossing my arms, only to see her arms are crossed. I immediately drop mine to my sides. Great. "H–Hey, Hiero, long ti–time no see!" I want to die.

"Likewise." She tilts her head. "Actually, I came here looking for you."

Probably to ask another dangerous and unsavory favor, but her words still catch me by surprise. I try to ignore how loud my heart is pounding as she steps closer. My mind flashes back to the gala, and my face heats. "Is this a–about what happened?"

"What exactly?"

"The bomb," I manage.

"Nooooo." Hiero's face falls, and she gestures for me to follow her outside of the ward. Her voice falls to a hush. "That should have never happened, sayev. You shouldn't have been there, and while it's not my fault, I'm sorry you were mixed up in it." There's a beat, then, "For all of it, actually." Hiero shifts her position. She stares at me, her gaze practically boring through my skin, begging me to face her directly. I glance up through my lashes. It's a rare moment when her facade of smug confidence melts away, but it seems to be happening more often. She's deep in thought, and looks almost regretful. I can only imagine what she's thinking about.

There's nothing I can say. I don't know for certain if the rebellion was behind what happened at my apartment. I don't know if I want to be involved with Rhine and his rebels any longer. Although I care a lot for the people I've met here, there are no outs left for me. For all I know, I'm on wanted posters in proc offices throughout Allowyn. I know too much to just walk out of the Airgon movement.

There's no other way to phrase it: I'm trapped. I'm forever going to be tied to a revolution I never cared about.

"I mean—" I exhale. "I-It's fine... I mean, it's n-not fine, but, you g-get the point."

Hiero keeps looking at me. I roll one shoulder back and clear my throat. Finally, she nods and adjusts her jacket. I watch as she starts to head past me for the other door. Bracing my forearms against the railing, I take a deep breath and close my eyes.

When I finally look over, Hiero is up ahead, waiting. "Are you coming?"

I blink. "Wh–What? To where?"

"I came to see you because I wanted to show you something. I thought that was clear."

Nothing is ever clear with Hiero. "I guess. You d–don't really show up j–just to say hi."

"Let's get going, then. Or would you rather wait around here?"

Kind of, yeah.

I abandon my spot to follow her. She doesn't react, just heads for the tunnels. They've taken on new meaning since the fire. No longer do they feel as ominous, nor does the silence bother me. Underground, surrounded by dirt and concrete, I'm beginning to feel safe.

When we exit the pub, Hiero stops me short, barring me with her arm as she glances down the road. The streets are busier than usual, with groups of friends or families completing errands for the day. My view is obscured thanks to Hiero, but I spot some proc barricades blocking off one of the main roads.

"Keep your eyes on my back and nowhere else. Act natural," Hiero warns. The hairs on the back of my neck prickle.

I don't know if Hiero is aware that telling someone to "act natural" is one of the worst things you can possibly do. As I follow at her back, I become hyper-aware of how much I rely on awareness of my environment. A man and woman in fancy outfits walk arm-in-arm, the man carrying a bag of bread. I catch the eye of a child who points at me and tugs on his mother's jacket. The dark reddish-brown weave of Hiero's coat is not enough to keep me from wanting to glance out of the corner of my eye at different people, or examine the procs blocking traffic. I'm probably walking funny, simultaneously too stiff and too loose with my movements.

Her words from our first mission echo in my head: "Try to relax, you're going to raise red flags." Keep it together, Artem. You're being way too obvious.

I must have made a noise, as Hiero stops in her tracks. She looks back casually, as if to check up on me. I bring my hands to my mouth. Unalarmed, she turns her head back and continues, saying nothing. We take a right onto an empty street, and she checks behind her again. Was it not something I did after all? She fixes the collar of her jacket, seemingly unruffled. Her expression is unreadable, her default when in the public eye.

I follow suit and look back. It doesn't look like we are being followed. What has her so on edge? Besides the extra procs everywhere.

She quickens her pace, voice low. "We have a couple blocks to go."

I clap my hand over my mouth again to hold in the strangled squeak working its way up my throat. These crumbling roads and boarded up buildings mean we're headed toward the Flooded Sector.

Years before I was born, there were seven sectors that made up Wellwick: Pollow, Peri, Kensing, Brunsel, Calken, Yisbel, and then the Flooded sector. It had a name once, but no one I've met has ever known it. Supposedly it was a bustling area, another housing sector, nicer than Calken, with the largest public train station. One day the dam there burst, due to heavy rains or sabotage. When the citizens of the sector reached out for help, they got none, and eventually everyone abandoned the area. High waters fill every roadway, and the whole sector's been sealed off to avoid flooding any of the surrounding areas. Aside from being used as a dump, no one comes to these parts.

We reach a high-walled section of thick iron and steel that cuts through the buildings in a jagged zig-zag. The metal has rusted, a sign the bearings are on borrowed time. It stands three-fourths the size of the tall buildings, and reeks of stagnant water and trash. Yet, instead of pausing, Hiero ducks behind a building, then balances on a discarded bin to hoist herself into the open window of a condemned house. I hesitate, just standing and watching her in disbelief, until she beckons me. With a deep breath, I scramble up after her.

Inside is a hallway, with stairs leading up and down. Hiero heads up, and I have no choice but to follow. When we reach the top, she pushes through a door, into a vacant apartment with a long wooden plank propped lengthwise along the wall. Hiero clicks her tongue. "How's your balance?"

"N–Not good." Nonexistent, really. "Why?"

"Well, it's a short enough distance, but..." She grunts as she struggles slightly lifting the board, and heads toward the window. "Only one way across."

"You w–want m–m–me to go i–into the Flooded sector."

"It's free real estate."

"No, wait." I hold my hands out in front of me. "Y–You're insane, Hiero. No one comes here, no one wants t–to come here."

She huffs and tugs at the bottom of her ponytail. "Just trust me, okay?"

I stare at her. Something about those vibrant green eyes of hers have me constantly forgetting my doubts about the woman behind them.

I gesture to the window. "You first."

Hiero raises an eyebrow but doesn't complain. She hoists the plank through the window, letting the other end fall in the window of another ramshackle building across the way, then secures the plank under a small notch on the windowsill and jostles the board a few times experimentally. Confident, she climbs up, then struts across just as gracefully as she glided through the gala. She hops inside the opposite building, then turns and waits.

Dreggar save me. It looks easy, but I know it isn't. With shaky legs and arms, I step up onto the board and cling to the sides of the window frame, glancing down. A pool of murky green water lies below, only the faintest of currents stirring its stagnant depths. It's about seven stories down from this thin hunk of wood, the only bridge between Calken and the Flooded Sector.

"This is the simplest way until we can get a path cleared underground," Hiero calls over. "Just run across and I'll be right here."

Run across? More like run straight to my genqii *death*. If I do this quickly, I'll just slip and fall. Maybe I can aedorpaddle a bit, but I don't trust that water, and it doesn't look like there's any way back up. I try to gauge crouching— maybe I could sit and scoot along the board. But the wood wobbles the moment I shift my weight, and I end up stumbling back into the windowsill with a surprised yip.

I'm going to die.

I stretch my arms out as far as I can and take the first step. Every part of my being screams not to look down. But as I wobble, my gaze drops to my feet. Maybe the fall isn't actually seven stories; it feels more like ten. Another step. I start composing my will: Esper gets everything except my tools, which will go to whomever needs them most. Who would need them though? Perhaps someone in the bunker, but everyone seems to be more well-equipped than me. I suppose I could have them sent to Mr. Connolly, as they were once his. As for my clothes, honestly, they should probably just be burned in a dumpster fire.

And then, somehow, I'm across. Before I know it, Hiero's looking up at me from the concrete floor of the new apartment, a hand open and ready. I take it, step down, and immediately crumple, my knees buckling beneath me. I stay on the ground for a minute, clutching at my chest. Hiero watches with a raised eyebrow. "Maybe this surprise won't be so great after all."

"Are y–you sure th–this is the only way?"

Hiero shakes her head, flicking her ponytail back over her shoulder. "Like I said, it's the easiest until I can get a path cleared underground. Something apart from the tunnels. It's going to take me some time."

I manage to get myself back on my feet. I don't know what Hiero is talking about, or why anyone would want to be over here. Yet, as my heartbeat settles, I can hear the sound of voices not far away. But isn't this whole place sectioned off? What would anyone be doing here?

Hiero starts walking again with me in tow. We head up another level onto a rooftop. The sight is one to behold; a shantytown built from large, sturdy planks and makeshift floors made of metal sheets. They connect from building to building, with ramps leading to higher- or lower-leveled areas. There are roofs constructed from copper piping and tarps, or heavy sheets of wood or metal. Most of the setups remind me of stalls at the market. People in worn clothing greet one another as they walk between the rickety, rusting bridges, which groan beneath the weight of passers-by. Many huddle beneath makeshift awnings, eyes darting cautiously up at the gray, looming sky. A huge, dingy white tarp, strung across the expanse of the marketplace, funnels down to a great stone well at the center of the market. One question answered, then; the people here collect rainwater. I start idly designing a more efficient system.

A few people glance over but don't say anything. One man waves in Hiero's direction, then returns to stripping meat from a gully carcass. Why aren't the people here panicking over strangers? If a proc came and discovered this, the whole sector would be shut down again. Maybe it's because they know Hiero, so anyone with her must be trustworthy.

Just how long has this community been living in the Flooded Sector? Given the size of the sector, couldn't the housing crisis be relieved if more people could live here? Other than the height, I wouldn't mind living someplace like this. The only issue I'd have is ensuring Esper wouldn't dive into the questionable water surrounding the entire place. That, and I don't know how they get enough fresh water without constant rainfall. Or how they receive food and supplies.

My answer awaits on the next rooftop: it's covered in rows

and rows of green, a large and thriving garden. A dozen or so people are tending to the soil, watering plants and scooping piles of fertilizer from worn barrels. It's smart— I wish I'd thought of something like it back when we lived in the apartments. It must cut down on the amount of food these people would need to procure from outside the sector.

I want to ask questions, to puzzle out all the logistics, but now doesn't seem to be the time. Hiero catches my eye again, nods, and motions for me to keep following her. I guess she was just giving me a moment to catch my breath and take it all in. I duck my head and follow behind her, glancing occasionally at the traders and the market folk.

The next platform feels more secure, though I still take my time crossing each plank. I can't help but feel judged for how I stare at my feet as I shuffle along to the other side. There's no avoiding it; I probably look like a hopeless wreck, especially to the folks who live here, many of whom trundle across the boards blindly from behind armfuls of boxes and goods.

A lot of the closer-together buildings have a flooring of sorts connecting them. Those are the easy ones to pass over. It's walking the long, narrow planks that's difficult. It's terrifying, crossing the length of a street with nothing but grody water a few stories below.

As if recognizing my inner turmoil, Hiero calls back, "Hey, everyone starts somewhere."

Yeah, except I'm starting at base zero in terms of agility and balance. There have been nights I've tripped over air carrying soup to the table. "What e-exactly is it w-we're doing?" I ask, trying my best not to whine. "Why do I–I need to b–be here?"

"Just up ahead, I promise."

"What's up a–ahead though? W–Why did you t–take me with you? What are we d–doing in the Fl–Flooded Sector?"

Hiero lifts an unamused brow. "Normally all the questions are kind of adorable, but it's a little late for them now. Save any and all queries for when we get there."

I'm not sure how to respond to that. Part of me wants to ask where is "there," but the gears get stuck on "adorable," and I end up just sputtering complete nonsense. Hiero laughs and continues along another plank, tucking some of her bangs behind her ear as she strides ahead.

I don't think all the time in the world could make me comfortable strutting rooftop to rooftop the way Hiero does. Technically that's all it takes, practice, but I know me, and I know I could never survive doing this day to day like everyone else here. Okay, maybe eventually; I'm improving, even if my legs are wobbly and my knees threaten to buckle. My lungs tighten as if I've been screaming the whole time. Maybe I have been. I check my jaw with my hands, but my mouth is closed. Apparently internal screaming is just as tiring.

"This is it," Hiero says finally, gesturing ahead. "Our stop."

A broken-down clock tower stands in all its glory one building over. It's half-submerged, like many of the other buildings around here, a wooden plank leading into a window surrounded by brick and sandstone. It's a miracle it hasn't sunken entirely into the ground, but there appear to be metal supports extending from parts of the tower to surrounding buildings. Perhaps the clock tower holds a certain significance to the people here. The clock face is stuck at three-thirty, and there are lights on inside.

A rotting plank sits off to the side. The last bridge, I assume. As terrifying as crossing these boards is, I'm beyond thankful someone thought to replace this one. Otherwise, though, it doesn't look as though anyone has set foot inside in a very long time.

I want to ask why we're here, but Hiero is leading the way again. I drop my shoulders and sigh, before shaking my head and following her. The board, though seemingly new, is as sturdy as they've all been, which is not saying much. The whole time I mumble a prayer to Dreggar under my breath and try desperately not to look down. Once across, she offers me a hand, and I hop down to look at the inside. The walls are peeling, and there's a thick stench of gullies and spoiled milk. A lone light shines overhead, casting deep shadows in the corners of the room. Two beds are set up, in good condition but without any obvious signs of use. It doesn't seem like anyone lives here, though. How is the electricity working? Why hasn't the rest of the community spread over to this area?

"What do you think?"

"What sh-should I think?" I ask, looking over at her.

She tips her head. "You should be thinking, 'Wow, Hiero, in this economy, you managed to find me and Esper a place to live? You're amazing!' Or something equally awed and complimentary."

A place to— "W-Wait, what?"

Hiero shrugs and kicks at the planking to demonstrate how secure it is, then takes in the room with a sweeping glance. "You can't live in the bunker forever, and it's hard to find anywhere to lay low. It's a bit hard to navigate, I suppose, but the tunnel between here and the bunker is still blocked off. Once that's finished, it'll only be three or four bridges to cross, but it's still something, and all to yourselves. Kranisky owes me a favor, and I had some help with the lighting and lugging furniture here. The stairway down should be blocked off from all the flooding, but I've been told the supports will keep it steady, like the rest of the buildings here..."

"Why would y-you g-g-go through a-all this trouble?" I'm not quite sure what to make of the gesture, other than it being overwhelming and oddly touching. "I don't un-under—"

"Kids shouldn't be forced to live in bunkers," Hiero interrupts, looking away. Her laugh sounds forced. "Maybe I just wanted to help. Make up for, you know, the... all of it."

I think I understand where Hiero's going with this. She feels obligated on some level to help me out. Hiero has a tough time voicing her feelings. She can joke all she wants to, but I do think she considers the two of us to be... something.

Without thinking, I wrap my arms around her in a tight hug, shutting my eyes. "Thank you." It takes a moment, but an arm wraps over my back, the other arm following shortly after. As soon as I let go, I look up at her; she gives me the briefest of smiles and turns right back around the way we came. She looks up toward the stairway and back toward me. "Take some time to explore a bit. Everyone here knows of the movement, you can get directions back to grab your things. I'd suggest you check out upstairs."

When she leaves, I take stock of the room, finding a living space with more chairs than back at the apartment. Across the way appears to be a bathroom— no tub, but I've dealt with worse. A makeshift kitchen lies one floor down, though everything beneath is sealed off. The stairs lead up a long ways, but everything's blocked off except for the very top floor. Through the grimy glass face of the clock, which serves as wall and window, I can see the whole of the makeshift sector, almost beautiful in the red and gold glow of the setting sun. The clock tower is bathed in the same fiery light, illuminating a couple of workbenches laden with more scrap metal than I could get my hands on in a month.

I'm more grateful than I can say, but I'm going to pay for this favor. I just know it.

CHAPTER 15

We spend the night in the ward again, since I don't feel comfortable navigating the planks with Esper in the dark. Eventually I'm going to have to get used to crossing the narrow wooden boards, but today is not that day. I tuck Esper into bed as he chatters on and on about our new home.

"It's in a clocktower?" His eyes are alight, and I have to keep adjusting his blanket as he wriggles beneath it.

"Yes." I smooth down his hair and smile. "Y–You're going to l–love it, Es'. It's got a great view, and we can drag our ch–chairs across the floor as loud as we want."

"That'll be awesome!"

"I know, rosh jul, and much more."

After one last little dance of excitement, he turns onto his side and closes his eyes. As I stroke his hair, I'm reminded of the song my father used to sing to put me to sleep, the one I used to sing to Esper when he was much younger. As Esper's breathing deepens, the song falls from my tongue in a soft sigh.

ĕ iix aberjii jĕ bulqet, rosh jul…

Listen to the wind, little love…

ilsam wĕliq, qes qa visii…

Hear it whistle softly…

d'rĕ sola iix sel adiisiq…

It rests down against the sand…

jeh ĕto ad ib qes jazod…

And curls into its sleep…

ĕ iix ba qen'm jĕ bulqet, rosh jul…

Listen to the waves, little love…

ro ib diit qariil qa visii…

Hear their gentle hush…

baxhĕq fashel qenalt…

They beat a quiet symphony…

jĕ ĕ ib lowil jĕ ubĕr…

To lull you to your peace…

iix qorig jĕ co fatzaq, rosh jul…

Do not fear the night, little love…

da sol qaves halod…

It whispers of only calm…

jeh ba qorig sam adiisa atzen…

And nights with an eternal rest…

ĕniq sol zan iix qorig nor qĕva…

Only in the night we are safe…

jĕ qĕva iix qorig hel ravod…

The night will keep you safe…

I furrow my brow as I stumble slightly over the last few words. I can faintly hear my father's thick accent, but I never realized how ominous that lullaby was…

I sit there a little longer, until his breaths come slow and even, before heading out of the room. Runa looks up from her desk and wrinkles her nose in question. "It's a little late to be working on the airship, Artem."

"I–I just need some fresh air."

"Hm." Runa absently brings her hands to her braid, tugging it forward and running her fingers along the intricate bumps. "If you run into Arek, can you tell him to stop by? He left something at my place."

I give a nod and step out onto the walkway. The nosy part of me wonders what Arek could have left behind. Certainly not his scarf, as he's always wearing it. It's not my business, though. I get the impression Runa and Arek are seeing each other, but it's not my place to ask such things. I run my hand along the railing and furrow my brow as my feet trace an absent track toward the tunnels.

Hiero gave me an entire clocktower, solely out of concern for Esper. Just thinking about having to pay her back makes my head spin. What else am I going to have to do? It's not like I haven't already witnessed terrible things: torture, fire, explosions. It's like everything I do winds up spilling blood in some way, and it's all my fault. On the other hand, maybe the little voice in my head saying these things is right.

Instead of heading for the tunnels, I wind down the staircase and into the workyard. With all the lights out— save the emergency ones— it's shadowy and foreboding. The hulking mass of the airship looming overhead demands my attention, and the air hangs thick and haunted with the ghosts of workers gone for the day. I shouldn't be afraid of a mere metal skeleton. Yet, the beams settle with a low groan, the craft practically shudders, and I find myself doing the same. My head whips from side to side, trying to catch movement in the shadows, but I find myself alone, chilled to the core.

I stumble back, hitting the wall, and reflexively rub the back of my head. It's childish, being intimidated by something not even alive. Still, my footsteps are quick as I make my way to the back room and turn on a lamp.

It's almost more creepy being in the dimly lit room, the shadows sitting thick beyond the doorway. If I close my eyes hard enough, I can pretend I'm in Mr. Connolly's workshop during the colder time of the year, when the sun sets earlier and we're closing shop for the day. That's when we'd work by candlelight and lamps. It wasn't so scary then.

Taking a deep breath, I unfurl my blueprints and look them over. I could get work done on the ship. However, I find myself turning the drawings to the side and beginning to take apart my audancers, noting down on spare paper the measurements and what needs fixing. Then I rebuild.

It's not the most complicated thing in the world. Once my ears were cut off by that proc in the marketplace, I had nothing but holes in the sides of my head. Around these, screwed into my head, are platforms built and installed by Mr. Connolly, to attach the bulk of the audancers, the actual listening components. There's one dial, in the middle of the "ear", that opens and closes the three outer vents that allow sound through, effectively allowing me to alter the volume of the sounds I'm hearing. A smaller switch runs along the top of the "ear", controlling the inner device, essentially a hearing horn, which lets me control the direction of my hearing. It's a simple design, but still just as finicky as any other model.

I usually close the vents when I'm working, which makes me effectively deaf, but it helps me focus, but my audancers have been having problems recently without Mr. Connolly around to help with maintenance. The switch that turns the small horn inside has been getting stuck more often than not, and there are times the vents will open on their own or not at all. The trick is finding the right materials, particularly ones that age well and fit nicely into place, so everything works fluidly. That, and it's hard to fix something you can't get a proper look at; I need to unbolt the audancers to take them off the frames, which is hard to do by myself... and I'm too self-conscious to ask anyone else for help.

Hiero gave me a bag of scraps and tools back when we first made up. I haven't had the chance to look at my audancers properly since then, but now is as good a time as ever. I manage to unbolt them with some difficulty, with the help of a small hand-mirror I've borrowed from Runa. I dump out the pouch and take inventory, only to huff in disappointment. Some of the jeweler's tools might be helpful— there's a tiny saw and some small sets of pliers that should work just fine— but I have no use for the little wire-cutters, or the gears mixed in with the metal scraps. Thankfully, some of the pieces are aluminum and copper, but there's not enough for all the repairs I need to make. If I were at the clocktower, maybe I'd have more materials. For now, I'll have to make do.

Before long, I find myself sagging against the desk, reassembling the pieces with fumbling hands. I utter a quick prayer that I won't need to worry about them for a few more weeks. The next thing I know, I'm laying my head down for a quick nap.

I'm on the skylines, but it's not quite... right. We're airbound: Esper and I, Hiero, and Rhine. Hiero stares at the floor, hands braced on her thighs. Rhine sits across the cabin, head high as he recites every Parvay law backwards.

All of a sudden, Hiero throws her head back and laughs, before looking directly at me. "Was she blonde too?"

She means the girl I once had a crush on in school, and at the moment I can't remember. I nod, and her eyes flicker with amusement. Behind her, something rushes up past the windows, but no one seems to notice. Everything smells of spice and honey, and I can't help but look around for my mother.

The colors and shapes outside the window shoot past even faster, and everything not nailed down in the cabin begins to rise. Hiero taps a finger against her lips, which are curled in a wicked little grin, as the ground rushes up to meet us. "What is it with you and flying, Artem? Are you so afraid to fall?"

I jolt upright and rub at my eyes. No matter how long I've been underground, it's still jarring not to hear the launauts chirping in the morning. As quickly as I come out of it, I can't help but cling to my now-fading dream. Why must everything involve airships and falling? Is it a premonition? Or just my anxiety over this project, not even letting me have peace in my sleep?

It's still dark in the bay. I glance at the clock; it's just before seven. Maybe it's worth going out to the market and getting some peaches for breakfast. I'm sure Esper would love it, and it'd be like a little celebration. New home, new start, new beginnings. Maybe everything's starting to be alright again.

I trudge up to the ward and peek in. Esper is still asleep, but Runa's awake, humming lightly under her breath as she organizes supplies. Did she even sleep? I pop my head back out before she can notice me and head for the tunnels.

I've been so paranoid about leaving ever since the gala. The reality is-- and I know this deep down— that I shouldn't be that worried about it. There weren't many people from Wellwick there to begin with; no one is going to recognize my face except for the MP and...

Roran.

He tends to hang around the market, but it's Pallock, so I doubt he'll be in the area. Still, I decide once I surface into the tavern to look both ways before heading down the street, and to keep as much to myself as possible. Not that I don't do that anyway.

There's something peaceful about coming to the market this early. The vendors are still shaking the slow roughness of sleep from their voices as they greet one another, and no one with any common sense is awake yet. One stall is selling qosa and colfe, freshly ground and brewed, and the scent is intoxicating. Beside it is a baker's booth, everything freshly made, the bread still steaming slightly in the chilly air. I hover nearby, tempted by the promise of unquestionable energy and exquisite pastries— I always have been a sucker for bread— but I keep my hand by my coin purse and shake my head.

The fruit vendor is surprised to see me, which is endearing but slightly alarming. "Glory be, girly! Long time no see! I was starting to think the portin got you."

"Gl–Glory be, Mr. Reldfin." I take out a couple of coins. "Two peaches and an apple, plea–please."

"Griplem?" He nods his head as I do, knowing the answer already, then whistles low as he takes the coin. "Splurging, I see."

I nod quickly, then duck my head. "We're cele–celebrating."

The vendor hands me a tiny bag, and I thank him as I head back the way I came. People are starting to trickle into the market, and the sun has begun to rise higher, peering just over the tops of the buildings. For a moment, it doesn't matter that I'm part of an underground rebellion, that my apartment was burned down, that I danced with Hiero at a high-class gala. I can just be a normal person— albeit still a Qorani— with no one questioning or pursuing me for just a couple of minutes.

It's almost laughable how hectic my life has grown to be within a matter of weeks, how much more of a target I've inadvertently become. Yet, here I am, buying peaches. In broad daylight.

I head back up the street the pub is on, but can't help but pause. Something isn't right. Is someone... following me? Each turn I take, the person behind me does the same, though I don't catch more than a brief flash in my periphery. Cautiously, I stop and turn my head, my stomach dropping as I lock eyes with Roran.

He stands right behind me, uncomfortably close, his head held high. He looks exhausted, like he's aged years in a matter of days. His stubble stands out like a stark five o'clock shadow, and heavy shadows ring his icy eyes.

"Roran," I yip, clutching the bag a bit tighter.

His voice comes out gravelly, tight and formal. "Ms. Clairingbold. We need to talk."

Talking is good. Not ideal, but better than meeting the edge of his blades. I swallow hard and nod as he motions me toward a nearby alleyway. Slowly I head in first, despite every cell in my body screaming to run, and he blocks off the exit, looming like a stone sentinel. With a ragged sigh, he brings a hand to his head, pressing it to his temples. He's shaking. Or I am. Maybe we both are.

"If thi–this is a–about—!"

"Artem." Roran shakes his head, holding a hand out. "What on Kristollen were you thinking?"

"I can explain."

"I don't want you to explain!" He stands up straighter, eyes narrowed. "The things I've done for you. I looked the other way with your... friend, I've helped out your brother countless times, and this is the thanks I get?"

"I–I never asked you to..."

"To what? Care about you? Because that's all I've done, Artem. Cover your hide because I care about you!"

I know I should just bite my lip and take it, but I can't help but squeak out, "So blackmail-mailing me to go t-to the gal-gala was caring about me?"

"You know why I asked you. But I never thought you'd be aiding traitors to the Crown." Roran shakes his head again, lowering his voice. "I can get you out of the rebellion. I know you, Artem, there's no way you'd be part of this if you knew what you were doing. I can keep you and Esper safe."

If I knew what I was doing? Just how dumb— naive— does Roran think I am?

Though... isn't an out what I've wanted all along? If it is, why does my stomach hurt at the suggestion? I just stare at him, waiting for the other shoe to drop. Roran stares back expectantly, like he wants me fall into his arms and thank him for his mercy.

"A–And what do I–I hav–have to do in ex–exchange?"

There's an almost fanatical gleam in his eye. "Come with me. I'll find a way to fix your papers. It can be just the three of us."

As tempting as the offer sounds, I don't like the implications. Before I can respond, Roran takes my hands so roughly I drop the bag of fruit. "Roran!"

"It can be like when we were kids! How I used to be your knight in shining armor. Just leave the rebellion, Artem! It's no place for someone like you."

"N–No." There's no hesitation. Roran jerks like I've delivered a physical blow, but his grip only gets stronger, his eyes narrowing into dark slits.

"What?"

"I said no, R–Roran." I try to pull back, but can't wrench my hands away. "I can't, I—!"

"Stop playing these games, Artem!"

"Roran, l–let go of me!" I squirm, and my breaths start coming short and fast. "I'm n–n–not playing a–any games! I c–can't back out o–of this—!"

"Artem, I don't want to have to arrest you!" Roran warns, tightening his grip. He's crushing my hands more than holding them now, and a twinge of pure, cold fear sparks in my chest.

This isn't at all how Roran used to be. When we were younger, sure, he protected me a lot from the other kids. Now he thinks he can do whatever he wants because of his uniform. It makes me sick. The special treatment, his entitled behavior, everything.

"Let m-me go, Roran."

"No." Roran grits his teeth, eyes widening. "No, you don't get to do that, you can't just bat your eyes and walk away this time. I should have taken you in back at the gala. I'm giving you one last chance, Artem. What's it going to be?"

My heart thuds in my chest. I try to find the right words, but nothing comes to my lips except a numb, confused, "B–B–B–Bat?" I'm stuck, that cold twinge of fear growing into a snarling beast that claws at my gut. I might die in this alleyway. Especially if that's another proc headed down the alley right now. I'm halfway through a prayer to Dreggar when the other man grabs Roran from behind, wrenching both his arms securely behind his back. Roran shouts, and suddenly Arek is beside me, yanking the blade by Roran's side out of its holster.

"Hi Artem!" Tristan greets cheerfully as he keeps Roran in place.

"H–Hi...?" I stand there, one hand on my chest, the other rubbing at my wrist.

Arek looks me over with narrowed eyes, hand gentle on my shoulder, a silent check-in. Before I can say anything or even nod, Tristan grunts as Roran struggles, managing to slip out of his hold. Arek stoops to pick up my bag and thrusts it into my hands, as Roran grabs the other sword strapped to his back. "Go. We've got this."

I hesitate and take a slight step back. There is no way this is happening. Roran would never escalate to this level. But as Roran steps to the side to face Tristan, readying a slash, Arek is already rushing forward. The two clash, Arek disengaging Roran's blade with a circular movement to point it away from Tristan, though he seems ready to jump in unarmed and wrestle the sword from Roran's grip. Arek turns his head toward me, his voice eerily calm.

"Get going."

I nod once and dart off toward the bunker. It's only once I'm alone in the tunnels that I take a moment to stop and breathe. My legs give out and I fall to my knees, shaking, clutching at my bag with numb fingers. If it weren't for Tristan and Arek.... Roran's changed a lot since he joined the procs, but I've never been scared of him. I never thought he would—

I don't know if I can ever walk that part of Wellwick alone again.

CHAPTER 16

The steam and gas engines are finished. The third one... not so much. I've made a prototype that runs on oil, but it's not going to work. It's too flammable; the ship would go down as soon as it managed to reach a decent height. The aerocraft is more delicate than I expected for something so big— it's more like a giant balloon than anything else. The gas engine is designed to inflate the balloon, while the steam engine should propel it, with excess steam vented out to inflate the rubber material hanging over the ship. It should propel it, at least... but even if it does, it will need more power. Steampower alone is not enough to power the rest of the airship. I need to try something else.

My options are limited. Oil is out, steam isn't going to cut it, and... quite frankly, I'm running out of materials and time. I wish I could talk to someone, anyone, about this project, but no one has the time to give, and even if they did, they wouldn't hand it over to me. Maybe Meno would listen, but he's busy enough as it is. I need someone who will listen and understand.

What I would give to see Mr. Connolly right now. I'd like to think enough time has passed that he'd listen to my explanations, give me another chance in the shop. I would do anything to be able to talk to him again, get his opinion, find out where I'm going wrong with this engine setup, or be reminded what power he was switching to for his own airship designs.

He wouldn't, though. Let me back into the shop. He's always been stubborn and held firmly to his beliefs. Maybe one day I can learn to do the same.

Esper huffs for the nineteenth time today. I sigh in response and refuse to look over. I know this bit far too well: the moment I cave and ask what's wrong, he'll deny and deny until his moping forces me to put down everything.

I get it. I may not have had the luxury of childhood for long, but I remember what it was like. So many nights spent just hanging off my mother's arm as she'd try to sew patches onto clothes, laughing and reminding me that Papa would be home soon. I'm guessing Esper's just as anxious to go back to our new home. The first time I brought him there, he was a ball of energy, dancing across every plank and excited, of all things, to have distance between our beds. Most of his night was spent exploring and playing pretend rather than listening to his radio. There's something about the view, presiding like lords over the makeshift sector, that he finds fascinating.

On cue, he groans and flops onto his back. "How much longer do we have to be here?"

"We're go–going home soon. I–I just have some work t–to finish up." Which might take me forever if I don't decide what to do about this engine situation.

"Why couldn't I go with Arek?"

"Because he was busy." I rub my temples. "You can't–can't go running o–o–off with everyone at the drop of a–a hat. I am su–supposed to watch you, you know."

More than likely Arek needed a break from Esper after taking him twice in the last two days. I don't blame him. It's difficult to spend more than five hours with him at a time, and that's on his best days. I love him, he's just... energetic.

Esper huffs and slumps his shoulders. I stop working and look over at him, then start sweeping my blueprints into a pile with a sigh. We've been cooped up in the same place long enough. There's not much else I can get done today, anyway.

Esper perks up as I start gathering my belongings. He bounds over to the door and hangs off the doorknob, rocking back and forth. I pretend to ignore his impatience and the wounded-aedor whine he's making and go about as I normally would. Each time he does something, I move a bit slower. After the fifth time or so, he takes the hint and stops altogether.

"Alright, let's get g–going." I wave my hand, and Esper takes off, ducking and weaving between people to make it to the stairs. I walk. As soon as I reach the stairs, he zooms up them, skipping every other step.

"When are you going to finish the engine?" Esper calls down to me.

"I–I don't know," I admit. "Hopefully soon."

"I thought you knew all about that kind of junk."

I hum noncommittally. "I th–thought I did, too."

At the top of the stairs, I spot Hiero, already heading out the door. Unfortunately, so does Esper. Before I can stop him, he's already pouncing on her. "Hiero! What's up? Where are you going?"

"Esper!" I groan and bring my hand to my head.

Hiero blinks a few times, offering a smile. "I've got a mission to deal with. Top secret."

"Doing what?"

"Top secret means I can't tell you, buddy."

I want to die again, either from embarrassment or from the excruciating softness of her smile. I feel my cheeks burn as I grab Esper by the shoulder and try to direct him toward the ward. The last thing I need is for us to leave at the same time through the same exit so that Esper can annoy me and Hiero simultaneously.

"Unless..." Hiero adds.

"Unless...?" Esper asks, eyes widening.

"Well, I suppose I could tell you if you came with me."

"N–No," I interrupt. "We're hea–heading home."

"I could actually really use another pair of eyes. Or two." Hiero takes a step closer to me, raising an eyebrow. I shrink back and clear my throat, but for the life of me can't think of what to say. Maybe something along the lines of not dragging

Esper along on something that's probably dangerous. She may play casual, but how am I to know she isn't looking to go back on the skylines to rob one of the cars? I know it's something about danger and not giving in to Esper every time he wants something, but as usual around Hiero, I just can't seem to find the words.

Taking my silence as agreement, Hiero nods her head and holds the door open for me and Esper. I hesitate, locking eyes with her just once before tearing my gaze away and following behind.

Esper hops along behind us. "Where are we going? What are we doing?" Hiero gives him a gentle hush, a reminder not to speak while in the tunnels. For some reason it scares me just a little bit more than usual.

As we make our way to the exit, my mind wanders. What would have happened if I had never flipped the sign to 'OPEN' back in the old shop? Would Hiero have tried to come in anyway? I might have never been part of this movement, might never have known a bunker existed below the city. My apartment would probably still be standing, I wouldn't be living in the Flooded Sector in Wellwick, and...

...and I also wouldn't have met Hiero.

She clears her throat as I stand immobile near the exit. They're both already up and waiting for me, peering down through the open hole. My face heats up, and I climb as quickly as I can with Esper egging me on to hurry. Hiero waits for me to top out before closing the sewer grate and adjusting her jacket with a huff.

I don't know this entrance; we must have taken another turn while I wasn't paying attention. Tall buildings surround us, a lower track for the skylines twisting around some buildings and through wide archways built into others. Many people walk by, all stiff-collars, some carrying fancy bags, most of them with nice jackets or sleek hats.

"Where are we?" Esper asks, louder than is probably advisable.

"The business sector," Hiero confirms.

"B–Brunsel," I add.

"I need to stop by a records office."

Esper groans. "Records?"

Hiero hums her affirmation. "I did say it was an important mission."

"I thought it would be something exciting!"

"Nothing's more exciting than paperwork, jo-må. You'll understand when you're an adult." Hiero shoots me a wink and leads the way. I push Esper forward and take up the rear. If I don't keep a staunch eye on Esper, he could get distracted and run off to who-knows-where.

We must stick out badly here. Maybe not Hiero, who always looks put-together, but Esper and I are wandering through unknown, high-class terrain in ratty clothes. It's almost as uncomfortable as the gala, and just as obvious that we don't belong here, in the world of the important, stylish, and well-off. I can practically feel the glares of those passing by. It's the unspoken question on everyone's lips: What's the Qorain doing here?

Hiero stops in front of a building and holds up a hand. I grip Esper's shoulder just as he turns to sprint off. "You can't wait o–one minute—"

"There's a bunch of people headed that way!"

"G–Good for them. We're helping Hiero out like you wanted, re–remember?"

"But Artem––"

"Esper." I turn to apologize to Hiero but she's already gone. I'm not sure what I'm supposed to do. Go inside? Stay put?

I opt to stay put as Esper huffs and puffs, eyes never leaving the urgent flow of the crowd. After a couple of minutes, the door opens, and Hiero ushers us inside. The main waiting area is empty, and there appears to be no one behind the desk. Hiero opens the door to the back and gestures with her head toward the restricted area.

"Wh–Where is everyone?"

"Distracted and elsewhere."

"Why didn't we see anyone leave then?" Esper asks. I was wondering the same.

"Back-room-type distracted." Hiero produces a key and unlocks another door to the side, revealing a staircase leading down into darkness. Esper leads the way, and Hiero flips a switch on the wall to light his path before blocking the doorway for a moment and looking down at me solemnly. "I redirect, not incapacitate, if that's what you're wondering. Some of us doing spywork aren't the barbaric type." There's a sneer on her lips that seems reserved for Aether.

"What's down here anyway?" Esper calls up.

"Keep your voice down," Hiero warns, then drily, "And considering this is a records office, I'd imagine records."

Rows upon rows of file cabinets take up what seems to be an expansive basement. There's little indication of how the files are organized, as the cabinets are labeled with some kind of esoteric numbering system. I have no idea what it is Hiero is looking for, but she gives a low whistle, as if impressed. I think she's actually intimidated, not that she'd ever admit it.

"We have maybe an hour at best. I need a lookout at the keyhole, someone with good ears..."

I know it wasn't meant to be a dig at me, but my hands flutter up to my audancers out of habit. Esper huffs and stomps his way back to the top, grumbling about this being lame, but seeing as he signed up for this, he doesn't really have a right to complain.

Not knowing what else to do, I follow Hiero as she looks through a few files from some of the closest cabinets. As if suddenly understanding, she shuts a cabinet drawer and quickens her pace down the aisles. "There's a method to this madness," Hiero explains with a grin.

"And wh–what is it?"

"It's categorized by city and sector, then by last name."

"Then why n–not label it by city rather t–t–than number?"

Hiero snorts. "Sayev, if I knew, I'd already have what I'm looking for."

I wring my hands together. "Which is what, ex–exactly?"

That earns me a side-eye. "Records."

"No, I m–mean—"

"I have a handful of names, but no Parvay addresses."

She continues along, then begins whistling a bouncy sort of song. She preaches about blending in and subtlety, then this-- my eye twitches. Here I am, wary of every step I make, afraid it'll draw attention to us, and here's Hiero, trilling a tune.

I jump as a set of boards propped up against a cabinet fall with a crash. Esper pops his head over to look at us and the mess he's created, before darting back through the maze of cabinets. Hiero remains unfazed, not even flinching, continuing with her song. I catch my breath, trying to ignore the small chuckle that accompanies her whistling.

"Esper, ca–can you please b–be more careful?"

"Did you really expect anything less from him?" Hiero looks back at me and I shake my head wearily. She turns her attention to a couple of boxes lying around and starts shuffling through them. If I didn't know any better, I'd say she was more interested in looting this place than looking for records, though I can't imagine what she'd find down here. There is work to be done, I guess, and she could be more dismissive of the conversation.

"I–I thought you wanted him o–on lookout?"

She picks up a book, turns it about in her hands, then starts flipping through the pages. A puff of dust kicks up, but she simply blows it away. Right into my face.

I start coughing, and Hiero stops, presses a finger to her lips with a smirk, then continues looking through. When she reaches the end, she places the book down off to the side, grabs another and repeats the process, her brow furrowed in concentration.

Before I can say anything, she neatly rips out a couple of pages, then places the book back. "He'll be fine. I honestly just wanted the company. These places creep me out."

I don't know how to take that. Is she joking? "Really?"

"Really."

"With ev–everything that you d–do?"

"I'm only human, Artem." Hiero walks down a row of cabinets, turning left. "And these catalogues are ancient. But this trip wasn't a complete waste. I have some addresses, and a little extra."

"H–How do you r–remember any of those?" I struggle to keep up, practically stumbling as she takes another sharp turn.

"What, the names? Addresses? I don't. I'm just taking what I need." I get a mental image of Hiero's inside jacket pocket pulling out into a mini file cabinet stuffed with scraps of paper and almost laugh.

"Are we almost done here?" Esper calls.

Hiero doesn't answer him. Instead she tugs open a cabinet drawer, thumbing through a couple of files, then freezes and pulls one out. Her expression is stone. Whatever it is that she's found seems to be important. I try to peer over to read what it is, but she simply folds it up, stuffing it away in her jacket with the others.

"Apparently, one of the Parvay members had a daughter who was almost wiped from the record," Hiero muses. "You might actually want to hear about this."

"What do y–you mean?" I ask.

Before Hiero can continue, the sound of a door opening forces our heads to turn. Esper's gone a little too quiet. Wordlessly, Hiero shuts the drawer and the two of us race our way through the maze of cabinets. The door at the top of the staircase is wide open. Hiero swears under her breath and starts looking around. I start heading up the staircase.

"What are you doing? Your brother—"

"—is aw–awful and probably w–went upstairs."

Sure enough, I catch the front door closing and follow suit, barrelling after him. Esper is ahead, trying to rush down the street. "Esper!" I shout. "Get b–back here!"

He either doesn't hear me or is pretending not to. It doesn't seem to make much of a difference. Everyone is headed in the same direction, including many people from the nearby offices, all streaming toward some sort of commotion.

Hiero catches my arm. "*Satch,*" she swears. "We need to go. Grab your brother and head for the sewers. Now."

"He's g–going that way— wh–what's going on?"

Hiero lets go with a hiss and starts running. I follow. We reach a big crowd, into which Esper has woven himself, most likely to get a better look. People are standing by watching another group, some faces I recognize from the underground, though not by name, protesting the skylines. A handful of procs stand protecting the station itself, armed with balistirs. Some of the people in the crowd are throwing rocks at the procs. Some are throwing them at the protesters.

I find Esper and grab him by the shoulders. "What were y–y–you thi–thinking?! We n–need to get going, now."

"I saw all the people running and wanted to see what was going on!"

"I d–don't care! That was dangerous! Th–this is dangerous! We're not get–getting involved in a pro–protest!"

Esper rolls his eyes. "They're not even doing anything. See?" In one fluid motion, Esper picks up a rock and hurls it at the nearest proc. My blood runs cold.

It's the last straw for the procier. Time slows heartbeat by heartbeat as he aims his balistir, the two procs beside him moving to restrain him. Hiero darts in front of us. A shot rings out. Hiero goes down. All I see are her green eyes flaring wide before she crumples to the ground in front of us. More shots. The crowd is screaming, swarming, many pushing the procs back into the building. I drop to my knees and drag Esper down with me, cradling Hiero. Her eyes are half-lidded, the runnel hole through her chest gushing scarlet, and my head spins. All I hear are screams.

CHAPTER 17

For once, my fervent prayers to Dreggar bear fruit. As Esper and I start dragging Hiero back toward the sewer grate, there appears a big friendly miracle: Tristan. He stands by the entrance to the tunnels, ushering in the fleeing members of the underground. His eyes widen when he sees us, blood-smeared and tugging along a ragdoll Hiero, who he scoops up on sight.

When we make it inside, there's a crowd forming near the ward. Hiero, eyes fluttering but stubbornly holding on to consciousness, makes a sound that could be an attempt at laughter but sounds like a strangled grunt. Tristan tries to shush her, adjusting his hold on her as I try my best to look anywhere but the wound. Anywhere but the blood.

One of the beds is occupied by a man getting his foot

examined. He quickly gets up and hobbles to the side as Tristan lays Hiero down in his place. She's drenched in sweat and blood, red, red all over, and everything about this is wrong.

Medics are buzzing left and right, some almost running in circles trying to organize triage. One man is knocked out, friends and med personnel trying to rouse him while examining his head. Another man whimpers as he is moved, his leg split open to the bone.

Runa is tending to someone else, but once an assistant catches a look at Hiero, a sharp word from her spins Runa's gaze our way. She spots Tristan and her eyes drop immediately to Hiero. Her face is a studied mask of professional calm as she marches over and starts undoing the top part of Hiero's shirt. All she says, in a tight, clipped voice, is, "Chest or shoulder?"

But she doesn't need the answer after only a moment's inspection; a few centimeters down from Hiero's right collarbone gapes a ragged-edged runnel hole. Gaqĕ. They must have been using the balistirs with the larger runnels. Roran always used a pipe balistir, claiming they were less messy. Now I see what he meant. I fight back the bile slowly rising in my throat. Yet, as concerned as I am and as much as I'm fighting back the urge to panic, I can't help but wonder: why use high-caliber balistirs at a protest?

Runa doesn't even flinch as she analyzes Hiero's injury. Her face is passive, even when Hiero yelps and swears as her arm is moved. Blood continues to gush from the wound. Red. Red. Red.

"Callista, grab the forceps." The girl leaves to retrieve

what she's asked. Runa puts on a pair of gloves and glances back at me and Esper. "I need you two to leave."

I nod and take Esper by the arm. Hiero lifts her head up slightly, her lips parting to speak. Then whatever it is is lost; she hisses as Runa presses into her shoulder, cutting bits of fabric from around the wound and peeling them away.

I've always been squeamish. Yet there's a morbid part of me that can't stand to look away. Hiero is hurt, and I want to stay by her side. Being hurt and alone is hard, and I wouldn't wish it on my worst enemy. Everyone deserves to have someone with them. But I don't argue with Runa. There's no logical reason for me and Esper to stick around. Esper shouldn't bear witness to such gruesome things. And as worried as I am for Hiero, I won't do her any favors standing around helplessly and getting in the way of Runa and the other medical officers.

As we leave, I find myself looking back, unable to keep from staring. Hiero's gaze is fixed past me, lost in the middle distance, yet those green eyes are burned into the forefront of my mind.

An hour passes as I just sit in useless, restless silence. I don't want to go back to the clocktower, but there's no way I could be productive right now. I do my best to fiddle around with something, do anything with the airship, but all of my thoughts are harried by swirls of red and green and an anxious clenching in my gut.

Esper has been in the side room, drawing and otherwise keeping to himself, aside from the occasional quip. I let him know I'm headed upstairs again and he barely bats an eye. I think he's still trying to deny what happened.

Waiting for an update about Hiero feels like the best thing to do, though it's also the most torturous. So I keep waiting, watching people pass from my seat on the ground. The metal has long stopped feeling cold, and by the time my shoulders start hurting, Runa is stepping out.

"H-Hey." I get up, and Runa turns, leaning into her hip slightly.

"Sorry, I haven't had a moment to use the toilet-- what's up?" Runa shifts again. I feel my face flush, starting to feel bad for even saying anything.

"Have things c-calmed down a-at all o-or—?"

"Hiero's stable. She's fine. You can see her if you want."

"Oh, well—"

"—Toilet." With that, Runa hobbles awkwardly off. I grimace, dust my shirt off, and return to the ward.

It's much calmer than it was, now that tensions aren't as high. Only a handful of people seem to have been hurt enough to need monitoring. The overall casualties aren't as bad as I would have guessed, and many folks are awake and talking with friends or doing their best to entertain themselves while waiting to be discharged.

Hiero is half-upright, awake but clearly exhausted. Two blankets cover her, yet she's trembling slightly, chilled by more than the cool bunker air. She's less out of it, and despite all she's gone through, looks as though she had the time to fix her hair.

Ever vigilant, she sits observing her surroundings and the people around her. I can only imagine how dull the conversations she's eavesdropping on are, but she seems interested enough. When she spots me, she seems to perk up a little, tilting her head up and shooting me the faintest of smiles. My stomach twists in knots.

"I didn't expect you to wait around." Hiero raises an eyebrow in question.

"I di–didn't expect you to get shot."

The words leave my mouth faster than I can process them. Immediately my shoulders scrunch up and my cheeks heat. Hiero's expression turns into one of amusement. "Touché."

An apology wouldn't matter. I'd like to think I've known Hiero long enough to get a sense of what might offend her. At the end of the day, most subjects don't bother her. Her eyes flicker as she waits for me to stumble out my usual apology. When it doesn't come, her lips quirk upwards in a grin, and she hums a faint, steady note of approval.

She nods her head at the end of the bed, and I hesitate before taking a seat on the edge. The blanket is coarser than it looks, and beneath it, I know, the linens are starchy. Part of me feels bad for Hiero having to use them. I can't imagine Hiero being the type to sleep in anything but fine sheets with high thread counts.

"These sorts of things happen when you start standing up to procs, start proclaiming contempt with Parvay," she tsks. "Eventually balistirs will come into the picture."

I shake my head. Hiero is the type that practically goes looking for trouble. Esper is the same way. It's no wonder he admires her. She purses her lips and appears to be deep in thought before continuing slowly. "I figured you would have gone home by now, fussed over Esper, and stayed up worrying about me until I dropped by." She pauses briefly, giving me a glance up from beneath her lashes. "I'm flattered."

I let out a soft "oh" and do my best to steady my heartbeat and not start babbling about being concerned for good reason. She looks entertained again, most likely from the delayed reaction. Does she like me questioning her sincerity? She grunts as she tries to adjust herself, struggling to sit properly rather than lay propped up. I lean forward to stop her from injuring herself any further, but my hands only hover above her shoulders. We lock eyes, staring back at each other. For once, her eyes, darting across my face, betray her vulnerability. It takes all my willpower just to pull back and tuck my hands safely out of range. Dreggar. I was right that Hiero was dangerous; I was wrong about how.

Though she doesn't try to move again, her arms remain braced at her sides. When the tension passes, she tucks her arms back under the blanket. We sit in brief, comfortable silence. For some reason, quiet moments with Hiero are peaceful. There's no pressure to fill the space with idle chat or forced conversation. Despite being shaken from the attack, I don't feel nervous like I might visiting an active medical ward.

Runa comes back and starts making rounds. As she makes her way toward Hiero, she slants me a look. I can't parse its meaning, but I blush anyway, and turn my attention quickly toward the exit.

"You're lucky that runnel didn't hit you any further down or to the left, otherwise we would be having a much different conversation." Runa flips through her notepad as she speaks. "Or be unable to hold a conversation in the first place."

Hiero clicks her tongue, shaking her head in faux-disappointment. "I suppose that's bad news for you."

Runa sighs, her brow furrowing as she jots something down. I bite my lip. "Your sense of humor is back. That's good. However, you still went into shock, and need to be monitored. We'll keep an eye on you overnight. Tomorrow you can go home and continue recuperating there. No strenuous activities or heavy lifting for a few weeks. I'll show you some exercises you can do in the meantime to keep your arm from getting too stiff."

Runa peels back the blankets. The bandages cover Hiero's entire upper torso to halfway down her right bicep. They are clean, save the slight rusty red that has leaked through, but her bleeding has definitely stopped. When Runa's satisfied with her examination, she pulls the blankets back up, practically swaddling Hiero. She leaves us alone again, but not before tapping my shoulder. I search for an explanation in her gaze, but Runa is already helping someone else.

Hiero's staring again. I'm reminded of her earlier, wanting to tell me something. Squirming a little, I clear my throat, trying not to be too direct. All this does is amuse Hiero further. I frown. "Why do you d–do that?"

"Do what?" she asks. I know she knows what I'm talking about, but I clarify anyway.

"You keep l–looking at me that way, like I–I–I'm just a subject for whatever social experiment you're conduct-conducting," I manage, huffing loudly.

Out of all the reactions I expect, I'm not prepared for surprise, or... hurt. It lasts only a moment, but she recovers quickly, her voice soft. "You're very interesting, Artem; one of the most intriguing people I've ever met."

I want to object, but her shifting under the blanket pushes whatever thought I had out of my head. "You n–need to rest," I say instead, lowering my voice.

"I am resting." Hiero sighs softly. "Your paranoia is getting the better of you. I assure you, you are not, nor have you ever been, any type of experiment. You're a bit odd, a downright curiosity at times, but if you think I only keep you around for laughs, sayev, you're sorely mistaken."

My throat tightens. She sounds genuine enough that guilt begins to pool in my stomach. I grab the bottom of my shirt and twist the fabric in my hands for something to hold on to. Unsure of what else to say, I nod jerkily, spin around, and head downstairs to gather Esper.

He doesn't fight me as we head for the clock tower. It's a long walk, and for once it's quiet the whole way there. It's only when we've crossed the fifth plank or so that he speaks up.

"Am I in trouble?"

"Huh?" I stop short of the next plank and scrunch my nose. "What d–do you mean?"

His head stays ducked. "What happened to Hiero, that was my fault, right?" Arguably. It was his fault, and it wasn't his fault. I'm sure he feels guilty enough. He doesn't need that heaped on top of him.

I hesitate for a moment. "No. Y–You w–weren't the one holding the balistir."

"I was just doing what everyone else was doing!"

"Which doesn't make i–it right," I sigh. "Esper, it's been a long d–day. Let's j–just go home. I'll make us s–soup."

"So I am in trouble?"

I sigh and shake my head. "No."

Esper doesn't seem thoroughly convinced, but he drops the topic. When we get home, he doesn't complain about my cooking, and he goes to bed just as the sun is starting to set. I head up to my workspace and fiddle with my audancers. The whole time, I can't help but question whose fault it was, really. Somehow it only feels like mine.

CHAPTER 18

"Artem!" The voice jolts me upright. "You should be working, not sleeping!"

"I know, s–sorry," I mumble. Verne walks off and goes back to barking orders at other people. I prop myself up on the engine casing I've passed out on and rub at my eyes. The insomnia isn't what's killing me right now. All my dreams are nightmares: Esper, shot through the throat, unable to scream, as I'm engulfed in a rapidly expanding pool of blood. No amount of colfe is enough to keep me awake; all my body wants to do is slip into a dreamless sleep.

This airship is also going to be the death of me, at the rate I'm working. I have three engines set up on the blueprints: one to power up the motor, one to fly the thing, and the other to power the rest of the ship. But every day people throw me new problems—the engines can't be contained one way, there are loose connections, that design is too difficult to operate, on and on and on.

I'm ripping my hair out over this third engine. I can't use coal, I can't use more steam, more gas, I can't use oil, I can't use, well, anything at this point. If I knew how to construct an engine that ran off a decently conductive stone like gitzen, this would be a different story. That's the perfect thing for an engine that might otherwise get overloaded. But the only person I know who's perfected the use of gitzen is Mr. Connolly. I've done my research, I've asked around, and everything points back to him.

I'm just getting frustrated now. All I want is to be able to talk to Mr. Connolly about this project. He wouldn't approve, of course; there's no way I could talk to him about the rebellion. Even if I could, somehow, convince him I was hired by a private company, Mr. Connolly was always one to hold grudges. Dreggar. I'd have to break into the shop.

I swipe the back of my hand across my mouth for any drool that might have slipped out. This is pointless. I need a break, where I can't doze off. I slide off the engines and trudge upstairs. By the time I reach the top, I'm out of breath, but not from the exercise. I can't help but huff and puff in frustration the more it dawns on me that I'm running out of time.

A hand claps my shoulder. I flinch, but it's only Christa. I decide to swallow the speech about sneaking up on me and drop my shoulders instead. "You look ready to deck someone," they note cheerily, by way of greeting.

"I f–feel ready to."

"I always took you as a pacifist."

"No. Just a sc–scaredy-ravlark." I bring a hand to my head and rub the space between my eyebrows. "I don't know what I'm doing."

Christa laughs, quick and sharp. "As if anyone does! Besides, if anyone's ready to pull any punches, I'd strike first and ask questions later. One of those days, you know?"

That gives me an idea. I take a step away from them. "You know," I start carefully, "I–I did you a favor, g–going to the gala."

"Yeah, you kinda did," Christa admits with a sigh.

"So you tech–technically... o–owe me one... right?"

Their expression hardens. "Where exactly are you going with this?"

"I n–need to break into Mr. Connolly's shop."

"Who?"

"Mr. C–Connolly. I used–used to w–work for him. He builds th–things. He worked on the–the skylines. I'm having diffi–difficulty with th–this airship, a–and if I can't talk to him, I kn–know he at least has b–b–blueprints for an airship h–he was designing, somewh–where. If I can g–get inside, a–all I need is c–confirmation on how t–to build a gitzen engine, a–and—"

"Slow down there!" Christa holds a hand out and stretches their arms. "First of all, this sounds like a Hiero- or Aether-type job."

"H–Hiero is—"

"I'm still talking. It sounds like a Hiero or Aether job. That said, Hiero's out of commission, and Aether hates your guts, right? Second, that's more of an 'I owe you two' situation, not 'I owe you one', if you catch my drift."

I don't want to catch their drift. I don't want to be on the hook for one more qiftin "favor". While I get that I don't have any weight in this rebellion, it'd be nice if I wasn't always running errands for everyone, and fixing anything slightly technical that no one else can be bothered with.

Taking a deep breath, I close my eyes and brace myself for the worst. "What w–would make things 'I owe y–you two'?"

"Just owe me one and we'll call it. That one I might need to cash out tomorrow, probably just handing off a package for me, or picking something up. Nothing huge."

That's it? I nod my head a couple times, before they can get a chance to change their mind on me. Christa sighs loudly and leans back against the railing, looking up at the ceiling in thought. There's no telling what they're thinking right now. After a moment they snap their head back in my direction. "There goes my evening, I guess. Best we go when the lamps are lit. We'll meet here. I'll ask Runa to watch Esper for you, if she's not already."

"She is."

"Wow, you're really putting me in a tough spot here."

There's no chance to apologize, because they're already off. Tristan is heading inside, and Christa runs up to greet him, hanging off his neck and kissing his cheek as he laughs and grins dopily. I don't know what they're talking about, but his smile disappears briefly as he glances over at me, before he shakes his head and starts trying to walk with them still attached to him.

I'm not exactly sure how it's a tough spot, other than

asking more from Runa. I don't know why paying people back around here always involves me risking my neck.

I spend the rest of the day pretending to look busy and helping out with minor tasks around the site. Once everyone goes home for the day, I head up to the ward instead. Esper seems to be organizing things for Runa while she tends to patients still hurt after the fiasco in the Brunsel sector. Hiero's already gone home, but I still make an instinctive, hopeful sweep of the ward. It's good to know Esper isn't sitting around bored. Mostly. Runa seems happy to have another pair of hands.

"Are we heading home?" Esper asks.

"Not yet. Y–You're going to be spending some m–more time with Runa."

"It'll be fun!" Runa promises, but even her unfettered optimism seems to be ineffective. He groans and continues what he's doing, and Runa throws me another of her countless appraising glances. "Artem, you look exhausted, maybe you should rest your eyes for a little?"

I guess I am still pretty tired. Maybe some more rest will do me good. I grab one of the spare beds and lay down, shutting my eyes. It seems like I've only taken a deep breath when I feel someone looking at me. Opening my eyes, I flinch as Christa hovers into my periphery, grinning.

"You drool quite a bit in your sleep." My hand goes to my mouth reflexively as they stretch their arms out. I almost expect them to break into jumping-jacks. "Alright, we've got places to be! Can't stay here all evening, unlike some."

"Christa," Runa warns.

"Runa." Christa sticks their tongue out and leaves.

I swing my legs over and follow, throwing a small wave and an apologetic look to Runa. She shoots one right back. Christa waits at the entrance to the tunnels, vaulted door wide open behind them, and gestures for me to lead the way. Next thing I know, we're in the tavern, and Christa is wheedling the barkeep into having a shot waiting when we get back.

It's weird going to Mr. Connolly's shop when it's so dark. Sure, there was a time or two I would stay long after hours just to get some work done, but this is different. I have someone with me, for one, and there are more procs patrolling the streets. It probably wasn't the brightest idea to have another Qorani accompany me after dusk to commit a crime. I keep expecting to run into guards at every turn. Every time we pass a late-night wanderer I pray to Dreggar I won't be looking up into Roran's face.

"We're okay with it, you know," Christa starts suddenly.

I jolt. Are we having a conversation? Since when are we having a conversation? "O-Okay with what?"

"You know, the fact that you're gay."

A yip squeaks its way free of my throat and my hand leaps up instinctively to cover Christa's mouth but ends up half-cracking against their cheek instead. Holy shit, that was not what I'd expected them to say. I pull my hand back like I've been burned and immediately start gibbering. "O-Oh, s-s-s-sorry, I didn't m-mean to— I d-don't— I-I'm not— why-why would you say th-that?!"

Thankfully Christa doesn't look mad that I've just backhanded them; they just rub their cheek, looking faintly bemused. "Relax, kiddo. I know the Crown isn't okay with it, or the church, or whatever, but, Runa and I don't care. Heck, we're rebels, screw the whole church thing, right?"

"H–How do you know I'm...?"

They give me a soft grin. "Hun. We all see the way you look at Hiero."

As much as I want to argue, there's no point. Since I was twelve, I've known I was anything but straight. But I didn't like to think about it or acknowledge it, especially with the way the Church of the Crown demonizes those outside of the bounds of heteronormativity. There have been many sanctioned hate crimes, procs looking the other way as couples get beaten or have slurs shouted at them. Last I checked, the official penalty for same gender attraction involved fines for public affection, though spiritually speaking, one could easily earn a ticket to eternal damnation.

But with Hiero, I'm not exactly sure how I feel. Do I have a crush on her?

Dreggar's sake, Artem, of course you do.

I don't know how else to respond. The rest of the walk is spent in silence, though I can practically feel the knowing look on Christa's face, as they wait patiently for me to admit my attraction to Hiero. Instead I mindlessly track the path to Mr. Connolly's shop, the weight in my stomach growing heavier the closer we get. It's getting harder to tell the good memories from the bad; more and more, they're less like memories, and more like reminders of every mistake I've made. I've imagined coming back here so many times, imagined that Mr. Connolly might forgive me, that we could go back to the way things were. But even though this place was once like a second home, now, standing before the window, I feel nothing but cold. It was childish to think I could ever just pick up my old life. Everything is different now. I'm different now. There are only ghosts left here.

The lights are off, the sign flipped to 'CLOSED'. A shiver travels down my back; it would have been so easy to have never met Hiero that day. She was the start of everything, for better or for worse, the storm that came crashing in and swept me out to sea. I wonder if Roran passes by here and thinks about that day, too. The day we met Hiero. The day his friend betrayed his trust and ripped his heart out.

Christa looks over the lock, pulling some tools from their pouch. I'm starting to think everyone in the rebellion carries around a lockpicking kit. Maybe I should, too. It seems to be the "in" thing to do, breaking into places. Christa raises an eyebrow at me. "Daydream later," they hiss. "Keep an eye out, will you? Last thing we need is to be going to prison over this, of all things."

I mumble an apology and turn around. The streets are empty, treading the line between peaceful and eerie. No music in the air, no travelers in sight. The lamps flicker occasionally, as if winking, and above there are barely any stars, the sky clouded over with industrial smog.

My audancers don't pick up the snick of the lock catching; Christa just swears softly under their breath, and when I turn to look, grabs me by the collar of my shirt and yanks me inside. The door rattles as it slams shut. On cue, a jitney sounds off its alarm, a proc-owned ML speeding by, and then we're left in darkness with the unnerving ticking of the half-dozen clocks.

"I told you to keep your eyes out." Christa runs a hand through their bangs with a huff. "Not stare up at the sky."

"S-Sorry, I-I—" I stop short as cold prickles run up the back of my neck. Something's not right. The plastered walls seem to shrink in, making the place feel smaller, and the moonlight creeping through the windows casts odd and shifting shadows. It reeks of rot. A mixture of feces and rancid meat, with a tinge of copper. It's familiar to me in the manner of a half-remembered childhood nightmare.

Christa notices, too. Their face is hard to see, but I swear they've gone pale, their voice dropping low as they take on a defensive posture, shoulders square and stiff and eyes narrowed at the unflinching darkness. "...I'm guessing it doesn't always smell like this?"

"No..."

Something is buzzing, high and close by, but I can't tell if it's just my audancers acting up or not. Christa walks ahead, glancing behind the counter, then winces and steps back, bringing their sleeve up in front of their mouth. "Does Mr. Connolly have graying hair?"

Why... why would Christa ask something like that? Pure, icy dread snakes up my spine as I take a few steps closer and try to sneak a glance.

Something that was once Mr. Connolly lies on the ground. The hardwood has been stained with a dark color, almost black in the creeping moonlight, and a handful of viseys buzz around his body, a few resting on exposed flesh. His skin has the pale flake of paper, and his neck is wrenched at an unnatural angle, the deep bruise of a bludgeon mark blooming dark near the base of his skull.

My stomach turns. I barely have enough time to spin around before the contents of my stomach force their way up. Tears sting my eyes as I heave helplessly, coughing and sputtering and praying to Dreggar that this is just another nightmare. Christa kneels by my side, rubbing their hand in slow, comforting circles on my back. I spit on the ground. Mr. Connolly's going to kill me for making a mess of his floor. Or, I guess not. I don't work here. He's dead. The world is spinning.

"You okay there?"

"N–No," I choke out, trying to keep from crying. "No, n–no, this can't be ha–happening."

"Did he have any enemies?"

I shake my head, then keep shaking it and shaking it, too caught up in the motion, in the grief, to stop. I don't know. He didn't seem like the sort. He may have been a grouch, but he had his good points. He cared, even if he didn't show it. This was the man who took me in as an apprentice at eleven because he knew my father. This was the boss who built my audancers and taught me basic repair. Mr. Connolly was the closest thing I had to a mentor... the closest thing I had to my father... and his last memory of me was losing an automaton and conspiring with rebels. Did he die thinking of me at all? Did I pass by his thoughts like Mrs. Connolly and his children must have? If I hadn't lost my job here, would it be me lying there dead instead? If I hadn't joined the rebellion... would he be dead at all?

Christa pats my back and tries to help me to my feet. I rub at my eyes and sniffle. They purposefully angle themself to block off his body and give me a helpless look. I don't expect them to understand, but I appreciate their efforts. They clear their throat, gaze flicking back over their shoulder. "I'd guess it happened a few hours ago. That's a four-hour-old body."

...I don't want to know how they would know something like that. I just push past them to the back room. Everything's scattered about. Whoever killed Mr. Connolly was looking for something, but it doesn't look like anything valuable was taken. I start sifting through some blueprints. He had been working on a new airship for the royal family, exclusive from the rest of the carriers that transport nobles. One time I had asked him how he expected anything like the sketch to fly.

"S–Surely something like that c–can't take off the ground."

"With a gitzen-based engine? Have you not been paying attention to what I've been saying?" he had chided, unfurling the print more and smacking the schematic with the back of his hand. "Gitzen could do the trick to provide and distribute more power. Even better than steam or gas."

"How could an–anything be b–better than steam?" I had asked, appalled by the very idea.

He hmphed. "You'll see, when you've got some experience. The mark of a great engineer is thinking beyond what works into what can work better. A dual-engine, using gitzen, that's the future."

If anything has what I need, it's those blueprints.

Christa just hangs around near the doorway. They don't know what to look for, and I don't think explaining it would help. They watch me for a moment, then grab a dusty cloth and disappear back into the other room.

Every wrong blueprint makes it harder to breathe. What

I'm looking for isn't here. I feel my shoulders slump in defeat. My eyes water. This was all for nothing. His death was—

No. I need this. I can't give up that easily. I head over to the cabinet and scrabble through paper after paper, blueprint after blueprint. I'm making a mess, throwing each dud behind me until they carpet the wooden floor, but it's not like it matters anymore. Tucked away in the back, I finally find something of value: the gitzen engine designs. I take a deep breath, rolling them up tightly and clenching them in my fist.

Out of habit I head for the back door, but as my hand touches the handle, it swings open. Outside sits a canister of what appears to be lepel oil. Qift. I think I'm shaking, but it doesn't seem to matter anymore. Whoever was here before came back, and they're planning on burning the place down.

I scramble back to Christa and find they've draped the cloth over Mr. Connolly and are kneeling by his body. They turn their head to me and look back down with a shrug. "I didn't know the man, but he deserves a prayer anyway. I'm sorry for your loss."

"Thank y-you." I bite my lip. "W-We need to leave. There's l-lepel oil out b-back; I think someone's go-going to b-burn this place d-d-down."

Their brows arch up and they stand quickly, brushing their hands together. "I don't want to know. The sooner I get back, the less of a lecture I'll get from Runa." I just nod and don't argue.

As we leave, another ML passes by, going in the opposite direction. We stick to the shadows, heading for the tavern. "Man, I could really go for that shot of knackle waiting for me right about now!" Christa fakes a yawn, but their attempt at light-hearted banter overshoots into almost hysterical bubbliness. There's no disguising the hesitance in their voice, though. They're just as uneasy as I am. "Tristan is probably wondering when we're going to be meeting up. I told him I wasn't going to outright cancel our plans, but..."

My thoughts are scattered: fire, the shop, my apartment, the explosive at the gala. Is this the work of someone within the rebellion? Why would anyone break in and kill Mr. Connolly? Were the blueprints I was looking for actually stolen? All I can think about is Mr. Connolly's shop bursting into flames. The world around us has grown so quiet I can nearly hear the crackling of the fire-to-be, my throat tight and airless with thick smoke and sorrow.

CHAPTER 19

"The skies are, uh, clear, sort of, the skylines that is! With the e-uh, evacuation following the Brunsel Massacre, it seems the-the procs are starting to retreat and hole up. Protests are, well, stronger than ever, with..."

Normally Leonard Kitts' soothing voice and awkward demeanor are enough to put me at ease, but right now it's making concentrating more difficult. I clear my throat politely; Esper's head pops up in attention. When I nod to the radio set, Esper gets the message, sulking over and shutting off the radio.

Whatever happened with Mr. Connolly was enough to scare me into isolation in the Flooded Sector. It figures: the moment I start to trust the rebels, I find more proof they're untrustworthy. That is, assuming any of my friends are part of the splinter within the rebellion. Who's to say, though? None of them condone the splinter's actions, but I wonder how Hiero seems to always catch wind of it.

Because it's her job, Artem. She's a great spy. Hiero would never do anything that would harm other people. You know that. She took a runnel for your brother.

I suppose there must be something deeper at work that I don't understand. It's not like anyone would explain anything to me anyway. I'm just a mechie, in way over her head. I can practically hear Aether telling me so right now, trademark sneer plastered onto her face.

For my sanity's sake, I've spent the last two days at the clocktower. It feels weird to call it "home", even if we've been here for a few weeks. Although, I'm starting to wonder if any place will ever truly feel like home. Regardless, it's where we're staying for now, and it has a workspace I can tinker in without having to go to the bunker and potentially be in the way. It's also a great spot for Esper, whose new hobby is exploring the clock tower and the surrounding area.

At the moment, Esper is drawing patterns into the fogged-up glass of the clock face as I pore over the notes for the gitzen engine for the umpteenth time. He hums a vaguely familiar tune under his breath, tracing his work with his finger as he illustrates what appears to be a monster attacking the rest of the sector. It's believable from the angle we're at, so high up, overseeing the makeshift town. I smile at his handiwork and watch for a few seconds longer than I should before turning back to my own work.

Mr. Connolly always writes in the most peculiar way. Oh, I mean... wrote. It was as if he didn't want just anybody to be able to read his blueprints. Were I an outsider, I'd have no way to decipher the symbols he uses, especially as he writes in such small script. But I happen to be uniquely qualified at reading and writing his style. I heard of a great inventor once who wrote all of his notes in code. And to think, I'm considered paranoid.

It wasn't easy, but I've managed to get my hands on some gitzen. It's an odd material, mined only in a specific region to the north of Wellwick, in a quarry near Myrlit. It's pricey, even under normal circumstances, but I talked Arek into providing me with some. After a rousing game of "I know a guy who knows a guy," I ended up spending a good chunk of my savings to fiddle with the metallic rock, and made a mental note to dip into my savings from the ship to purchase the rest.

However, there's no point in buying up as much of the mineral as possible until I can confirm a gitzen engine is doable. As it is, whenever I work with it, no matter how thick my gloves, I end up shocking myself. On top of it all, Mr. Connolly is the only one I've heard of to have perfected a gitzen engine. His handwriting is a bit more frantic in these blueprints than usual, and I'm having a hard time telling some of the glyphs apart.

Esper sighs loudly and rolls onto the hardwood. I shake my head at him, bury myself deeper into the blueprints for a moment, then come up for air to adjust my current rig. In the center of another table sits my attempt at a gitzen engine, the encasing complete and output set up to a series of bulbs. All that remains is to put the gitzen inside of the chamber and secure the tubing.

"There's nothing to dooooooo."

"C–Complaining a–about it isn't going to–to do anything."

"Can't we go into town here?"

"Esper," I warn. "This is a–a–a really, r–really important project I'm working on r–right now. I promise w–we can do something together i–in an hour."

He huffs and scrambles to his feet, trying to peer over my shoulder.

"What's so special about this engine, anyway?"

"I–It cost a good chunk o–of our savings."

"So what are we going to do with it?"

Test it. Maybe sell it to someone in the Flooded Sector who could use it. I'm not entirely certain, honestly.

Somehow my lack of an answer is entertaining, as Esper snorts and fiddles with a knob. Immediately I bat his hands away and fix him with a stare. He blinks back with deceptive innocence and scuffs his foot against the floor.

It's about time I try running my test. Carefully, I pick up the small amount of gitzen and place it inside the chamber. It sparks at my touch, and I flinch at a particularly sharp sting before I can get it contained. I move the dial back, pull the lever to start it, and take a step back.

It whirs, chugging along, and vibrates. The metal inside sparks a few times, before a puff of purple smoke comes billowing out of the exhaust. Hastily I switch it off and open up the chamber, coughing as the room begins to fill with the stuff. It's probably only slightly toxic. I'm sure I've inhaled much worse in my lifetime working at Mr. Connolly's shop, or even just being in the bunker.

I groan and bring a hand to my head as the smoke begins

to dissipate. Another failure added to the chalkboard. Back to the basics.

"Can I help?"

Esper's suggestion is just as shocking as the gitzen. He's never shown an interest in engineering type stuff. Or mechie stuff. I wrinkle my nose slightly as it occurs to me he's asking out of boredom. Or to create more chaos. It could go either way.

"You n–never want to help."

"Well, there's nothing else to do!"

I prop an elbow on the table and lean my weight into it, looking him up and down for a moment. Somehow he still has an abundance of energy he doesn't know what to do with. At his age, I was already overworked enough to not even think about what it meant to be a child. Come to think of it, I was Esper's age when I found him and took him in.

Of course, those were the days before the price hike in living expenses, and I had already aged seven years in the span of one. But I suppose, were my circumstances different, I'd be the same way. What that is, exactly, I'll never be able to name, but I need to find a balance between giving in and pushing him aside.

"A–Alright, if I t–take a break, w–will you please let me f–finish this?"

Esper brightens, nodding his head enthusiastically. I push my materials to the side to clear some space up, as if it might do anything. "Deal!"

"We have f–fifteen minutes. W–What do you w–want to do?"

"Um," Esper stalls for a moment, looking around in thought. "This doesn't count as part of the time!"

I shake my head, stifling a laugh as I run a hand through my hair. The motion just reminds me how long it's been since I've actually washed it. Maybe I should do that later tonight. It's feeling kind of grody. A haircut wouldn't hurt either.

Finally, Esper slams his hands down on the table, pinpointing what it is he wants to do exactly. "Let's play a game!"

"W–What kind of g–game?" I ask, offering a smile. Inwardly, I'm just praying it's not something destructive.

"Hide-and-find!"

That's a game I haven't played in a while. It was something Esper liked to do when he was younger, and better at hiding in small spaces. The older he got, the less he wanted to play games like that. Not to mention, there were only so many places to hide in the alleyways and apartment, back when we used to venture farther than our room.

Slowly, I nod my agreement. "We c–can do that."

"Not it!" Esper shouts, and tears out of the room. I sigh, crossing my arms as I stand up straighter and close my eyes.

As I count, I hear his footsteps hammering down the stairs. After a beat, it grows dead silent. The moment I open my eyes, I'm hit with an almost eerie feeling. I never realized just how quiet it was here, so far away from the rest of the community. The rain hits the building with enough intensity to cause a hollow echo throughout the entirety of the clocktower. The few candles burning to provide light flicker, casting the slightest of shadows across the walls.

I start down the stairs, absently humming a tune under my breath. They creak every third step, and my hand trails down the railing lazily behind me. It's almost calming, the feel of the cool metal against my skin, and I briefly miss the summertime, when I don't have to wear gloves.

"I-I hope you f-found a good spot!" I call out, glancing at the main room. I wait a second, trying my best to listen for him. Unfortunately, he doesn't seem as noisy as he used to be.

The standard spots are empty. No hiding under the bed, not behind any desks or bureaus, and certainly not tucked into the corner with the couch. The bathroom, or what we've been calling a bathroom, turns up empty as well. I furrow my brow and bring my hands together in thought. Either I'm worse at this game than I thought, or Esper's hiding in one of the blocked off sections to the clocktower.

The downstairs isn't completely flooded, merely blockaded. There are roughly two levels below, boarded up, or locked without a key. After a certain point, the staircase is blocked off entirely, though we have to come down with a mop every so often to get the water that trickles through.

Could Esper have managed to squeeze through one of the semi-open floors? My head pounds at the thought. Maybe hide-and-find was a bad idea. Especially with how crafty Esper's gotten.

I head back down the stairs, pausing by one of the locked doors. It doesn't seem disturbed in any way, and I nudge aside some broken boards to try the handle. Locked, still.

Stepping back, I cup a hand around my mouth. "Y-You got me! I g-give!"

Silence. I groan, bringing my hands to my face. There's no need to panic. He's just playing a trick again.

The longer I stare at the door, I can't help but notice how odd the keyhole looks. Tilting my head, I crouch and try the handle again, giving it a better look. It's hard to tell from just looking at it, but it looks like it takes a smaller key than most doors.

I'm hit with an odd sense of déjâ vu, like maybe I had a dream of this. My hand goes to my necklace, slowly pulling out the key hiding under my shirt. I turn it over, running a finger along the teeth. It couldn't possibly fit inside, could it? I grasp it a bit tighter, and--

"Roar!!"

I yelp, letting go of the key and scrambling back against the wall, as Esper pops out wearing the world's biggest shit-eating grin. "E-Esper!"

"You give up too easily! I win!"

"Wh-Where..." I close my eyes, trying to steady my breathing. "Where were y-you hiding?"

"You'll have to find out next time."

Fair enough, I guess. I sigh, ruffling his hair as I head back up the stairs. Esper whines, but doesn't complain as I head back up the tower.

Walking away from projects can be beneficial. The moment I look at the gitzen engine, I realize exactly what the problem is: the wiring is wrong, and I flipped one of the switches the wrong way. I fiddle with it a bit, then splash a little water onto the gitzen before closing the hatch. I say a prayer, and flip the switch.

It pops a few times, fizzling and sparking. Flashes of

electricity fill the chamber, as slowly the glass turns a dark purple and the engine hums to life. The lightbulb attached to it glows brightly, only to shatter from the intensity of the gitzen.

"Y–Yes!" I shout, jumping into the air and bringing a hand to my mouth. "I–I got it! It w–works!"

"You did it?" Esper asks, hanging upside-down from the railing at the top of the stairs. I'm too giddy to even yell at him.

"I–I did!" I laugh, shutting off the engine, then take a deep breath. Some minor adjustments will need to be made, but I can draw the energy needed from the gitzen, and it is more than powerful enough.

"Cool." Esper rocks back and forth on his feet. "We should celebrate."

I knew this was coming. I shake my head with a smile, bracing my forearms against the table. "We–We should."

Esper shouts something incomprehensible, though I can guess as he runs off that he wants something sugary. I suppose it wouldn't hurt my wallet more than the gitzen did. I eye the machine, taking mental measurements for the new engine and preparing for the build I'll need to get started on tomorrow. Should everything go the way I plan, the construction should only take two to three days.

And yet, the moment I finish my work with the rebellion, what will I do? Where will I go? I shake my head firmly and fix my tie. I can worry later.

Tonight, we celebrate.

CHAPTER 20

The blueprints have helped. The engines should work, though I'm worried they won't do what they're supposed to do: make the ship fly. But my job is just to get them running. The entire ship is almost completed, the rooms sectioned off by actual walls and doorways, down to the oval hatch leading inside to the expansive main chamber. All that's left is for me to connect everything together. No one's even attempted to cover the wiring, I think partially as a courtesy toward me. With any luck, within a few days I should be able to wash my hands of this airship entirely. The steam engines are secure; all that's left are the finishing touches on the gitzen engine.

I tighten the bolts to the frame of the firing cylinder and take a step back to look at it. From what I understood of the blueprints, gitzen is meant to be heated like coal, using only a coil and excess steam from the engines. From there the output is an electrical current that could power half the bunker, and will certainly have no problem powering the ship. The only problem is just how flammable the engine is, but I've installed a spray system for coolant, just in case. I really hope Mr. Connolly knew what he was doing when he designed this.

Someone clears their throat and I spin to see Christa, holding a letter. Right. We had a deal, and I guess that deal means playing delivery girl. I take the envelope and look it over, finding no address. "Wh–Where is this going?"

"128 Lancarne Lane, Apartment 201. Should be in the upper right of Calken Sector. Hiero Heroux."

"Wait." I shake my head. "H–Hiero? Hiero Hiero?" Her last name is qiftin *Heroux*?

"The one and only. Figured you might enjoy the trip." Christa winks as they walk off. I stand awkwardly, fighting the blush in my cheeks. Tucking the letter away, I scurry up the stairway and out through the tunnels.

It's been far too long since I was last in the Calken part of Wellwick. The last time I was anywhere near here, we were fleeing the fire with half the proc force on our tail. After that run-in with Roran, I feel as though I'm always being watched, like I have to check behind me every few blocks. I'm always expecting the special forces to be right around the corner, ready to rip up my fake papers when I stutter the alias I was given, and throw me in a cell or worse. In reality, there's never anything more threatening than a launaut or a beggar.

I end up not even five blocks away from where Esper and

I used to live. I never expected Hiero to live in Calken. I always assumed she lived in Peri, where the housing is larger and nicer, and families can afford to take up whole floors. Though I suppose this is still a nicer part of Calken than I'm used to: only some of the paint is chipped off the buildings, which look roomier and less cramped. They stack up against one another, about a foot between each building, generous compared to the suffocating closeness of my old apartment block. The top rooms here are actually occupied— a woman airs out a towel from one of the windows. I stop in front of a building made entirely of red brick, with a window on either side of the door. I take a moment, stuff the letter into my pocket, then brace myself as I head inside.

It's a huge improvement on my old building. There are two apartments on each floor, and a staircase leading up to the other levels. The hallways are clean, and there's no shouting, or doorways blocked by broken glass or wooden boards... but comparing this place to what is no longer mine is pointless.

I clutch the letter in my pocket for comfort and try to steel myself as I head up the stairs. There's no way she could know I'm coming by, so what if she doesn't want me to be here? I didn't think this through.

On this floor, the first door is set up right in front of the stairs. The next flight up obscures my view of 202, but I imagine it must be just around the corner. The apartment is marked "201" with silver-painted numbers that gleam against the otherwise plain wooden door. I knock. A few seconds pass before I catch a very distant and muffled voice calling back. It sounds sort of like "Come in," so it must be okay. Sure enough, the knob turns easily and the door swings right open.

I'm greeted by a bland living room; there's a weathered blue couch against one of the beige walls, a half-assembled bookcase filled with miscellaneous junk, and a table with a couple of scattered papers. The items on the bookcase are all fairly ornate, like a fancy-looking sugar bowl, and jewelry-encrusted knickknacks. A ratty blue plush chair is pushed into a corner with a side table holding a cup of qosa and a newspaper half-folded against the armrest. It seems to be a shared space for only one or two people rather than five or eight. Luxury, to my eyes.

"Who's there?" Hiero calls out.

"Me," I answer. "Ar–Artem, I mean."

There's a vague laugh choked off by a cough. "Of course it is. Just straight ahead."

"Crown's he–health."

She's tucked into bed. Once again, I'm underwhelmed by just how simple everything is, from the single cot separated from the corner by a nightstand, to the dresser adorned only with a few cosmetics. Otherwise, the only things that stand out are framed ticket stubs on the walls, and a particularly fancy pocket-watch with a red ruby in the middle on a table near the bed. On the desk sits a bastrina, though not particularly shiny or new, amidst a nest of papers, a few old Airships Monthly folios, and what appear to be more useless but nice-looking trinkets. Two books are stacked up by the table, with a third left on the floor, leaning up against the table leg.

I never took her as a reader; the thought almost slips past

my lips before I think better of it. I settle for a small hum of acknowledgement and look at Hiero. She's not surprised, merely curious as I just stand there for a moment trying to figure out what to say. It's a lot more awkward than I thought to face someone who took a runnel for your brother.

"Can I g–get you a–anything?"

"No," she says. "I'm sure when my uncle gets back he can give me a hand." I must look as dumbfounded as I feel, as she goes from slightly amused to snorting at my expression, before clutching at her shoulder and wincing. "*Jos.*"

"I di–didn't know you lived with anyone."

"It'd be a waste of that second room if I didn't." Hiero sinks further into her pillow.

"Sorry, I–I–I just, why don't I get you s–some water?"

"Really, it's fine."

I walk out anyway, pressing a hand to my suddenly aching head, the beginnings of a headache pulsing right behind my eye and deep within my temples. Can embarrassment cause migraines?

To the left is the other room, which can only be her uncle's, and to the right are the kitchen and bathroom. Same as before: not much to look at. More junk that doesn't seem to make sense being there. Perhaps it holds value, though it's hard to tell by the box of pocket-watches on the floor, some of which are rusted over and none of which match.

I look through a couple cabinets, finding them bare, save for sparse cookware. Most items are in pairs, but there's always an odd difference between each. One glass might be tall and slim, the other short and stout. They have a third fork, and one of the spoons seems to be made of gold. Everything is out of place.

It's bothering me, honestly, how much Hiero has and yet how little. Compared to where I used to live, she's doing much better, which I always figured. Yet, at the same time, a part of me was certain she would be living in a fancy building, with ornate furniture, extravagant curtains, and red silk linens on her bed.

I slam the cabinet shut with a little more force than I expected, and Hiero calls out from the other room. "Everything alright?"

"Fine! Th–Thought I saw something was a–all!"

"Might have been Reginald."

"R–Reginald?" I ask, turning the faucet. Orange water comes out of the tap. I shut the water off and check the fridge. I manage to find a jug of water, pour her a glass, then join her. As I place the glass down, she continues.

"Uncle Jak insists on naming the portin. He's always had a soft spot for them."

Uncle *what?*

"D–Does he like vermin?"

"They're basically family." She takes a sip of water, furrowing her brow.

I watch her, waiting until she's finished to ask the burning question on my mind: why is she living with her uncle? An uncle she's never even mentioned.

Before I can, Hiero waves her good hand dismissively and pushes herself to a sitting position. "What brings you here, exactly?"

What does bring me here? I nearly admit I've forgotten and make a fool of myself, but my hand goes to my pocket.

Right. Letter.

I pull the envelope out and hand it over. Hiero furrows her brow and starts to get up. I don't think she should be up and about, at least without help, but I swallow my concerns. In the letter is an auscript; she hobbles to her bastrina, winding the perforated page into the feeder and hitting play. A voice crackles over the script, the sound of whirring and clunking almost overpowering the message.

"Info leak; someone talked. The bunker has been discovered. It's only a matter of time." Hiero's good shoulder slumps at the news, and she swears softly but wholeheartedly under her breath. "Satch." My heart thuds in my chest. I need to get the ship flying now more than ever.

I do my best to stand as a support as Hiero eases herself back onto the bed. She falters slightly and reaches out, grabbing my forearm as I stumble, somehow managing to catch myself before I can fall on top of her. It takes me a moment to register how close of a call that was, how she could have gotten even more hurt.

Hiero blinks a few times, dazed. I stand upright and adjust my tie, looking around the room, at anything other than Hiero. "When w-were you going t-to tell me you had family?"

"You never asked. But I suppose fair is fair— you've told me about your situation, I could have told you about mine." Hiero gestures to a chair in the corner. I grab it, pulling it closer to sit by the bed. She grunts but manages to situate herself where she's still comfortable, then sighs and begins to speak.

"Let's get the obvious out of the way: Sertalis has a handful of verbotkå—green-eyed bastards born in brothels. Sailors, royalty, who knows. I got dumped onto Uncle Jak when I was a kid, and he taught me everything I know. Sertali got boring, so I left."

Hiero pauses and shifts her gaze towards the window. She seems lost in thought for a moment. It's also Hiero, so, who knows, she could be taking a moment for dramatic effect. Either way, I'm a little lost.

"S—Sertali?" I furrow my brow. "Where's th–that?"

Hiero tsks, crinkling her nose in disgust. "Sertalis. Ingwell is incomparable at butchering languages, don't you think?"

She has a point. Qalqora is treated like a joke in Ingwell. The difference between Qorani and Qorain is one thing, but most folks don't even know Qorani originated from Qorar. Mr. Connolly always referred to it as Qorailt. My cheeks burn at the thought. Hiero clicks her tongue then continues.

"That's when that failed uprising happened a few years back. Uncle Jak got involved, and, well, point is he can't exactly take care of himself anymore. So, I'm repaying him, letting him stay here to play with portin and wander around as he likes, saints protect him. Playing informant only pays the bills so much, though."

I sit quietly through Hiero's story with my hands in my lap. When she finishes, I take a moment to digest the information. "S–So why are you with Rhine's m–movement?"

"I don't know," Hiero sighs. "It's complicated. I do genuinely believe in Rhine's cause, and I hope it will all work out. At the end of the day, it pays rent in a way that doesn't make me feel like a terrible person, and it makes the old man happy to think his prodigy is also anti-establishment. I'm in deep now, though, so I guess that's that."

So we're in somewhat similar boats, huh? A sad smile tugs the corners of my mouth, and all at once I'm overwhelmed. I move to leave then stop short, turning on my heel to stare at Hiero for a moment. She gives a questioning hum, tilting her head.

"The ot-other day, in the r-records office..." I furrow my brow. "What was it y-you wanted to tell me?"

Hiero twists her lips and stares at the ceiling. A few awkward seconds pass, and I wonder just how annoyed she is, but finally, she answers. "It was about your file."

My file? Dreggar, I didn't even know I had a file. I thought she was looking for officials in Parvay? I squirm at the thought of anyone being able to find confidential information on me— or the idea there might actually be information on me. Last I checked, no legitimate papers, no legitimate file. There wouldn't be a lot, as Hiero said, but it still makes me uncomfortable.

"W-Why w-were you in my f-files? I tho-thought you were l-looking for something impor-important, with o-officials and stuff."

She's so close to sleep that even her blinking has slowed. "Well, not your files, per se. You said you never legally adopted Esper because of a papers issue. I think I know now why your papers don't seem to exist."

So I don't have a file after all. My heart skips a beat and warmth rushes to my cheeks. I stand frozen for a moment, unable to say anything. Hiero was trying to fudge my papers? So that I could adopt Esper for real? No one has ever tried to do anything so thoughtful for me, nothing— nothing like that. I start to feel bad about every doubt I've had about Hiero, about how suspicious I've been while she's been working to regain my trust and correct her typist thinking. She's changed so much more in the past few months than I've given her credit for.

"What did y–you find?"

"Maybe now isn't the time."

"Hi–Hiero," I beg. "Please."

She lays back and closes her eyes with a sigh. "I think I found your grandfather. You have family, Artem, and he's one of the people screwing up Parvay."

She trails off from there, and I get the sense she's said her piece. My breath leaves my lungs and I clench my fists as the news circles through my head.

Gaqĕ. I have a grandfather. I have family. I have family.

There are more questions I want to ask, but I don't even know where to begin. How much has she dug up on me to even piece that together? Is he in Lindsor? Where was he when my parents were struggling? Does he even know I exist?

Any words die on my tongue when I glance back to Hiero, looking tired and fragile. I can wait for answers. Right now I have a ship I need to get flying, a revolution to aid. I get up from the chair and push it back into place, then step back over to the side of the bed to say my goodbyes. Hiero lifts her head, clearly a bit confused that I'm leaving so soon, but I've already overstayed my welcome, and I should be getting back to work. Or at least, home to watch Esper. Her eyes are starting to flutter closed anyway, as she fights the urge to sleep. The action makes her look soft, almost childish, and I nearly laugh.

She blinks over at me, the green of her eyes nearly lost behind her drooping lashes, and she catches my hand in her own. "Ålaynik," she sighs.

I stop short. "I–I'm sorry?"

Another sigh, soft and weary, and her hand drops back onto the comforter. I instantly miss her warmth. "You're always sorry."

"N–No, I m–mean, I didn't ca–catch that," I admit, twiddling furiously at my audancers' knobs, as though it would help. "What d–did you say?"

There's a long breath of silence before she speaks again, slipping her arm back under the covers. "Go," Hiero answers dully, her eyes shuttered closed. She almost sounds... defeated. Most likely she's just tired and doesn't want to have to repeat herself. I'd feel the same way.

In the moment I stand hesitating by the bed her eyes fall closed all the way and Hiero begins to snore softly. I've... never seen her so vulnerable before. I tiptoe closer to tug the blanket over her shoulders, pausing for a moment. She looks so peaceful. I wonder just how often she truly gets to rest. It seems like all she's ever doing is running around. I hesitate, then take her hand and give it a squeeze before leaving.

I don't see Jak on my way out, or Reginald either. I head straight back to the bunker and gather what belongings I need. Back in the clocktower, Esper eats, then fiddles with the radio. I sit in my makeshift workshop and wonder about tomorrow. The bunker has been discovered, I have family still alive, and I have an airship to get off the ground.

What could possibly go wrong?

CHAPTER 21

There's added pressure now. I've gotten the information I need to keep working on the engines, but there's no denying the tense air in the workyard today. Or maybe that's just me.

Nobody else should know what we heard on that message. There's no way anyone could know. Maybe I'm just being more paranoid than usual. Everyone is usually buzzing about anyway; the only difference is that now I know this could crumble at any minute.

It's for the best that Esper stayed home today. He's been spending so much time with Runa in the medical ward that he's getting bored, but I can't have him nearby when I need to get down to business working on the ship, and especially not when we're so exposed. I'm so close to getting these engines finished, I can nearly taste the victory colfe. It's because I am so close that I need Esper to keep his distance, just for the next few days.

Besides, worst comes to worst, I've given him Hiero's address, and he has his fake papers. He should be fine. I hope.

Rhine hovers nearby, a little too close for comfort. I always hear about him working from a remote office, on more important matters. Today, however, he's made a surprise visit to the bunker, and an unsettlingly surprising visit to the engine room of the airship.

"How's it coming?" Rhine steps inside, eyes narrowed as he inspects every corner of the airship, addressing the nearest of the mechanics buzzing around the site.

"Excellent, sir. All that's left is to make it fly."

"And where are we in terms of that?"

Oh, Dreggar. I tighten my grip on my screwdriver as I try to put the finishing touches on the gitzen engine. Technically, the ship is ready to fly: the gas engine has been running, and the air bladder— the balloon-like material up top— is fully inflated. The only thing keeping the ship tethered is a series of weights. All that's left to finish is the gitzen engine, which will power the rest of the ship. The mechanic's response fades into the distance, and I stop what I'm doing to fiddle with my audancers, just as they walk in.

Great, now I look like I've just been standing around clutching at my ears. I let go and stand at attention, hands stiff by my sides. "M–Mr. Toberts!"

"Miss Clairingbold. How goes your work on the engine? Is this ship ready to fly?" A rhetorical question, considering the ship is hovering a hair above the ground.

"En-Engines, sir. I'm finishing u-up the last one r-right now, then it's a-a matter of con-connecting everything t-together. It should b-be able to fly to-tomorrow, once I test the propulsion."

He rearranges his expression into an apologetic moue. "Change of plans, I'm afraid. We need this ship to fly today."

Jaq? Jĕs? The deadline is....

Suddenly my paranoia is justified. My mind races back to the message on the bastrina, and there's no disguising the tremor in my hands as I bring them together awkwardly around the screwdriver I'm clutching. My voice rises to a squeak. "T-Today? Today w-wasn't—"

The apology falls from his face; now he just looks impatient. "—I am well aware that this was not part of the schedule. However, you've done substantial work, I've heard, and that engine looks complete to me." He nods at it, and I shake my head furiously.

"The tests ha-haven't even been d-d-done yet! I need to fi-finish connecting everything. Why w-would it need to run t-today?"

Rhine doesn't answer. His second-in-command leans over to whisper something to him, and Rhine's lips tighten into a thin line. Without saying anything else, he leaves the engine room. The other man continues to stare at me expectantly.

I don't know what he wants me to say. I shrug, but he stays put, waiting. Waiting for what, I'm not sure. I turn back to the engine and get back to work; after about a minute, he leaves. My breaths start coming sharp and fast, and I pause for a moment to steady myself, clutching at the key around my neck like it might magically calm my jangling nerves.

Is there something I don't know about? Is the bunker going to be stormed tomorrow? Today? Is that why Rhine wants so badly to get out?

I finish and secure the covering to the gitzen engine, then flip the switch and stand back to take in the sight. It's not a bad job, though Mr. Connolly would have done it better. Still— not too bad for my first engine solo, let alone a triple engine setup. The whole process would have gone a lot faster and more smoothly had I found the blueprints for the airship Mr. Connolly had been designing, but this will have to do. All I know is that the steam engines should be fine... it's the gitzen one I'm concerned about.

Right now would be a good time for a systems test. I head to the front; a loud bang echoes through the bunker. I try to peer out, but one of Rhine's men— Nateb, I think he's called— steps close enough to entirely block my view of the bunker. I jolt back and he moves a bit closer, forcing me into the ship.

"Wh-What's going on?"

"You need to make sure everything is connected. Now."

"But I-I don't u-understand—" Another loud bang, and the rising shriek of voices. I flinch, my eyes drawn to the open door, but Naneb presses closer, blocking the way with his wide shoulders.

"Move. Now. Let's go."

He hustles me away. I catch, as we pass doors and windows, brief, frenzied glimpses of people running by. Everyone is rushing, desperate, many starting to head for the airship itself. I'm not even looking where I'm going now; my neck cranes this way and that to catch what's going on in the hangar. Naneb propels me along, pushing at my back until we finally reach the control room.

Rhine stands behind one of the chairs, gripping at the top of it as I enter. He nods at me, then directs me to the underside of the control panel. There's no affable charm left in his voice now, just the bark of someone who expects to be obeyed. "Everything else has been set up, all that's left is your last engine. No one else is available and we're running out of time. You need to connect the controls now."

"But I-I don't kn-know how t-to—"

"You're going to have to know how to do it. The bunker has been compromised."

As Rhine speaks, a large cranking noise groans overhead, the sound of machinery that hasn't been operated in years. I watch as a few people move to unanchor the airship. That's great, but if this ship is going to go anywhere but up, it needs to have working controls. I hurry underneath the panel to find a mess of wires. Everything is thankfully untangled and easy to trace back, but that doesn't mean I understand what's going to connect the engines to a switch. I suppose the rest isn't all that important right now, so long as the ship can get started and fly as well as land.

It takes me a few minutes to get my bearings, during which there's another loud clang. One of the vault doors seems to have been slammed open, and the bang of runnels being shot echoes through the bunker. Rhine's second-in-command announces that the doors to the airship have been sealed. Someone asks me what's taking so long. I do my best to grit my teeth and blot out the screams, fumbling for my crimping tool as my hands continue to shake.

By the time I twist two ends together and cap them, the shouting has moved to right outside the ship. I stumble to my feet and grab at the levers I need. Inwardly I pray. Dreggar, I hope that this works. Otherwise, a lot of people are going to die. Who's to say people haven't already died? They can't have all fit in the airship....

I throw one switch and the panel comes online. Another, and the anchor falls away with a loud clang. I choke back a sob of relief as I'm pushed off to the side. The controls are taken from me, and slowly the craft begins to rise. Outside, the ship's hull rings with balistir-shots.

Curiosity drags me out of the front room and over to the side. Many people are huddled together, but I start to realize just how few we are. None of them are familiar faces; all have pins showing their high ranking within Rhine's forces. These men are all soldier types, hiding out on a ship rather than taking control of the chaos outside. There's no sign of Christa, Runa, Tristan, Arek— no sign of anyone I know, other than Aether. She stands calmly near the door, keeping it sealed.

We only appear to be a foot off the ground. I'm not even sure if the ship will fully fly, but we should at least be letting more people in to keep them safe! As I move to open the door, Aether throws her hand out to keep hold of the lever. "What do you think you're doing?"

"Th-There are p-people dying out th-there! The pr-procs are everywhere! We c-can hold more people!" I insist, trying to reach past her.

Aether kicks me square in the stomach, and I go skidding, clutching my gut. "I have my orders, you have yours," she says sharply. "You're not even supposed to be on this ship, Artem. I suggest you thank your lucky stars and stay out of the way."

Orders? What orders would leave our people to the mercy of the procs?

I head to the window again; we seem to have gained more air. Right outside of the door, on the boarding platform, is a body, laying with arms outstretched toward the ship. I'd recognize that face anywhere: Meno, eyes glazed over and lifeless.

The sharp hail of runnels against the ship only forces my panic further. I don't know how stable this ship is or how it will do at greater altitudes. Yet we continue to rise, higher and higher, and soon all I can see are the dirt walls around us as the airship travels up.

A warning sounds, and a loud grinding grates overhead as a hatch opens and we soar up through an abandoned factory. We keep drifting up, through the open roof, as the tiny figures milling around outside the factory gaze up at us. In a moment, it all fades into a distant haze: the sectors, the city, Allowyn, everything. All that surrounds us are the clouds. The sky is greenish this high up, the clouds like strands of cotton floating in the breeze.

My thoughts remain sunk beneath the surface of the city. Below ground there are still dozens of people, procs and rebel alike, falling under a flurry of runnels as the bunker is flooded with people, desperate to get in or out. Just how many people are dead? Did anyone manage to escape?

All I can picture is Runa's body draped over her medical cabinet, or Christa drowning in their own blood. Arek probably is dead, as is Verne and Gewell. Everyone, except for Aether. Then there's Hiero. I have no clue if the bunker being compromised meant her home has as well, if she had a contingency plan, if she could even carry one out in her condition. Then there's the clocktower. And Esper. A sob catches in my throat.

I manage to crawl into the warm darkness of the engine room and curl up into a ball. I'm starting to think I'll never stop shaking. Part of me wants to get sick, ruining my clothes, forgoing any decency. Another part of me wants to cry and never stop crying. But I've never been so paralyzed, so helpless.

When I try to speak, it comes out a gasp. "Esper— oh fuck, Esper—" If I had taken Roran's offer, could I have avoided this? Would we be safe somewhere, far from this violence, all these deaths? I don't know. Suddenly, any path that didn't lead here—thousands of meters up in the air and far away from Esper— seems better.

I don't know where this ship is headed or when we'll land, but I'm going to make my way back to Wellwick, even if it kills me. Forget about the others, about the rebellion, about any of this. I don't care about this movement, and I don't care about the procs or the Crown. I care about keeping what family I have left safe. All that matters is getting back to Esper.

This fight is far from over.

GLOSSARY AND TRANSLATIONS

Serkek

Ålaynik (uh-LIE-nik)— Stay (imperative)

Åneysh (uh-NAYSH)— Goodbye, a shortened form of "tevå aneysh" (TEV-uh uh-NAYSH), literally "safe travels"

Jo-må (jo-MUH)— Little one

Jos (JOHs)— Moderate swear

Kashø (KA-shoo)— Really/ seriously/actually

Kivesh (kih-VESH)— A crass equivalent to "crown-licker"

Poshi-må (PO-shee muh)— "Little apple"

Satch (SAHTCH)— Major swear

Sayev (SAI-ev)— Term of endearment akin to sweetie or darling

So sabi taknik (SO SAH-bee TAHK-nik)— Tell me the truth

Tesht (TESHT)— A moderate insult

Vashtet (VAHSH-tet)— Dummy

Veså (VESS-uh)— Certainly/ of course

Qalqora

Aberqen (uh-BEAR-ken)— Airship

Aqiil ĕnem? (uh-KEEL AY-nem)— Are you well?

Gaqĕ/ Genqii (GAHK-ay/ GEN-key)— Exclamatory and descriptive version of a minor swear, a lesser version of qift/ qiften

Jaq (JAHK)— What

Jĕs (JAYs)— Why

Maro (MAH-ro)— Please

Pasha, e vâlĕ qev'niin ĕnem (PAH-shuh, ey VAI-ley KEV-uh-neen AY-nem)— Thanks, you're a life-saver

Râ jĕ qavesii (RAI JAY kah-VESS-ee)— Calm yourself

Rosh jul (ROHsh JOOL)— Little love, common term of endearment

Qa visaq! Maro qa visaq! (KA VEE-sahk! MAH-ro KA VEE-sahk!)— Help! Please help!

Qes jaq ĕnav? (KESS JAHK AYnahv)— What is it?

Qift/ Qiften (KIFT/ KIFT-en)— Exclamatory and descriptive version of a major swear

ACKNOWLEDGEMENTS

I would like to thank:

Heather Staradumsky, RISD graduate, who worked tirelessly on the illustrations and cover for this project. I told her my idea for this book when it was a very rough concept eight years ago. All I had was a character design or two, a potential plot, and a vision. Without Heather, my dream would remain an untold story. She also has been immensely patient while details have changed for some visual elements, as well as helping catch an inconsistency or two. Thank you for your artistic prowess and for inspiring me to pursue this project.

Kaden Whitman, my editor, who I would trust with anything. A fellow graduate from Rhode Island College, we shared many classes together where Kaden would mercilessly critique and correct my writing, forcing me to continually strive for better. (Reader, this too has been edited by them; that is how much I rely on their input.) They are also responsible for the handling of pronouns and correct terminology for my non-binary character, Christa, as well as for constructing the fictional languages (Serkek/Sertalin and Qalqora) within the book.

Maple Intersectionality Counseling, my secondary editor for cultural sensitivity. Given some of the topics in this book, Leona helped immensely with making sure I was approaching the concept of culturalism appropriately and even coined the term. Thank you for your guidance on handling the xenophobia within the book.

Maddy Riorda, an alum of RISD and classmate of Heather Staradumsky, my metal guru. Maddy was not only the first person to read Hidebound who wasn't working on the project, but ended up joining because of her knowledge with alloys, as a gifted metal fabricator. Thank you for help, and for your knowledge in engineering and metalwork.

Tyler Carter, who this book is dedicated to, for being my constant emotional support. Tyler helped me brainstorm ideas for the book, which led to the creation of a few characters. She has also stood tirelessly by me while I continued to rework ideas and encouraged me to keep chugging along. Thank you for being my confidante.

Lastly, this book would not be possible if it were not for my mom. After all, I would not exist, and though perhaps Hidebound would exist in some other form, as according to the theory presented in Tom Stoppard's Arcadia, it would not exactly be the same. I also have to thank my dad for supporting me all these years. Thank you both for always encouraging my creativity, even if it didn't always come out in the best of ways.

ABOUT THE AUTHOR

A. Oliver Noel has always loved the art of storytelling, with a deep fascination with complex characters and realistic dialogue. A graduate with a degree in Creative Writing, he has written plays and been published for non-fiction pieces covering his journey as a transgender man finding his voice. He has a passion for fantasy and science fiction, but takes issue with the lack of LGBT adventures. A. Oliver Noel has set out on a personal mission to create tales about LGBT folks for LGBT folks by someone in the community. His interest has always been to lend a voice to those whose representation is often overlooked in fictional settings.

CPSIA information can be obtained
at www.ICGtesting.com
Printed in the USA
FSHW020951080221
78321FS

9 781665 510646